EDEN DISCOVERED

EDEN DISCOVERED

LEXI POST

Eden Discovered

The Eden Series, Book 3

By Lexi Post

Animal lover Jaelene Upton doesn't expect to lose sight of her sister when she follows her through a bizarre travel portal, but that's exactly what happens when she's distracted by a cute baby porcupine. Lost, she asks for directions, only to be nearly assaulted by one naked man before being saved by another. Her best guess is she's landed among a native tribe in the middle of a jungle….but odd reflections and energy sources have her questioning even that assumption.

Theron misses his home in Loraleaf and the brothers of his heart Konala and Rekah. His new home, a lonely cave, is his escape from seeing the woman he loves happily bonded to Loraleaf's leaders. When he saves Jaelene from lawbreakers, he finds himself drawn to her intoxicating curiosity and despite his best efforts, he falls for her. But no matter what his heart wants, he can't offer her anything but safety and a reunion with her sister. Unless…

If Theron can interest Konala in Jaelene as well, then he would only have two more obstacles to conquer, Rekah and Jaelene herself. But Rekah, hurt by Theron's betrayal, wants nothing to do with Jaelene and when she discovers Theron's past love, she refuses to be his consolation price. As the battle with the lawbreakers grows near, Theron realizes this time he may well lose more than his heart.

For updates, sneak peeks, and special prizes, it's easy to sign up to receive the latest news from Lexi at http://eepurl.com/D3MqT

ACKNOWLEDGMENTS

For Bob Fabich, the man who has always put me first. Thank you for showing me what true love can be.

For Paige Wood who gives me the confidence to keep writing.

I must say a special thank you to my critique partner, Marie Patrick, for giving up her weekends so that my book could be the best it could be.

I also want to thank my readers for their loyal support and interest in my books. Without you, I'd have no reason to tell my stories. I hope you enjoy *Eden Discovered*.

AUTHOR'S NOTE

Eden Discovered was inspired by Emily Dickinson's poem, *The Goal,* or so her editor titled it in 1867. Thomas Wentworth Higginson and Dickinson's friend, Mabel Loomis Todd at the bequest of Dickinson's sister, edited and published Dickinson's poems after her death.

This poem speaks of a goal, perhaps silent or even unconscious in a man's or woman's mind, but there nonetheless, fragile yet enduring, and maybe not ever obtainable in life, but another chance will be given in immortality.

What if a man on another planet thought his failed goal was all there was? Could he open his heart and mind to it once again while still alive, or would he be lost until his death? What if a woman continued to hope that she would one day find the love she sought, even if every time she tried she was pushed aside? Would her constant search turn her bitter or would her never-ending curiosity lead her to the attainable and even unbelievable?

The Goal

Each life converges to some centre
Expressed or still;
Exists in every human nature

A goal,

Admitted scarcely to itself, it may be,
Too fair
For credibility's temerity
To dare.

Adored with caution, as a brittle heaven,
To reach
Were hopeless as the rainbow's raiment
To touch,

Yet persevered toward, surer for the distance;
How high
Unto the saints' slow diligence
The sky!

Ungained, it may be, by a life's low venture,
But then,
Eternity enables the endeavoring
Again.

CHAPTER ONE

Theron followed the tracks through the jungle, certain he was close to the lawbreakers. There were only three men, but he had no idea what abilities they might possess, so he kept silent.

This was an area outside the city of Naralina that he wasn't familiar with as it was closer to the exile settlement of Haven than to that of Loraleaf. As he gained on them, he heard voices. The men stopped between an opening in the trees.

Theron crept forward, careful not to make a sound. Hopefully, none could sense emotions like Rekah. A dull ache started at the thought of the brother of his heart who he'd left behind in Loraleaf. He missed Konala too, but he couldn't go back. Not yet. Maybe not ever.

Ducking beneath the weeping branches of a salish bush, he studied the three men. One dark-haired man frowned and pointed at a small man whose eyes never stopped moving, nor did his body. The third, a blond man with his back to Theron, lifted his hand and the small man slumped to the ground.

He didn't like the look of that. What Kindred could cause that kind of reaction?

The blond moved, stepping to the side of the unconscious

man. As he raised him in his arms, he flipped his long hair out of his face. Theron froze.

Sandale!

Theron's body practically hummed at the possibility that his former leader was not dead. The last they'd known, Sandale had been dying and had disappeared, possibly dead or taken by the lawbreakers.

Now, Sandale's face, usually full of kindness and reflecting the humor he was quick to find in the smallest of things, was hard, his lips tight, brows lowered in anger. Was he held by some force against his will?

The urge to help was impossible to resist. He could project a reflection of himself to catch the attention of what appeared to be the leader and then grab Sandale away. He had to act quickly while it was only the three of them.

He studied the trees on the other side of the break. He could have his image come from there and then turn and appear to run back inside. Ducking back from underneath the bush, his long hair caught on a branch. Quietly, he untangled it and backed away to gain a better vantage point.

The view from his new angle did not reassure him. The two men were arguing and Sandale pointed across the clearing, his voice raised. When the other man shook his head, Sandale dropped the unconscious man on the ground.

That was not the man Theron knew. He waited and watched.

When the leader saw Sandale wouldn't be swayed, he picked the small man up and headed off, away from both hidden settlements of the exiles. But Sandale remained watching the trees in the direction of the city of Naralina.

Noise coming from that direction caught Theron's attention

as well. That's what Sandale was waiting for. Maybe he planned to bring down an animal like he had the small man. From the sound of it, it was a larger animal.

Determined to gather as much information about Sandale as he could, Theron moved to get a better view. When he found it, he stared in shock.

Walking across the clearing with her head down and muttering to herself was a lone woman dressed in a short-sleeved shirt and long pants he'd learned were called jeans. Her black hair fell far below her shoulders and her skin was as pale as the white walls of the city of his birth. She was halfway to him before she noticed Sandale staring at her.

"Oh." She stopped then quickly turned her back to him. "I'm sorry. I didn't realize you were there. I mean …um, that you were naked. Is there any chance you can help me? I'm totally lost."

Sandale's gaze raked over her, the lust in his eyes appearing predatory, but she didn't see it. He took a step toward her. "I can help you."

"Oh, good. I followed my sister into this jungle, but she and her husbands, yes I know that sounds a little hard to believe, but she does have two, sort of the opposite of—never mind. What I mean is my sister and her husbands were kissing and it's just—eew. So I turned away."

As the female spoke, Sandale stalked closer.

Everything in Theron's blood told him this wouldn't end well for the young woman.

"That's when I saw this really cute animal that looked like a baby porcupine and I followed it, but then I lost my bearings. So maybe you could put on some clothes so you can…" She yawned.

"Oh my, I'm feeling really tired. Do you have your clothes…" She yawned again and fell to her knees. "on yet?" She turned her head to look. When she did, she scrambled backward.

"What are you doing? Why are you…looking at me like that?" She reached back but her arm buckled out from under her. "Don't…come…near…me." Her words formed slowly.

Sandale was using his ability to calm people to turn her helpless, and from the state of his cock, he seemed to have forgotten every rule of Eden. He was no longer the man Theron respected.

He couldn't allow him to have the woman. Gesturing to the trees on the opposite side, he projected an image of himself walking toward Sandale.

The man spun. "Who are you?" Sandale took two steps toward the reflection. "Never mind. I don't share." He lifted his hand to make the reflection sleep.

Theron kept the image of himself still while he watched the woman take advantage of Sandale's distraction, pleased to see she wasn't frozen with fear.

He backed his reflection toward the trees.

"What?" Sandale's hand came down in anger. "You can't resist me." The tone of his voice was so guttural, Theron barely recognized it. It was as if Sandale was in a state of barely controlled rage. It was so completely opposite of how the man used to be that Theron almost missed the woman standing up. To keep Sandale's attention, he turned the reflection around and had it start running into the woods.

The growling sound that issued from Sandale sent chills through Theron's body. But when Sandale raced into the trees on the other side, Theron turned his attention to the woman headed right for him.

When she ran into him, he wrapped his arm around her head and covered her mouth.

Jaelene didn't know whether to laugh or cry to find herself escaping from one naked man intent on rape only to run into the arms of another naked man who wanted who knew what.

"Shhh, we must be quiet if we don't want him to find you."

The soothing baritone voice did more to slow her panic than his actual words. She nodded against his arm and he lifted his hand away.

"So in other words, don't scream." She raised her head to look at the face of the man that held her and sucked in her breath. His eyes were the deepest brown she'd ever seen. They reminded her of dark chocolate, one of her biggest weaknesses. His cheek bones were prominent and his lips full. The only imperfection was a small bump on his nose.

Those lips lifted slightly. "Yes."

Wow, she needed to focus. She didn't know this man any more than the blond guy.

His hold on her loosened. "We need to leave here. He will soon tire of chasing my reflection and come looking for you."

"Your reflection?"

"Later. Can you run?"

"If you mean fast, then no. I think I have small lungs, but if you need help lifting something…" her gaze moved to his arms. "Never mind."

He turned his back to her as he grinned.

He found her amusing, but she was used to that. No one took her seriously except her sister and her boss.

He bent his knees, and spoke over his shoulder. "Jump on my back. I'll carry you."

She looked at his broad back, the muscles tensed for her weight. A glance below it showed a hard rounded butt and thighs the size of her head. Oh, the man was built. "Are you sure?" Now that was a dumb question.

"Yes."

She glanced back where she'd last seen the blond man headed into the jungle. What choice did she have? At least this man was nice. And seriously hot. She wrapped her arms around his neck and hiked her legs onto his waist. He grabbed a hold of her. She attempted to ignore the sensual feel of his large hands wrapped around her thighs.

He immediately set out at a run.

She tried not to bounce against him too much. She hadn't ridden piggyback since she was eight and she was pretty sure her last ride didn't smell nearly this good.

She inhaled slowly trying to place the scent. It reminded her of hot cocoa on a cold New Jersey night. Maybe she was just hungry.

She tried to keep track of landmarks but it was hopeless. It appeared as if she'd landed in a never ending jungle.

Her moment of triumph when she'd followed her sister through the travel portal was short-lived. She's guessed there was something secretive about how quickly Serena had come and gone, but she'd never imagined the technology actually existed to move around the world so fast. Either Jahl and Khaos were scientists, which she doubted, or they had some working for them.

Losing them had just been stupid on her part. Here she was in a strange country and she follows a cute animal out of earshot of the threesome in the middle of a jungle. Serena was going to kill her.

The man beneath her continued to run, his pace with her on his back faster than she could run by herself. They certainly grew men strong around here.

"Where are we going?" She whispered close to his ear. She didn't want anyone to hear, especially the angry blond man.

The hunk beneath readjusted her weight on his back. Was that a bad sign? Was he tiring?

The woman's whispered words sent a cascade of longing through Theron's body. Holy Bendis, he needed to find her agapaytos soon. It was bad enough he'd fallen for Serena, his leaders' beloved. Even just feeling lust for another taken woman would be hard, and her sweet nutlike scent already had his thoughts straying in that direction. He had to return her to her filoz before he became attached.

He pulled his focus back to her question. "We are going to my secret home."

The need to protect her, even if she was someone else's beloved, had been drilled into him at an early age. It was the way of Eden and part of Dickinson law. For Sandale to ignore it meant his mind must have been severely altered by the lawbreakers.

Her hold on him tightened. Was she afraid to go with him?

"Just until I can return you to your filoz." That he'd caused her fear bothered him. "You will be safe until then."

She didn't exactly relax, but her arms no longer strangled him about the neck. "My filoz?"

He took a moment as he ran over rocks across a small stream. "Yes, your filoz. You have one, don't you?"

"I don't know what a filoz is."

Theron slowed, but didn't stop running as his mind flipped through a number of reasons why she wouldn't know that term. "Yes, your filoz. The men you are connected to. They call it married on Earth."

He felt her silent giggle. "Oh, I'm not married. Why do you say Earth as if we aren't there?"

By the Crius, had the woman landed on Eden by herself somehow? It was impossible to contemplate. There had to be a reason. Every set of men, be it two or five that formed a filoz, watched an Earth woman for years before bringing their chosen one to Eden. That's how it was done. Women didn't simply appear on his planet.

He turned his head to the side slightly. "I will explain everything when we are safe."

"Okay."

Her easy acceptance calmed his own turbulent thoughts, even as his body continued on the path to safety.

He would ask her which Edenists opened the portal that allowed her to step through. It took two Eden men with a Crius chip under the skin beneath their arm to open a portal. Unfortunately, he didn't have anyone to help him open one to help her return to Earth.

She must be a new chosen one separated from her filoz. They would be anxious to find her, unless the lawbreakers had killed them.

Even as the tragic thought formed, a noise above had him stopping and he scanned the trees. With the lawbreakers venturing farther into the jungle, he was on constant alert. It took him a moment to find the object that had made the noise, but when he did, he relaxed. It was only a purple-winged elseire settling into her nest.

"What is it?"

He pointed up. "Nothing to be afraid of. Just a bird coming home."

The woman on his back moved her head. "I don't see it." Her disappointment was evident.

"It's not important." He immediately started running again, but felt her twisting, still trying to find the bird. He didn't know how he would react if he was transported to a new planet and confronted with danger. He doubted finding a native bird would be one of his priorities.

As he neared his lonely cave, he slowed. When he stopped, he bent his knees and let go of the woman's legs. She slid off his back. He turned to speak, but his words failed at her look of admiration.

Clearing his throat, he focused on their situation. "I want you to stay here behind this boulder while I make sure everything is safe."

She nodded as if in a trance.

Gently, he led her to the monolith he'd pointed to and made her crouch down. Then he moved toward his cave and checked for prints of either Edenists or animals. Finding none, he proceeded into his new living quarters.

Satisfied all was safe, he returned outside, pleased to find the woman where he left her. "You can come in now."

She looked around at the trees and the rock formation that showed the entrance to his home. "Come in where?"

"Take my hand and I will show you."

She didn't hesitate, which sent a glow of warmth into his heart. He quickly squashed it. She belonged to others. He led her to what looked like a solid wall of stone, very similar to the one he'd had her hide behind. "Duck your head."

She did and he walked her through the reflection he'd created by linking his ability to create reflections with the eyllen energy stones beneath the ground. It wasn't nearly as elaborate as the one he'd helped create for Loraleaf, but since he now lived in the jungle by himself, he didn't need anything larger.

"Oh wow." The woman stopped, pulling her hand from his. "This is amazing."

Now that he had a moment to look at her, he agreed. He'd felt her breasts pressing against his back and her strong legs around his waist, but her face was lovely. Framed by long, black as night hair, with a pert nose and wide dark blue eyes, she was everything feminine and fragile.

She was a vision for dreams.

Jaelene stared at her surroundings. Walking through stone was something in and of itself, but she'd never expected to find a comfy bungalow inside. The walls had bamboo accents and there were mats thrown on the floor. Along the far wall were bamboo doors. One was open and she could see a large bed inside.

She quickly averted her gaze, still unsure exactly how safe she was. Instead, she turned toward her rescuer to find the outside wall was also bamboo with a large opening as an exit. How could that be?

She moved toward it but the hunk grabbed her arm. "It's not safe out there."

She gazed into his dark eyes and tried to discern if she could trust him. She found his features so distracting, she had to look away. At least he was nicer to her than the angry blond man.

She nodded and stepped back when he released her. If she wanted to leave, she could always go while he slept. He must sleep at some point.

"What is your name?"

She returned her gaze to his. "I'm Jaelene." No need to tell him her last name, just in case. She didn't need a stalker at her heels though her gut said he would never behave so poorly. She lifted her chin a notch. "What's yours?"

He smiled kindly, the corners of his eyes crinkling. Shoot, he was far more handsome than any man she'd ever dated. She lowered her gaze to his muscled chest and felt heat flood her. She'd have to be dead not to be attracted to his rippled abdomen and mounded pectorals.

"I'm Theron of the Kindred of Light."

He pronounced his name like he was the king of a foreign country. "What is this Light Kindred?"

He pointed to the back of his right wrist where there were two parallel lines bracketed by an angled line on each side and three dots near the top between each line. It wasn't black or colored like a tattoo. Instead it was brown like a birthmark.

"This symbol marks me as part of the Kindred of Light. It means I have the ability to control light in some way. It wasn't until I went through the change that I figured out I could reflect it to create existing images."

Okay, so the man thought he could create reflections. Things sounded a little more cultish than she was comfortable with. It was probably best to humor him. It figured she'd find a super-hot hunk only to discover his mind wasn't quite all there. "I see. I've never heard of that, but it sounds fascinating."

His lips quirked up for a second. "I know you don't believe me, but it's not important. What is important is who brought you here. You are not safe without them. Do you know their Kindred?"

He must be speaking in a foreign language. Maybe there were some English words that didn't translate exactly. She pretended to think and took a quick glance at his cock. While it was large, he didn't appear to be aroused, so she remained calm. She finally looked him in the eye. "Okay, so I'm not exactly sure what you mean. Does this Kindred come through that travel portal?"

His eyes lit with excitement. "No, but that is how you got here. It took two Edenists to open it. Do you know their names? If I know them, then I could return you to them."

Now she was getting somewhere. "Of course I know their names. I don't follow strangers into strange places. They are my sister's husbands, Jahl and Khaos."

Theron took a deep breath to steady his suddenly speeding heart. He couldn't bring Jaelene to Loraleaf.

"So do you know them?" She looked hopeful.

"I do." Though he wished he didn't, just for a moment.

"Excellent. That means I can get back with my sister." Her smile faltered. "Of course, she's going to kill me for following her. I knew she was hiding something from me, and she never does that, so I spied on her. I can see why now. If our government knew that some other country had this travel technology, they would be all over her."

"Planet."

"I mean, it's like the kind of space travel she's always talking about in those movies she works on. She blows up — wait, what did you say?"

Theron hesitated. He should let Serena explain, but part of him resented her happiness while his heart was in shreds. "I said, planet. You are on the planet Eden."

She chuckled uncomfortably. "Of course, the planet Eden. I should have known." She winked. "Listen, I wasn't born yesterday. It was more like twenty-eight years, two hundred and eleven days ago. Not that I'm counting. So you can skip over the joke and tell me where I am."

Maybe he should do what Jahl and Khaos had done with Serena and let Jaelene come to her own conclusions. Then again, Serena had been chosen as a beloved because of her belief in life on other planets. Jaelene wasn't chosen, which meant she might not even think his world was possible. "Don't you believe there can be life on other planets?"

She looked down in thought. When her deep blue gaze returned to his, he almost forgot what they were discussing. Her eyes reminded him of the Latzeran Sea, its dark blue waters so beautiful that people were known to ignore the dangers of its depths and drown.

"I never really thought about it." She shrugged one shoulder. "It would be a bit egotistical to think Earth had the only living beings, so I guess I can accept that somewhere out there in another galaxy, there is life."

She held up her index finger. "But I don't accept that there is a portal that I can step through and suddenly be on another planet." She shook her head, her long black hair swishing over her shoulder. "Nope. I know I'm still on Earth. Heck, it was a porcupine that got me lost in the first place. I doubt there are porcupines on other planets." Jaelene crossed her arms as if she'd solved the most important problem in the universe.

There was something endearing about her complete confidence. He liked it. "That was a welchet."

"A what?"

He grinned. "It's a welchet. It looks like a porcupine as you noticed, but it has two tusks that grow down from its bottom jaw for digging up grubs and it has six feet."

She looked at him a moment then shook her head. "Nice try. What I saw was a porcupine. Maybe you just call it something different."

Theron studied her. What would she think when she saw her sister's pet welchet? What would she think of Loraleaf? A stab of longing sliced through his heart at the thought of her seeing his home. He missed it more than he'd thought possible, but just imagining going back caused another pain altogether.

"So will you bring me to my sister?" Jaelene stepped closer and her scent wafted over him again.

His body took notice. She wasn't a chosen one and therefore free for the taking, but every woman must have at least two agapaytos. He had left Konala and Rekah in Loraleaf so it was a moot point. Besides, she had not been chosen, and like Serena's friend, was not attached to any filoz…yet.

She squinted at him. "What's the matter? Is something wrong?" Her eyes widened. "Jahl and Khaos aren't criminals are they?" She grabbed his arm, her small hand pale against his bronze forearm. "She's not in trouble, is she?"

He covered her hand with his own and held it against his arm before looking into her worried eyes. "No, she is fine. She is treated like a queen since Jahl and Khaos are the leaders of Loraleaf."

Jaelene's eyes widened in surprise. "A queen? Shoot, she's going to be impossible to live with now." She stepped away, taking her soft hand with her as she walked deeper into his living area and flopped down on a chair. "So where is this Loraleaf?"

He turned away, not willing to let her see in his eyes how much he missed his home and the brothers of his heart. Instead, he moved to his food cabinet and pulled out a jug of cool water. "It is a day's run from here."

"Oh, then I guess going there today is out."

When he turned, he found her looking down at her hands, her shoulders slumped forward. It took everything he had not to offer to bring her to Loraleaf immediately. "Would you like some water?"

She looked up at the glass he held. "Is it safe to drink? I know in some countries the water can make you sick. What country is this again?"

She cocked her head, looking at him curiously, but she didn't reach for the glass.

He'd been so enraptured by her eyes earlier that he'd failed to notice her small mouth with the bottom lip fuller than the top. It made him want to pull her close and suck on it. Blinking, he moved his gaze to the water. "You won't become ill from drinking this."

At his reassurance, she took the glass from him without touching his hand. "Thank you, I *am* thirsty."

He watched her throat work as she swallowed the cool liquid and he found himself pouring a glass and taking a sip to wet his suddenly dry mouth. When she wiped her lips on her shirt sleeve, he took a gulp.

"That hit the spot." She set the glass on the small bamboo table he had made. "You didn't answer me about what country I'm in."

He turned toward the cabinet again. This was Serena's sister. He needed to respect that and forget that he hadn't had a woman in six years. He spoke over his shoulder. "I think it best if your sister answers that question as I'm sure you will have many questions for her when you see her."

He finally faced her and leaned against the cabinet, his glass in hand. It was his turn to ask the questions and he had many. "Will your sister be happy you are here?"

Jaelene tried to keep her gaze on Theron's face and not rake it over his muscular body, but his face was just as much a distraction. She looked past him in an effort to concentrate because she was far more interested in his body at the moment, which wasn't the norm for her. Then again, it wasn't every day she had a conversation with a naked man either.

"I'm sure she's going to be pissed, but I also think she'll feel a bit relieved that she doesn't have to hide her life from me anymore." At least that's what she hoped.

"And will you ask to have your man to come as well?"

She laughed. "Man? Oh, I don't have a boyfriend, unless you consider Bumble, but he's sixty pounds of mutt."

"Mutt?"

It must be the language thing again. "A mutt is a dog that isn't pure. In this case, Bumble is mostly St. Bernard, but instead of having brown fur, his only color besides white is black, so he may be part black Lab or Border Collie or maybe even Dalmatian. So he's a mutt."

Theron was staring at her with a look of disbelief that made it clear he thought she literally had sex with the dog.

For some odd reason that seemed funny to her and she waved her hand. "Oh no, I was joking about Bumble being my boyfriend. He doesn't even live with me. He's my parents' pet. It's just that he's the only male in my life who gives me unconditional love besides my dad." As he opened his mouth she held up her finger. "Before you ask, my dad simply loves me. There's nothing weird going on there either."

"That's not what I thought." He sounded affronted.

She shouldn't care. She didn't even know him, but she didn't want him to be insulted. He had saved her and could take her to Serena. "I'm sure you didn't. I was just making it clear. I think we have some language issues between us."

He appeared appeased which made her feel a lot more comfortable with him. She'd seen some pretty sensitive men take umbrage at the slightest thing and then hold a grudge. They were the ones she worked with and she doubted very much that Theron was into interior decorating, though his home had a great theme to it. Now, if she could just get him dressed.

"Do you think you could put on some clothes? As hot as you are to look at, it's a little disconcerting to try to talk to you without looking in certain areas."

His lips turned devilish and she sucked in her breath, anticipating his reply.

"I have no problem with you looking at all my 'areas.'"

Shoot, now all she wanted to do was stare at his cock. She

forced her gaze to the two doors that were closed. "*You* may not, but I'm not in the market for a boyfriend right now. My life is way too busy." She pressed her lips together at her bald-faced lie. "So could you put your clothes on?"

"No."

At his refusal, she snapped her head around and frowned at him to hide her nervousness. Yes, she was in a foreign country, but to have a man refuse to clothe himself had to be a danger sign. "Why not?"

"I don't own any clothes."

She stared open mouthed for a second before snapping her jaw shut and scanning the room. "Are you saying you are too poor to buy clothes when you obviously had the money to furnish this place?"

Theron shook his head. "That is not how our society works. We don't have rich and poor as you define it. This furniture I made. And as for clothes," he shrugged, "we don't wear any."

She crossed her arms. "So you're trying to tell me that your country doesn't use money and no one wears clothes?"

"Exactly." He smiled, obviously missing the sarcasm in her voice.

This was just plain bizarre. Then again, a naked man living in a cave that looked like a bamboo hut inside wasn't exactly normal.

Was the man a hermit? Maybe he was mentally unbalanced, though that would be a shame because he had the body of a professional soccer player on steroids. "I'm sorry, but this is all very strange for me. Is there a woman nearby I could talk to?"

Theron's face lost its enthusiasm. "No, there isn't. The closest settlement is Haven and we couldn't make it there before nightfall. It is too dangerous to be in the jungle at night."

"But it was only just after dinner when I came through the portal."

He hesitated to answer her which made her nervous. Was he trying to figure out what lie she might believe?

"Daylight fades early this time of year."

Her growing panic steadied. "Oh, so we must be on the other side of the equator. I can understand that."

Was it her or did he look relieved?

"Let me show you where you can sleep."

Her panic started growing again. "Sleep? I can sleep right here."

Theron's face grew serious. "No. I cannot allow you such an uncomfortable accommodation. You must sleep in my bed."

Okay, that was it. Jaelene stood up. "Let's get something clear. I'm not sleeping with you, even if you *are* the most attractive man I've ever laid eyes on. I don't know you from Adam and I'm not *that* kind of girl."

Theron's brows drew together in confusion. "I do not know who Adam is, but I don't want to sleep with you. I just want you to sleep in my bed. I will sleep here. What kind of girl do you mean?"

She felt her cheeks heat with embarrassment. Of course he didn't want to have sex with her. Men often asked her out based on her looks and small talk. Once they had a real conversation with her, they lost interest and she and Theron had had nothing but *real* conversation. Now who looked like an egotistical diva? "Never mind."

He continued to look puzzled and she couldn't resist trying to explain.

"I think it's just another language issue. In my country, when someone wants to sleep with someone else, it means they want to have sex. I based my reaction on your words, but I see now that is not how you would refer to, well, you know."

His face cleared. "I would like to have sex with you, but I know that it can take women a little while to adjust to our pl—pleasant country." He smiled encouragingly.

She wasn't stupid. He'd been about to say something else. Place? Pleasurable ways? Plague? Now she was over-reacting again. "Why just women? Don't men need time to adjust if they are from another country?" She crossed her arms, not happy with what appeared to be some machoism going on.

Again, Theron avoided her gaze and walked by her toward the open door. He stopped before entering. "Foreign men do not visit us."

At his statement, he continued into the next room, shutting the door behind him.

No men came to his country? Only women? It sounded like a cult again. Would she ever get to leave? Her body started to rev into panic mode again.

She strode toward the outside door but paused as a thought occurred. Serena had come home to visit, so leaving *had* to be an option. Her heart slowed to a more normal pace.

It was like riding an emotional roller coaster. As much as she shouldn't trust Theron, her gut told her she was hundred percent better off with him than with the blond dude. Everything would be better once she united with her sister, or rather after her sister stopped yelling at her.

Jaelene continued toward the door, watching outside. The landscape was amazing, especially with the sun setting. It reminded her of the time she went ziplining in Costa Rica, but in this jungle, everything was bigger. The trees were taller and wider, the leaves on the bushes as big as her head, and the grass thicker. At least it wasn't more humid or she wouldn't be able to breathe.

There must be serious nutrients in the soil here. A bird with the appropriate large wing span caught her attention as it flew by, its feathers a bright shiny purple that complimented the purple sunset. "Oh wow." She watched as it landed in the top branches of some kind of deciduous tree, folding its wings against itself until not a single purple feather showed, its body the green color of the leaves surrounding it.

Now that was amazing. She couldn't wait to tell Serena about it. She'd ask Theron what type of bird it was. She glanced back toward the closed door of his bedroom. Faint sounds came from behind it as he moved around. What was he doing in there? Maybe his room was a mess and he was cleaning it up just for her. Now that would be a first.

Movement outside caught her attention and it took her a moment to figure out what it was, but when she did, she shivered. It was a huge cat of some sort. She'd never seen anything like it. It was like a chameleon, its fur blending with the environment, changing as it moved between a green bush with brilliant pink flowers and the brown dead tree trunk on the ground.

"Wow, you're beautiful, but I'm glad I'm in here and not out…" she swallowed hard as the cat turned and looked directly at her. It could see her? She looked at the little bamboo door with its big window. If that cat wanted to come in, there'd be no stopping it. She kept absolutely still, hoping the animal wouldn't catch her scent, but when it started to stroll toward her, she lost it.

"Theron!"

CHAPTER TWO

He must have heard the fear in her voice because the door behind her was thrown open and in less than a second he was by her side. "What is it?"

She pointed to the cat, her stomach in her throat, making it impossible to form more words.

Theron put his hand on her shoulder and squeezed it gently. "It's okay. That's Talia."

She snapped her gaze to his face. "Talia? You know this tiger, cat, whatever it is?"

He nodded calmly. "Yes, I do and she's friendly. Would you like to meet her?"

She stared dumfounded at him for a moment as his words registered. A big cat the size of a sabretooth tiger was friendly?

She looked back toward the approaching animal. It didn't look friendly, but the opportunity to touch such a unique beast was too much for her to resist. She nodded.

"Good. Come." Theron took her hand and it felt like a magnetic pulse flowed from him to her, gluing them together, but that had to be her imagination.

Opening the bamboo door, Theron walked her a couple feet in front of his cave. She stared as the cat approached, squeezing Theron's hand harder and harder as Talia came closer.

He chuckled. "Trust me. She won't hurt you. I would never put you in danger."

The sincerity of his words took the edge off her terror and her own anticipation had her excited, but her human instinct wouldn't let her fear back off.

"Good evening, Talia. Have you come for your combing?" A rumbling started in the big cat's chest and Theron chuckled. "I thought so."

Was the cat actually purring? Jaelene watched as Theron held his hand out and the cat pushed its large head, which was stripped green like the grass at the moment, against Theron's hand. She stared, fascinated as Theron rubbed Talia behind the ears.

"I want you to meet my new friend. Her name is Jaelene." He lowered his voice. "Hold out your hand so she can gain your scent."

Hesitantly, she did, but forgot to be afraid as the cat's fur started to sport pink polka dots, the color of her nail polish. After a cursory sniff, the large head bumped against her hand and she immediately started to pet her.

"She's so sweet." The cat must have sensed an animal lover as it pushed its body up against hers and she let go of Theron's hand to give the now blue jean colored fur a good scratching.

"She comes by every evening, just before the darkness. I think her sleeping nest must be nearby."

Jaelene wanted to hug the big cat, but despite her excitement, a little common sense prevailed. She heard of tiger and lion owners being attacked by their animals after years of trust being built. "Did you say she sleeps in a nest, like in a tree?"

The cat moved back to Theron and his larger, stronger hands and he gave her a back massage.

"Yes, but it's not like a bird. It's much lower in the trees and is formed by the tigran scratching deep into the branches and trunk to form a hollow for sleeping."

She grinned as Talia stretched her paws out and lay down, fully expecting Theron to continue rubbing her. She reminded Jaelene of a big tabby she'd found with a broken leg. That animal had been orange, and stayed orange, but even after the vet added a splint, he still managed to lie just like Talia to get his back brushed.

"She reminds me of a house cat, only a dinosaur version."

Theron gave Talia two final pats on her back, letting her know he was done. Stretching as she stood, she sauntered away without even looking back. With the coming darkness and her color change, Jaelene lost her within seconds. "I love her. Does she have a mate? How many times does she breed? What does she eat and why didn't she want to eat us?"

Theron grinned and took her hand. "First, we go inside where it is safe. Then I will answer your questions."

She liked that he held her hand and the tiny buzz she got from it.

He led her toward the big rock. She only remembered to duck after he did. Walking through a rock was a new experience for her. She'd have to add that to her list of questions for him. How did he figure out the rock wasn't solid and how come Talia saw her, even though she couldn't see inside the cave from outside?

After they entered, he turned, closed the door then fastened what looked like dead vines across it and around hooks.

"Is that how you lock your door?"

He nodded, though he didn't look at her, his focus on securing the door for the night. She didn't exactly mind the view. As he tugged on the ropes, his back muscles rippled and his biceps flexed. She couldn't help letting her gaze wander over his backside, which was taut as he leaned. Even his calves bulged with tension until he completed his task and turned around.

She quickly switched her gaze to the cabinet he'd stood against earlier. The darkness outside reminded her of exactly how dangerous a situation she might be in. Sure Talia was sweet, but other animals, even humans, might want in. "Will those vines hold if the blond man finds us?"

Thereon stepped to her and laid both his hands on her shoulders. "You are safe with me. Nothing will harm you while I breathe." His face, so serious, relaxed and he gestured with his head. "The infragile vines are unbreakable once they've been separated from their original plant for a full day."

It took her a minute to focus—his yummy scent and dark gaze caused her mind to wander. His willingness to protect her with his life when he knew so little about her was overwhelmingly kind. Without thought, she leaned forward and kissed him on the cheek. "Thank you."

Theron's surprise was obvious as his mouth opened, but his dark eyes seemed to reflect a light from within him as he stared at her.

That was too weird. "It's getting pretty dark in here. I don't imagine you have electricity out here."

He removed his hands from her shoulders and moved to his cabinet.

She missed the warmth of his touch. For such a big man, he was incredibly gentle.

Theron spoke over his shoulder. "No, we don't have electricity like you have on your, ah, in your country. Here we have mineral energy. That is what powers this shiner." Light appeared to glow from his hand, but as he turned, she could see it was some kind of lantern.

He moved to a hook drilled into the ceiling and hung the light on it.

"Wow, that lights up the whole room." She could actually see a lot more than she had while there was still light filtering through the window in the door. She glanced at it, fearful the light might give them away, but the window was covered with bamboo. Still, light could seep through. "Will the light show outside?"

Theron shook his head. "No. It is being reflected back in here."

She couldn't see how, but she'd take his word for it. It wasn't as if she had any choice.

"Would you like something to drink?" He'd opened the bottom of the cabinet.

"That would be great. What do you have?" She moved to get a closer look. From her viewpoint, it seemed everything of any use was in his floor to ceiling cabinet.

"I have ambrosia. It isn't as good as what is served in the settlements because I am not an expert at making it, but it is passable."

"Ambrosia?" It sounded like it would put her out like a date rape drug. "Is it strong?"

He frowned. "I'm not sure what you mean by strong. It's sweet and refreshing. What you call sugar is very rare here, so this is considered a treat because the fruit and nut give it a semi-sweet taste."

They didn't have sugar? She shrugged her shoulder. "Why not? I like trying new food and drink as long as it won't make me sick." She raised one eyebrow in question.

Theron poured some of the orangey-pink clear liquid into a red glass. "I'm beginning to think in your past you had food and water that your body did not like." He handed her the glass. "But no need to worry here."

She held the glass to her nose and sniffed. It reminded her of suntan lotion, a coconut-mango scent. Hesitantly, she took a sip and then another. "Oh wow. That is delicious. There's a bunch of flavor in this and—oh, a spicy kick in the after taste. This could be addictive. Is there alcohol in it?"

Theron shrugged. "We don't make anything here called alcohol."

She took a good swallow, letting her mouth enjoy the after-taste before she tried to explain. "Alcohol is a liquid that will cause a person to act differently than normal and if too much is imbibed, he or she might stumble as they walked and even fall down and pass out."

He gestured to the chair she'd sat in earlier and she walked to it, pleased to discover no ill side effects from the delicious drink.

"We do have drinks that can make you excited or relaxed and they can affect how a person acts if too much of one kind is imbibed, but ambrosia has none of those ingredients." Theron sat on a large cut log that looked like part of a stump.

She hadn't noticed it before. But she did notice that his package hung down between his spread legs and she quickly took another sip of ambrosia, focusing on the glass in her hand. If it did have alcohol in it, she'd be all over him in about ten minutes. She was a true lightweight.

"You had a number of questions about Talia. I will try to answer them, but Konala would know a lot more."

"Who's Konala?"

"He is part of my filoz. I have two brothers of my heart in my filoz, Konala and Rekah. Konala is very good with animals. He's Kindred of Eden and can communicate with them."

Excitement streaked through her. "Oh my God, that's so amazing. I love animals, like ridiculously. I was always bringing home a stray. My parents made me find forever homes for every single one because if we had kept them all, they said they would have had a zoo."

She grinned at the memory of her mother's face when she had said that the first time. "And they would have. I saw nothing wrong with it until I was much older. I adore animals. I even volunteer at the local zoo. I thought about being a vet, but I could never take a knife and operate on an animal." She shook her head for emphasis.

"Then you will enjoy talking with Konala. He can tell you about every animal on this p—land. What I can tell you is that most tigran are friendly to people, though they can take down a feroon in the blink of an eye and those are very big animals, about the size of your elephant. Tigran have a harder time with direlots because they are so ferocious and cunning."

"If tigrans can be so aggressive, why do they like humans? I would think they would want to eat us. Our tiger, which is half the size of Talia, would just as soon have us for dinner."

Theron shook his head. "We are the only species that can rub their fur. The changing colors of their coat can make the skin underneath stiff. Except for rubbing their backs on trees, which they don't do very well, tigran need us to scratch them."

"That is beyond amazing. What about babies and mating for life and food and—"

Theron raised his hand as he chuckled. "You will have to speak to Konala about that. What I know is from him, but I didn't ask nearly as many questions."

"I'm sorry. When it comes to animals, I get a bit carried away." And this is why she didn't get second dates. Her mouth ran off without her brain.

He took another sip of his drink before responding. "Actually, I find it refreshing. You make me aware of how much I don't know."

So in other words, she made him feel stupid. Now she felt like an idiot. Maybe they should talk about something he did know. "You said you had two brothers, but you didn't call them that."

"They are the brothers of my heart which means they are very close friends and we have committed to live together and when we find our chosen one, she will complete us."

Jaelene paused, her glass halfway to her mouth. "You mean three husbands to one woman?"

Theron nodded, but looked away.

What wasn't he telling her? "Who is your other brother? What does he do?"

"His name is Rekah. He can sense people's emotions."

She may not have Rekah's empathy, but it was clear that Theron was uncomfortable talking about his family or filoz. If he had such a great family, why was he living in a cave by himself? She had to ask. "So why are you here and not with Konala and Rekah?"

The sharp pain in Theron's chest was too much to bear in front of a woman. He stood and strode by her toward the door at the back wall of the cave. "I forgot something you will need tonight. I will return."

He closed the door behind him and the darkness of the cave surrounded him. Looping a piece of infragile vine over a peg, he locked it.

He walked past some of his stored provisions and moved deeper into the cave which burrowed under the land and split off in various directions, none of which he'd explored. Over the last three months, he'd focused on making a home for himself, trying to blot out the pain he felt. Usually his labors helped him sleep, but Jaelene's simple question in the dark of night brought his pain to the surface.

"Theron?" Her voice was muffled by the sturdy door and the space he put between them.

But it reminded him he couldn't go far. She was his responsibility now. Serena's sister.

Serena.

His heart ached as he pictured her, but his shame at having fallen for the chosen one of his leaders twisted deep in his gut. He'd done the only thing he could do.

Leave.

Which meant he'd left the brothers of his heart, the men

he'd grown up with, the men he had expected to share a beloved with.

But if he had stayed, every woman they suggested would have been compared to Serena. He fervently hoped that Konala and Rekah would find a beloved and be happy. He'd hurt them when he left, but to stay had been impossible. To see Serena happy with Jahl and Khaos would have driven him insane.

Theron took a deep breath and forced his fisted hands to relax. He'd made a home for himself and despite his anguish, he'd made the right decision.

He would be alone the rest of his life, but that wasn't completely unheard of. The members of the Triad in Naralina did not belong to a filoz or take an agapayto. As the moral mentors of society, they had to be free of family connections that might impair their clear judgment.

Not that he was such a stellar being. He snorted. Men like those who served on the Triad did not fall in love with their leaders' beloved.

"Theron? Are you still here?" Jaelene's worried voice broke through his self-flagellation.

She was totally dependent on him until she reunited with her sister. He would not fail her as well. He raised his voice, forcing his throat to relax. "I will be there shortly."

The door jiggled. "Okay."

He pressed his palms against the cool wall of the cave. The minute vibration that flowed from it and into his body calmed him. It had been this property of the cave that enticed him to make his home inside it. He didn't know what caused it or how it worked, but it had given him the peace he needed when he most needed it.

He stepped closer and leaned his forehead against the wall as well, feeling the need to fortify himself against his own mind. After he'd left Loraleaf, night had become the hardest part of the day for him.

After minutes of calming, he finally stepped away, staring into the darkness as if he could see the wall. With his emotions once again under control, he headed back toward his new home, the light filtering in from the living area pointed the way like a warm beacon.

Before opening the door, he rummaged through his baskets to find what he'd been bent on getting for Jaelene, a piece of fruit with sleeping properties that would help her rest.

He must keep her needs and wants at the forefront of his mind if he was to reunite her with her sister. The question was, how to do that without returning to Loraleaf himself?

He unlooped his lock and stilled as his hand gripped the door latch. Of course! He would connect with one of the patrols sent out to watch for lawbreakers and bring her to them. Hopefully, the patrol would not consist of either Konala or Rekah.

Theron opened the door and stepped inside. Jaelene stood no more than a foot away, her blues eyes filled with concern.

"I'm sorry if I upset you. I didn't mean to pry."

He forced his lips to curve upwards. "You did not pry. You just reminded me that I wanted to give you this." He held out his hand, palm up so she could see the luscious red of the kerasi fruit.

Her eyes widened. "I've never seen a fruit this color." She picked it up and turned it in her hand. "Oh wow, it changes. I thought it was red, but now it looks yellow." She moved it again. "No, it's red. Does everything here change color? I mean first Talia and now this—what did you call it?"

His smile came easier this time. "It's a kerasi. It will help you relax so you can sleep well."

She slanted her gaze up at him. "What do you mean, sleep well?"

She was definitely cautious about what she ate and drank. He tried to think of something from Earth that would equate to it. "I'm not sure, but I believe it is like Chamomile."

Jaelene lifted the fruit to her nose and sniffed. "It doesn't smell like anything."

He enjoyed her curiosity. "No, it doesn't. If it did, the animals might eat it and lounge around forgetting to hunt for their dinner."

She cocked her head. "Really?"

He chuckled. "No. It's just how the fruit grows. You don't have to eat it. I only thought of it because you have had a disturbing day and may want something to relax your mind so you can rest well."

Her mouth opened slightly and her gazed softened. "That's so thoughtful of you."

He shrugged. "I'm not the expert. Rekah would know exactly what would help you sleep." Theron had used the fruit on more than one occasion when he'd first left Loraleaf after escorting Serena's friend Toni to Naralina. Now Konala was in charge of communicating with Toni via the animals. He hoped all was well with that endeavor.

Jaelene yawned, putting her free hand in front of her mouth, but she still hadn't taken a bite of the kerasi. Maybe she didn't need it after all.

"Here," he opened his arm toward the bedroom door, "let me show you my room so you can go to bed. Tomorrow will be an arduous day traveling to reunite with your sister."

She hesitated to move, the indecision clear in her eyes. At least he didn't need Rekah to understand what she felt.

"I promise, you will have the room to yourself. There is a loop of infragile vine you can use to lock the door. I will sleep out here and keep you safe."

Jaelene smiled shyly. "I'm really glad *you* came to my rescue." She laid her hand on his arm pulling him down and rose on her toes to kiss his cheek. "Thank you." She whispered the words against his face then let go and turned away, but he caught the blush on her cheeks.

As the door to his room shut behind her, he raised his finger to the spot where she'd kissed him. Comfort filled his soul as he stared at the closed door.

Her first kiss had surprised him. This second kiss did as well, but once she'd touched his arm and the buzz of connection skidded through his body, he'd known what she would do. It had taken more willpower than he'd expected not to turn his head and capture her lips. He may be in love with her sister, but his attraction to her was undeniable.

He would deny it though. It was imperative he protect her but keep her at arm's length. He must have been born under an unlucky star to have first fallen in love with the wrong woman, and then be attracted to that woman's sister while being forced to keep her safe.

Anger at his situation Eden began to build in his heart until Jaelene's words floated back to him. *I'm really glad you came to my rescue.*

Where would she be right now if he hadn't been tracking the lawbreakers and recognized Sandale and his ability to do her harm?

The Crius must have been smiling down on Jaelene today and now he must see his "rescue" through. Knowing he was meant for a better purpose quelled his rising frustration.

He reviewed the furniture in the room, the two chairs, small table and short shelf. None of it was conducive to sleeping. There must be something he could use in his supply room. Taking his shiner from its hook on the ceiling, he opened the third door off his living area and scanned the shelves and baskets on the floor.

The light reflected off the basket of siris webbing, causing it to glisten. The webbing was soft and he planned to weave pads for his furniture with it, but in the meantime it would make a bearable bed. Placing his shiner on a shelf far from the very flammable webbing, he picked up the basket and brought it to the living area.

After retrieving the shiner and placing it on the counter of his main cabinet, he quickly spread all the webbing he had. It was only the length and width of his body, but it would do. He walked to a peg in the cave wall near the door and lifted the clear hesta from it. The thin blanket was warm, but he didn't plan to use it as a blanket.

Theron folded the hesta in three and rolled it up. He placed it at one end of his makeshift bed before returning to the shiner. After extinguishing the light, he waited for his eyes to adjust to the blackness.

He lay down on the siris webbing and silently sighed. His day had not gone as expected, but for that he was grateful. Closing his eyes he focused on Jaelene's myriad expressions and drifted off to sleep.

Jaelene finished the eggs Theron had cooked her for breakfast. A man who could cook was one thing, but a man who cooked naked was in a whole other category, as in the drool-worthy category.

She took another sip of the kafez that tasted an awful lot like coffee to her, but a bit stronger. Luckily, Theron allowed her to add water to it and didn't look insulted. She had the feeling he found her amusing. There were worse things he could think.

She'd locked the door when she went to bed, just as a precaution. She doubted Theron would do anything to hurt her. She was only concerned about him making a move on her. She doubted she could resist. They grew their men big and strong in this country. It was like walking into a gym of men working out, except these didn't have any clothes on.

The kerasi fruit had soothed her nerves as well last night, so she'd slept like the dead and felt refreshed. She was an early riser, but not as early as Theron. When she walked out of the bedroom, he was already cooking her breakfast at the counter with the cabinet. The counter pulled off and beneath was some type of heating element.

He'd scrambled the eggs with spices she'd never had before and she'd actually asked for seconds. He seemed pleased that she liked them.

The view of his hard butt and play of muscles in his back as he worked had provided her with sweet entertainment. So much better than the morning show she usually watched before heading to work.

Now, Theron was out "scouting," as he put it. She couldn't wait to see Serena and tell her about everything she'd learned, especially about Talia and the bird with purple wings that Theron said was called an elseire.

She brought her plate to the cabinet and found a tub of water. She'd just dropped her plate in when the door opened.

"We will have to wait to leave." Theron's frown discouraged her excitement.

"Why? What is it?"

"There are lawbreakers very close by. It would be too dangerous for you."

Her heart sank. "Are they the same ones from yesterday?"

He nodded. "I need to follow them and see where they are going. I won't take any chances with you."

The thrill his protective attitude sent through her was quickly squashed by the idea of Theron leaving her alone, which scared her more than she cared to admit.

"I want you to stay inside the cave while I track them. As soon as I'm sure they are headed in the opposite direction from where we need to go, I will come back and get you."

"What if you get hurt?"

He shook his head. "I won't. My first duty is to protect you."

She'd never heard of such a thing. The man didn't even know her but he would put himself in danger for her? "What country is this again?"

He hesitated. "Naralina is the nearby city."

The name didn't ring any bells, but she wasn't exactly an expert on cities.

Theron turned back to the door and pointed to the ties on the side made from the vine he said was unbreakable. "Loop these in place after I leave and don't open it for anyone except me."

"Okay." She wanted to run to him and get a hug before he left, but that was silly. She was a grown woman and she barely even knew him.

Theron didn't open the door though his hand was on the latch. He appeared to be thinking. Unexpectedly, he let go, strode to her and hugged her to him. "Be safe."

She barely heard the words whispered into the hair on top of her head, but she squeezed him back, thankful he'd intuitively known what she needed.

She loved the warm, cocoa scent of him. It reassured her. Of course the strong arms wrapped around her certainly didn't hurt either.

After a couple minutes, he pulled back and placed his hands on her shoulders. "Better?"

She nodded and gave him a small smile. The man was a genius.

He nodded once. "Good. Now I must go. The sooner I track them, the faster I can return and bring you to your sister."

"Good luck."

He thought about her words for a moment then nodded once again. "Thank you." He immediately strode back to the door, opened it, and disappeared into the jungle.

She didn't want to find out what would happen if someone were to stumble upon the cave, so she quickly "locked" the door.

She'd already tried to break the vine that served as the lock. There was some of it on the other door in the bedroom, the one that led to an odd bathroom, but she hadn't been able to make a dent in it. She hoped it would hold against anyone stronger trying to get into the cave.

She busied herself with cleaning the dishes and discovering

where they belonged. Then she straightened up, swept the floor, which seemed to have tiny sparkles on it that she hadn't noticed yesterday, and investigated everything in the cabinet, including what appeared to be a small fridge. In between her activities, she anxiously looked outside.

When there was nothing else to do, and Theron still had not returned, she started to explore. She ignored his bedroom, as tempting as it was, out of respect for him, and instead opened the middle door in the back of the living room.

The other side was as dark as a black hole in space, something Serena was fascinated by, but not something she was in a hurry to become acquainted with. She could use the lantern Theron had lit the night before, but she'd looked it over while investigating the contents of his cabinet and couldn't figure out how to turn it on.

She opened the door wider, hoping some of the daylight from outside would pierce the darkness, but except for the first few feet where baskets of various fruits lined one wall, she could see nothing. It must be another room, maybe like a root cellar. She listened and could hear a faint trickle of water.

That had to be it. Caves were usually cool and damp, though she'd noticed in the "bathroom" that the water trickling from the wall into the ingenious stone sink was warm. That alone had impressed her. The water was a continuous trickle and the sink was plugged at the bottom, but it had an overflow hole a couple inches from the top and the water went down it when it reached that high. The soft sound of the water had lulled her to sleep.

She glanced back over her shoulder to look out the window. Still no sign of him. She wasn't sure she missed him because she liked who he was or because she wasn't usually alone, despite living in her own apartment. She had lots of friends.

Stepping back into the living room, she closed the door. Her friends were going to love her stories about this place. She just needed to know which country she was in so she could look up a few supporting details on the internet when she got home.

She strode to the door and looked out. The tree leaves moved a bit as a soft breeze blew, but other than that, she couldn't see anything moving. As tempted as she was to open the door and listen, she didn't dare. She knew nothing about the area and if Theron said to stay inside for her own safety then she would.

Turning away from the door, she scanned the room. "One door left." Moving toward her target, she envisioned what might be on the other side. A den? A hot spring? Maybe a laboratory. She opened the door and stared. "Another storage room."

Though a little disappointed the room wasn't something more unique that she could talk about with her girlfriends, she busied herself with reviewing the contents. There was everything from food to tools in the room. What was strange was how rudimentary some of the items were, yet others were so modern she wasn't exactly sure what they might be used for.

As she picked up what looked like a drill but there was no cord to plug it in, she heard a sound coming from outside. She set down the tool and listened.

There was definitely something out there. She ran to the window. The noise was louder now, like a moan, and it came from the right of the entrance, but she couldn't see what caused it. It sounded like someone in pain. Theron?

Worry and fear for him tightened her chest. What if he was

hurt and couldn't get back into the cave? Her hands began to sweat and she nibbled at her bottom lip. Should she call out? What if it was one of the criminals and Theron had wounded him. If he wasn't dead, he could still do her harm.

The noise came again. It was clearly more a whimper this time and less a moan. She moved to the far side of the door and tried to see around the corner. At first she didn't see anything, but then what looked like a cow's tail on the ground rose and fell with the whimper.

An animal was hurt!

She might be able to ignore a wounded criminal, but an animal was a completely different story. She'd also learned from experience, when she'd been bit and scratched by a raccoon with a broken leg, that no matter how much she wanted to help, an animal in pain could be dangerous.

She scanned the contents of the living room but didn't see anything she could use to shield herself. She grabbed the small cloth she'd dried the dishes with and looked around for a weapon, just in case. There had been something in the storage room.

Throwing the door wide, she spotted what she was looking for. It reminded her of a fireplace poker, but it wasn't metal. It was more like a finely honed spear. She strode to the corner of the door and peered out to see if the animal was still there. She couldn't hear anything, but she caught the telltale swish of the tail.

Cautiously, she unhooked the infragile vine and opened the door.

CHAPTER THREE

Jaelene examined the immediate area for any threat. Nothing moved but the breeze and the tail. She listened for voices but could only hear the chirps of birds and the sound of leaves rustling in the very tops of the trees.

The animal whimpered again, ending on a moan and her heart contracted. *The poor thing.* She took two steps away from the door and paused.

Now the beast was in clear view and it was huge. It looked like a bison lying on its side, only without all the fur, just a shiny smooth brown hide with splotches of black on its legs. The enormous stomach rose and fell rhythmically except for when the animal gave out a low moan.

Jaelene swallowed. She was no vet, but she might be able to help. Her worry for the beast easily outweighed her fear, so she moved slowly toward it. She didn't want to scare it and cause more injury.

The animal's stomach hesitated in its breathing and a massive head lifted from the ground to look back at her.

She froze. Holy guacamole with jalapenos! The thing looked like it had crawled out of the primordial abyss.

Its head was bigger than a bison's and had the horns of bull. Its face was a big flat rectangle dusted with a smattering of fur and two small eyes placed far apart. The weirdest feature was that its top lip appeared to fall well over its lower lip and flopped about as it turned back to lay its head down again. The large stomach rose with a breath that ended in a whimper.

The poor thing was not only ugly but hurting. She sincerely hoped it was more like a docile cow than a bison. She'd never seen anything like it and she'd seen a lot of animals. Every night she flipped back and forth between her favorite animal channel and the one on international living.

She crept forward, not wanting to startle the animal and have it get up and charge her. Approaching from behind was not a good idea, so she made a wide arc around it, splitting her attention between it and the jungle around her.

She didn't like being outside the cave without Theron, the memory of the lethargic feeling she'd had around the blond man still very fresh in her mind, but that was probably because of some plant she'd been standing in. This beast was clearly suffering.

As she made her way to the front of it, its eyes focused on her for a bare moment before closing and it let out another moan. Usually, a hurt animal was wary, but this one reminded her of a beached dolphin, helpless.

She continued her walk around, trying to figure out why it lay there. She saw no blood and its four legs didn't look broken. Maybe it ate something poisonous. She walked back toward the head, a little more confident that it was definitely down and out.

"What's wrong, sweetie? Are you in pain?" She kept her voice soft and low, but still the eyelids snapped up.

Konala grabbed a vine and swung over to the highest wooden walkway that ran along the length of Loraleaf, high up in the trees, anxious to tell Rekah the good news. The henny had hatched all six of her eggs. Not only was she happy but very proud.

He'd worried about her after the last two clutches he let her sit on didn't hatch. Rekah's idea to let her sit on more to help the odds had worked better than anticipated. The news should bring at least a glimmer of a smile to Rekah's face.

Konala nodded as a man strode by him, a certain jaunt in his step. Everyone in Loraleaf was excited about finding their beloveds. Everyone but Rekah.

Theron's leaving had hurt, deeply, but Konala was too far in tune with animal life and the life cycle of Eden to hold onto the hurt.

Living days were limited and he wanted to have what Jahl, Khaos and Serena had, but every time he got Rekah to open the portal and look for a possible chosen one, Rekah didn't pay attention or found problems with every possibility.

He rubbed the top of his head, still getting used to the shorter hair he sported. It was even shorter than Rekah's, but then again, Rekah had let his grow. He'd even let his beard grow. There had to be a way to jolt Rekah into life again.

The man rarely smiled anymore and the rest of the men were in no hurry to seek his counsel unless they were equally saddened. But that was rare because Jahl had given permission for every filoz to start looking for a beloved from Earth. Now that Serena was a permanent part of Loraleaf, she could help new women adjust as they were brought to Eden.

Konala stepped into the lift and sent it down past two more levels of wooden walkways. The lack of men seeking Rekah's counsel didn't help matters either. Rekah liked to give advice and he was good at it.

His gut told him that Rekah was hoping Theron would return. He continuously volunteered for patrols, especially when they were to confer with Haven's patrols.

They were supposed to be watching for signs of lawbreakers and any indication their missing leader, Sandale, had survived, but Konala was convinced Rekah only went out to seek news of Theron.

That was the last time he saw the brother of his heart smile, when he spoke to a Haven man named Mykl, who told him he'd met Theron and had traded with him. That was over a cycle of Selene ago, and since then there was no further word. Edenists were a social collective species that depended on one another for survival, which meant the chances for Theron surviving on his own were not good.

He secretly hoped, for Theron's sake, that he joined with someone from Haven.

Stepping off the lift, Konala strode to the entrance of their home. As he opened the door, the scent of feroon stew hit him. Rekah liked to cook, which Konala had no problem with. "It smells great in here." He stepped into the meal room to find Rekah stirring the contents of a pot on the heat top, his movements practiced.

"No one has been to see me all day, so I decided to get our meal prepared." Rekah's voice was monotone, more proof that he continued to go through life's motions, but wasn't actually involved.

Konala pulled out a chair and straddled it. The position gave him a good view of Rekah's profile. "I have good news. Our henny hatched all six of her eggs. If they live to adulthood, we can start sharing the produce. We will probably lose one, but we can let the mother sit on a few more if that happens."

"That's good."

He watched Rekah closely. They had been friends since they went through the change to manhood. He may not have Rekah's ability to know other's emotions, but he'd known the man long enough to read body language and he didn't like the story Rekah was radiating.

His body was far too relaxed. Every muscle in his back, ass and legs barely moved as if it was too much effort. His sadness was taking a toll. He'd even gained weight, which was rare in Loraleaf.

Konala purposefully kept his tone upbeat. "Have you thought of any new dishes you could make with the eggs we're going to have?"

"*If* we have them."

Konala didn't know if it was Rekah's answer or just that he was tired of being the only one in the filoz to move forward, but Rekah's response to the henny's accomplishment pushed his temper over the edge. *He was done.*

He pushed the chair out from under him, scrapping it across the wood floor and slammed it back into place.

At the noise, Rekah finally faced him, his usually trim beard looking scraggly.

"When are you going to start living again? We've been hoping the henny would hatch babies for half a year now and you treat it like it's another breath of air. By the Crius, Rekah, Theron is gone!

He's not coming back. I've been patient, letting you grieve the loss of our brother, but it's enough."

Rekah's eyes widened in shock before he scowled. "There is no limitation on grief. You talk of Theron as if he's dead. He's not. He's out there struggling to survive when he should be here with us." He threw the ladle on the counter. "He could walk through that door at any moment. That's called hope, Konala."

He sneered. "Hope? Is that what you call it when you sleep until mid-day and you shower but once every three days?" He pointed to Rekah's beard. "You look like a lawbreaker. If Theron *did* walk in that door, he would be saddened to see you like this. How do you think it makes me feel to lose one brother of my heart to the jungle and the other to grief? I've lost my filoz in three short turns of Selene. Maybe I need to search out another."

"You can't." Rekah's scowl slipped.

Konala fisted his hands. "I can and I will if you don't join the living again. Theron may prefer to be alone, but I don't. It's your decision and I suggest you make it quickly."

Rekah's mouth opened but he didn't speak.

"Let me know when you do. In the meantime, I'll be at Libations and after my lunch I'll find somewhere else to stay. If you want to be alone in your grief, I'm happy to accommodate you." He turned on his heel and strode out of the room.

Though his heart ached to hear Rekah say something, his wish was left unfulfilled as he slammed the front door and headed for the lift. Maybe a few mixed drinks of red and blue would help him cope.

He didn't care how impaired his brain became. The more the better. His hope was that come tomorrow, he'd have the courage to do what he had to do. After the lift stopped on the third level, he strode into Libations. Stepping up to the counter, he ordered a Sunset Song and took it to a table in the corner where a pleasant jungle scene played on the walls.

As he sipped his drink, the mixture smoothed over the edges of his anger and sorrow. Then the scene on the walls next to him changed to an ocean of blue with layfeenya playing in the warm waters, their gray bodies arching over the waves as their rounded noses dove back in.

Theron. He had worked with Paxon and created the changing illusion on the walls. Too bad the man couldn't work with Rekah and create the illusion of a healed heart. Gripping his glass hard, Konala threw back the rest of the drink.

He wasn't sure which was worse, Rekah's indifference or Theron's abandonment.

"I'm not going to hurt you. I just want to help." Jaelene moved slowly, trying to project a feeling of calm despite her nervousness around the strange beast.

The animal's small nostrils, which she hadn't seen until she'd stepped closer, wiggled as it tried to sniff her.

She crouched down no more than a couple yards away, using the spear to steady herself.

"You're not feeling well, are you?"

The beast sighed.

Oh wow. She hadn't expected that. "Would some water help?"

The animal lifted its head about a foot then dropped it back down.

"Oh, you poor thing. Just hold on." Slowly she rose and walked around it. Once nearer the cave, she ran inside and soaked the towel she held. She'd let the water drip onto the animal's massive lip. Once the towel was soaked, she dropped the spear and held the material with both hands, moving a bit faster this time.

"Okay, I'm going to give you some water." A few drops fell from between her fingers and the beast licked its upper lip with a tongue the size of her thigh. What the hell was she thinking?

As if it guessed her hesitancy, the animal whimpered, its brown eyes staring at her hands.

She stepped closer, her hands outstretched with the soaked towel. "It's okay."

"Jaelene, stop!" The yell froze her in place and sent shivers through her body.

She looked near the cave. Theron ran through the jungle on the other side toward her.

"I'm just giving it some water." She kept her voice soothing as she took another step toward it.

"No!"

At the fear on Theron's face, she paused, frowning, but the movement of the beast had her swinging her head back in its direction. It rose on its feet at the same time it curled up its massive upper lip to reveal a double row of teeth to rival a great white shark.

Its massive mouth opened and it came at her just as she was pulled off her feet and slammed to the ground. Theron jumped up, pulling her with him. "Run for the cave!"

She'd barely taken a step when a loud snap resounded behind her followed by Theron's shout of pain. She turned back to see the beast's hoof on Theron's thigh as he lay on the ground.

Oh God, this wasn't happening. Theron tried to crawl out

from under the animal, but its lip curled back again. She couldn't just stand there, but she had no weapon. The image of a fight scene in a movie she'd seen came to mind and she crouched down, scooping dirt into her hands. Swallowing more fear than she'd ever experienced, she ran forward and threw the dirt in the beast's eyes.

The growl that came with the shaking head had her running for the cave. She didn't look back until she'd reached it, but the beast wasn't behind her.

It had Theron backed against a tree, where he stood on one leg. Why hadn't it chased her?

She ran into the cave and grabbed the spear. When she came back out, she was pushed over as another body bounded by her.

Talia!

She jumped up and ran after the big cat.

Theron had kept the beast at bay with a huge log, but the beast bit through it and spit it out before catching Theron's arm with its teeth as he tried to roll to the side of the tree. Blood sprayed and Theron let out a howl of pain.

Talia bounded onto the beast's back, her claws sinking in deep as she bared her fangs and sunk her teeth into the thick neck. Blood gushed and the beast pivoted, bucking, trying to dislodge the big cat.

Giving the two animals a wide birth, Jaelene sprinted to Theron. She whipped off her blue short-sleeve shirt and wound it around his arm to slow the blood flow. At least she still had her black tank on.

"No! Get back." Theron wasn't happy to see her. "Go to the cave."

"Lean on me."

"Jaelene, you must be safe."

She ignored him and wrapped his good arm over her shoulder. "Come on."

Theron gritted his teeth against the pain and his need to keep Jaelene safe. Every instinct in his body screamed at her to run, but his gut told him she would only stay and argue. The fastest way to get her to the cave was to limp along beside her.

He kept his eye on the boarox and Talia. He'd grown fond of the big cat over the last few months. She seemed to have a handle on the situation, showing no sign of letting go. Tigran usually slept during the day, only hunting for food at dawn and dusk. She must have heard his shout, and like all cats, curiosity led her from her nest.

They made it to the cave, thanks to Talia. He sent a prayer to Helios to watch over her and ducked inside. Jaelene started to bring him into his bedroom and he balked. "No, that's your room."

"It doesn't matter whose room it is. You're hurt and the only way I can help you is if you lie down. Now stop fighting me. It's not helping."

He couldn't see her face but he heard the frustration in her voice. Acquiescing, he limped to his bed and sat hard, his broken leg coming out from under him. "By the Crius, that hurts!"

She gave him an odd look before fluffing his head puffs and pulling at his shoulders to lie back. He did as she indicated, gritting his teeth as she helped him lift his leg onto the bed. Once he was down, the pain eased in his leg, but his arm began to throb.

Jaelene's brows were lowered in concern. "We need to get you to a hospital or a doctor at least."

"The Healing Center is in Naralina and the closest healer is at Haven. It wouldn't be safe for you if we traveled there in my condition."

"Not to mention you might not make it." Jaelene shook her head. "You need to know that I'm no doctor. I'm an interior designer with a love for animals, so what I know about the human body is only in how it is similar to critters and even then that's only from my experiences volunteering at a wildlife center."

She pulled in her luscious lower lip after this quick speech and Theron was distracted from his pain for a moment. But the pounding in his arm reminded him of his predicament. "You sound just like Konala."

Giving him a half smile, she pulled over the chair he'd just made two days before, and she examined his arm. "I think the blood is slowing. I will need to bandage it with something other than my shirt. Do you have any other sheets or material I can use?"

He had no idea what sheets were, but he did have material. "In the room off the living area there is a basket of siris webbing."

Jaelene cocked her head. "What's that? Is it like gauze?"

"It is the webbing the siris insects produce in the spring. It's white and reflects the light."

"Okay." She didn't move, just stared at him. "I'm not sure something from an insect would be the best thing to cover an open wound."

He wasn't either, but it was the closest material he had to the binding he'd seen Konala use on his animals. "It's all I have."

"Then I guess it will have to do." Jaelene turned and strode from the room, her narrow hips swaying with her gait.

Theron closed his eyes in an attempt to focus on the blood pounding in his arm instead of on Jaelene and how close he'd come to failing her. He should have never left her alone. When he'd seen the Boarox rise to attack his heart seized inside his chest even as adrenaline flew through his body.

Only the sight of Jaelene rising from the ground unhurt had released his mind to refocus on the beast. They didn't usually wander to this area of the jungle, preferring to frequent the Jade forests outside of Kif. The beasts had been one of the reasons the Crius had left the portal chips for his ancient ancestors.

"Oh wow, this is beautiful." Jaelene's voice from the other room brought him back to his situation.

How could he protect her if he was wounded? Luckily, Edenists healed fast, but his injuries were the worst he'd ever had and he had no idea how long they would take to mend.

Jaelene reentered the bedroom. "This isn't just beautiful, but I think it will act like gauze."

"Lock the door."

"Huh?" She cocked her head.

Theron cleared his throat. "You need to lock the outside door. It isn't safe."

"First, I need to bandage your arm. You've lost a lot of blood."

He grabbed her wrist with his good hand as she moved toward him. "No. First, the door."

"Fine." She dropped the siris webbing on the chair and went back into the living area.

Theron listened to her mutter under her breath and his lips twitched. She may be stubborn, but she was intelligent and understood a little of their danger.

Jaelene reentered the room. "It's locked. Now can I wrap your arm?"

He nodded. "You may need to close the wound. There is needle and thread in the cabinet in the bath."

"You mean I might need to stitch it?" Jaelene's already pale skin turned a shade lighter. She swallowed. "I'm not sure I can do that."

"It may just need to be wrapped very tight, but just in case, before you see what's beneath your bandage, you should probably get the needle and thread."

Jaelene didn't say anything. She just nodded and rose before walking hesitantly toward the bath. Once in there, she seemed to come alive again.

"Oh, I'll need to clean away the blood as well. I'm going to use this small cloth I found on the sink. Is that okay?"

"Yes." He heard the cabinet door close and she re-emerged.

"Got it. I love that warm water sink. Very ingenious."

"Thank you." He couldn't tell if her off topic conversation was due to nerves or just her own curiosity, but he was glad for it. He hadn't spoken to another person in almost a cycle of Selene.

He did wander near Haven on occasion and talk to the patrollers there. He'd made friends with Lennix and Mykl, who he'd met before when running messages for his leaders. They weren't in the same filoz. Patrols were never one filoz because of the dangers in the jungle.

"Okay, I'm going to untie my shirt from your arm. I'm really hoping the blood has slowed from coagulation and not from the pressure."

As Jaelene reached for the bandage, she worried that full bottom lip of hers, something he found himself wishing he could do instead. But as the pressure eased from his arm, the blood flowed again.

"Shoot." She pressed the wet cloth against his upper arm.

He turned his head to watch what she did. "It will need to be closed. Konala does this when his animals have such a wound."

"Are you sure?" Her fear registered in her voice. "Take a look."

She lifted the soaked cloth and blood flowed fast, immediately covering the large gashes made by the boarox's teeth. She covered the wound and pressed her blood soaked shirt over it as well.

Theron placed his hand over hers. "You need to close each cut. I will hold this." He looked up at her to find her face even whiter than before. If she lost consciousness, he could bleed to death. "Jaelene. I need you to do this for me. I cannot do it by myself."

She nodded silently but didn't look at him. Turning, she picked up the thread made of sable worm silk and attempted to push it through the eyehole of the needle. "It won't go."

Her hands were slippery with his blood, making her task that much harder. She could faint at any moment. He needed to distract her. "I know it's hard. You should have seen me the first time I had to put thread to needle. All I had to do is fix a hesta, but they are see through which made finding the tread even harder."

"You had to repair see-through material? Why? If it's see-through, can you actually see the hole?"

He watched her fingers steady as she attempted the eyehole again. "The hole was barely visible, but I had to repair it, otherwise the ties would rip off next time it was worn. It was a cape and the hole was at the base of the tie."

"I got it." She looked at him in triumph.

"Good. I knew you could." He smiled, hoping to give her

encouragement. "I will hold your shirt over the other slashes while you start with the outside one."

"Okay." Her hesitancy prepared him for a painful mending.

He'd only had to have a wound closed once and it was small and quick. Maybe if he kept talking it would help her focus on something beyond what she did.

"The hesta was for my mother and I had been the one to tear it." The needle pushed through his skin and he took a deep breath, forcing himself not to flinch. "She was always cold and wore one every time we left home."

The needle pulled his flesh together as Jaelene pushed through the skin again.

"My fathers used to tell us children that they had to take her in the bedroom and warm her up. Of course—" He hesitated as the needled dove through his skin again. "My brother and I didn't catch on until we learned about sex."

She pulled the thread through faster on the second stitch. "You have brothers?"

"Yes, but I was the youngest, so I was the brunt of my brothers tricks, but the favorite of the family."

"I'm the youngest too." She pushed the needle into his arm with more confidence which helped lessen the pain just a bit.

He swallowed, thinking of her older sister. "Did your parents dote on you, too?"

She shook her head, but continued her work. "At first, but then Serena moved away and I stayed nearby so they made a bigger deal about seeing her." She shrugged one shoulder. "I didn't mind though. Serena always stuck up for me. I envy her, her confidence."

Jaelene tied a knot and Theron moved his hand from the

largest gash. Blood began to flow instantly and he covered it again. "This one will be harder. Can you do it?"

She moved her gaze from his arm and nodded. "Like you said, I have to." She took the small knife she'd brought in with the other sewing materials and cut the thread. "Are you ready?"

He grinned, hoping to encourage her. "I am if you are."

"Okay, just keep talking."

He chuckled inside. She knew exactly what he was up to, but if it saved his life and therefore hers in the process, he didn't mind that she'd figured it out. "I thought I would never find men to form a filoz with because I had such outstanding brothers."

Despite her frown of concentration over the largest gash, she continued stitching and followed his conversation. "So a filoz is like a family of your own. Does that mean you have sex with your friends? I mean, it doesn't matter to me, I'm just curious."

Her sudden blush told him her curiosity embarrassed her, but she still asked.

There was a lot of strength in her that he hadn't noticed immediately. Like the fact she'd come to his aid despite the boarox still being just yards away. "We don't have sex with each other. We will have sex with our chosen one together and sometimes separate, but not without her." He spoke as if he would return to Konala and Rekah, but that was impossible.

"What is a chosen one?" Jaelene worried her bottom lip as she pulled together the widest part of the gash.

Keeping his arm still was a study in torture and his brow began to sweat, but he forced himself to remain absolutely still. "It is similar to your idea of a fiancé. Once we have formed the bond then we are agapaytos or what you would call husbands and wife."

Jaelene tied off the final stitch on the largest gash and sat straighter, rolling her shoulders. She looked at him with a half-smile on her face. "Actually, we don't have anything like a wife with multiple husbands in our country, but we have the opposite in a few places. To tell the truth, I like your way better." She winked.

At that moment, she appeared the prettiest woman he'd ever seen, sweet, innocent, curious, and strong.

"But then again, I'm a little strange." She picked up the thread again, patiently pushing it through the eyehole of the needle.

Her concentration was absolute and he found himself appreciating the curve of her cheek, the point of her nose and the long black lashes that framed her brilliantly colored eyes. "I like strange."

She glanced at him. "That doesn't surprise me. You walk around naked and live in a cave. Of course you would." She flipped her hair over her shoulder with a shake of her head then pushed his hand away so she could see the next cut.

He blinked, gritting his teeth as the needle plunged into his arm again. He needed to keep his mind on his predicament. She was Serena's sister and he'd already embarrassed himself with Serena. His only interest in Jaelene had to be to keep her safe.

A full throated bellow sounded outside.

"What was that?" Jaelene's eyes were wide.

"My guess is we just heard the death throe of the boarox. Talia must have completed her kill."

Jaelene shivered and he didn't blame her.

Death of any kind was tragic, even for a boarox who had done only what its instinct told it to do. "At least Talia will have food for a few days without having to hunt. Don't be surprised if the next time she comes by for a pet, her stomach is dragging on the ground."

Jaelene gave him a small smile and returned to his cut up arm. "So you said you would tell me later what you meant when you said that blond guy who was after me would tire of chasing your reflection."

Scrat, now he was wishing her mind wasn't so sharp. How to explain it without revealing she was on another planet? "It's just a talent I have. Like Konala is good with animals and Rekah can understand how someone is feeling, I'm just good with reflections."

She paused in her stitching and looked at him. "You make reflections? You mean like mirrors?"

He searched his memory of lessons about Earth. "Yes, exactly. Only mine are more complicated, like the one at the entrance to this cave."

She turned her attention back to his wound, not saying anything until she'd tied the knot and cut the thread. Then she gave him her full attention. "You mean the door that blends in with the rest of the rock so it looks like you are actually walking through stone."

"Yes." His relief was short-lived at her next question.

"How?"

Chapter Four

Jaelene stared at Theron, her curiosity full blown now. If she could learn how to create these type of reflections, she would be the most sought after interior designer in all of New Jersey. Maybe even in New York.

But as she gazed at him and caught his pained stare, his physical state squashed her enthusiasm. Here she was drilling him with questions when the man had to be in agonizing pain. She'd put in at least eighteen stitches and there were still cuts under the blood soaked mess that had been her shirt.

Theron's face had lost its deep tan color and his brow was furrowed. His chest was covered in scratches and his long brown hair was matted with twigs and grass. "Never mind. We can talk about that later. I really appreciate you distracting me though."

She threaded the needle again. She needed to finish this, splint his leg and wash him up so he could rest and recover. She would have plenty of time to ask him all kinds of questions because it was obvious neither of them was going anywhere any time soon. "I just want you to know, I'm no doctor. I can't guarantee your arm will heal okay. I can't even be sure my stitches will hold. I've never stitched a human before."

Theron didn't reply right away and she spared his face a glance. His eyes were closed, but his jaw was tight. Shoot, he had to be in a lot of pain. She needed to finish this quickly, but every time he moved her bloody shirt, he revealed another gash. He must have lost a lot of blood.

Finally, she reached cuts that weren't as deep and had stopped bleeding. Putting aside the needle and thread, she gently took her bloodied shirt from his grasp and dropped it on the floor. Next she pulled a swatch of the webbing, as he called it, and wrapped it around his biceps, tying it carefully to keep it in place, but without it being too tight. She sat back and stared at Theron.

He opened his eyes. "Done?"

She nodded, laying her hand on his good one. "Yes, with your arm, but I need to splint your leg somehow." She rose to look for a piece of wood or something, but Theron grabbed her wrist.

"No. Not now. I need to sleep first."

She wanted to argue, but his color was so poor, she bit back her words. "Okay. Let me just immobilize your leg so you don't hurt it in your sleep."

He nodded slightly as if even that was too much of an effort. The poor man had spent all his energy talking to her to keep her calm and now had nothing left.

She rolled the light blanket at the end of the bed and as gently as possible, placed it against the outside of Theron's leg. Then she took the second pillow on the bed and the rest of the webbing and piled it against the inside of his leg, which wasn't easy without looking above his knee.

When she was done, she glanced at his face to find his head to the side, his lips slightly parted and his eyes closed. She watched his muscled chest rise and fall rhythmically for a few moments before she relaxed.

But then her gaze wouldn't behave and she stared at his package. Even in its limp state it was impressive, and she'd seen a few to compare it to. She rarely had a second date except for her high school sweetheart. She had enough nights with Mr. Wrong while looking for Mr. Right. And Theron was definitely unique.

Heck, he walked around the jungle stark naked. And he saved her, twice. His first thought seemed to be her safety.

And there he lay, his arm gashed to pieces and his leg broken in who knew how many places. All for her. No one had ever done so much for her and asked for so little in return. Her heart swelled.

It was her fault. If she hadn't gone outside and stayed put like he'd told her, they would be trotting merrily through the forest right now toward her sister.

What the heck was she doing in the middle of some godforsaken jungle in who knew what country with a strange man who almost died for her?

Tears blurred her vision. She couldn't even be sure he knew her sister. It could be just a ruse to hold her captive. But even as she contemplated the possibility, she rejected it. If she was safe anywhere besides with Serena, her instinct said it was with Theron.

She should have never followed her sister through that portal.

She'd figured out that her sister wasn't telling her everything and was determined to find out where she lived because it sounded like a cult. Who ever heard of a country where women were expected to have more than one husband?

All she wanted was to have one lover who was interested in more than sex. She wasn't greedy. Just one. Okay, so she used to fantasize about having sex with two men, but that was just sex. What she wanted now was an actual relationship. Was she really that odd?

The image of the beast opening its mouth to show her all those sharp teeth floated across her weak brain and her tears began to flow in earnest. Her body shook as the fear she'd kept at bay with Theron's help bulldozed through her. She crossed her arms over her body, but it was little comfort.

Instinct, more than any conscious decision making process, had her climbing carefully onto the bed and lying next to Theron. She tried to stop shaking and crying, but her heart forced the tears from her.

"Jaelene?" Theron's concerned whisper only made it worse and she started to sob.

"Come here, Khityki." He lifted his arm.

The comfort he offered was too needed. She lay her head on his shoulder and moved her body against the side of his.

Theron's arm wrapped around her, holding her against him. "You did well. Now rest. You are safe."

It wasn't his words so much as his soothing tone that helped her stop shaking. As the warmth of his body penetrated through her clothes, her tears slowed. She closed her eyes, the heavy arm wrapped around her back comforting, keeping her safe. She let herself fall asleep.

~~*~~

Theron woke to pitch darkness. He blinked in an effort to

pierce the blackness with his gaze, but to no avail. Had he gone blind? He started to move his left arm when pain sliced through it. He let it drop to his side, the cushion beneath it clarifying his location.

Jaelene? He moved his other hand to find it tucked into the waistband of her jeans. Her breathing remained even and he became aware of her head on his chest, her arm across his stomach and her nutty scent calming him. No wonder he'd dreamed of lying on a bed of siris webbing in a nest high in the trees with her against him.

He liked the feel of her smaller body cuddled up against his. He would have preferred it if she were naked, but then he'd be far too tempted to enjoy her body as much as he enjoyed her mind. She was off limits in that sense, but her trust in him resurrected a bit of his self-worth.

Unfortunately, he had to urinate and if he ever wanted to have use of his leg again, he probably shouldn't get up. Plus they were in the midnight blackness of the cave without the shiner and that meant moving about would be difficult at best.

Though loathe to do so, he extracted his fingers from the warmth of Jaelene's soft skin, not ashamed to enjoy the feminine softness as he slid his hand out of her waistband. He grasped her arm with his hand. "Jaelene. Jaelene. Wake up."

"Huh?" Her head moved on his chest and he felt her jaw open as she yawned against him. "It's so dark."

He ran his hand up and down her arm. "I know. It grew dark out while we slept and we didn't have the shiner on."

"So maybe we should just go back t—" A rumbling sound coming from her body interrupted her. "Never mind."

He grinned. There was so much about her he found amusing. "We need to take care of a few bodily functions, don't you think?"

She nodded against his chest. "I guess so." Slowly she sat up.

Despite the addiction of her soft skin, he forced his arm to move away. "You will need to get the shiner."

"The what?"

Even in the blackness, he pictured her turning her head to look at him, probably cocking it.

"The portable light."

"Oh, the lantern. You know what? I think your language makes more sense than mine." She moved on the bed and when she next spoke, he could tell she stood next to it. "This isn't going to be easy. I know where the 'shiner' is, but I'm not sure I remember exactly where all the furniture is in the living room.

"If you take an immediate right out of this door and follow the back wall, you should be able to avoid the chairs and tables."

"Good point." She walked slowly toward the door, his ability to tell where she was based on her hand tracing the bed. When she got to the end, she paused. "Okay, I'm reaching for the door frame."

He listened as her feet took tentative steps across the floor.

"Found it." The triumph was clear in her voice.

The smallest things made her happy. She would make someone a perfect beloved. His mind raced ahead. Would Jahl and Khaos, Serena's agapaytos, allow Jaelene to go back to Earth without agapaytos? Or would they require, as they did of all women, that she join a filoz or a Pleasure Temple.

The thought of innocent Jaelene in a Pleasure Temple bothered him greatly and he found his leg and arm throbbing with his reaction.

"Ow. Oh heck, I left the stupid door open."

"Are you hurt?" He wished he could help her, his immobility making his mood worse.

He heard a door close. "I'm fine. I just walked face first into the storage room door, which *I* left open. I swear if my head wasn't attached I'd forget that too."

For some reason, Jaelene's strange wording had him relaxing again.

"Got it. Yay! Now how do you turn this thing on? I tried to figure that out earlier today in the daylight and I was stumped."

"Do you feel the round cylinder near the top that is no wider than your finger?"

"Round cylinder? I'm not sure—wait, I think I have it. So now what?"

He could sense her anticipation. "Hold the shiner in your left hand and turn the cylinder with your right hand toward you a finger's width."

"You measure a lot with your finger, don't you?"

He grinned. "Yes, I do."

"Okay, here goes nothing."

Light from the living area filtered into the bedroom.

"I did it!"

Theron felt his body hum with Jaelene's happiness. Such a small accomplishment, but one she celebrated. Rekah would greatly enjoy being around her for that reason alone. The man was far too serious for his own good.

Jaelene walked into the room. "I did it. If I turn the cylinder more, will it get brighter?"

"Don't." He held up his good hand. "Don't open it more than that or it will blind you permanently."

"Okay. So it would be like staring at the sun? What's in here? I don't see a light bulb and there's no cord or place for batteries. Is it some type of chemical reaction? Not that I would know anything about that because I wasn't very good in school when it came to—"

"Jaelene." He stifled a smile as she snapped her head up to look at him instead of at the shiner.

"I was rambling again. Sorry."

"I enjoy your rambling, but I need your help."

She set the shiner on the chair next to the bed. "Of course. What do you need? Water? Food? A blanket? I'm at your service. After all, you saved my life. It's the least I can do."

"I need a cup." He'd never had to urinate in bed before and he certainly had never had to ask a woman for help with it, but his need was pushing the limits of his ability to be polite.

"Oh, I saw one of those in the cabinet. Did you want water in it?"

He shook his head. "Just the cup."

She cocked her head but didn't ask and instead grabbed the shiner and went back into the living area. When she returned, she held it out to him. "Okay, here's the cup. Now what?"

Scrat, there was no way around it. He would not only have to tell her, but he'd also need her to empty it. He took a deep breath and met her gaze. "I need to urinate in it."

"Oh." She blushed before turning around and walking to the door. "Of course."

Theron felt his own cheeks redden. Hopefully, she wouldn't tell her sister about this particular episode of her travels.

Carefully, he wedged the cup between his legs and held his cock in position to avoid any spillage. It was not a large enough cup, so he had to stop. "Jaelene, I have to ask you to empty this in the bath and return it to me."

She came back inside and took a firm hold of the cup, walking carefully into the bath. Without looking at his cock, she came back with the empty cup and walked out of the room without another word.

Three more times he had to call her before his bladder was satisfied, but with that necessity out of the way, he focused on her and her rumbling stomach. He directed her to where the food was and in particular the meat he cooked yesterday before he stumbled upon her.

It wasn't long before Jaelene walked in with two plates and handed him one. "Okay, I'm pretty good at putting things together so they look good, but I can't vouch for how these will taste together."

He bit his tongue to keep from laughing aloud at her choices. Instead, he smiled. "This looks beautiful."

"That's what I thought too." She sat in the chair next him, having hung the shiner on the hook he had in the wall.

He avoided the vegetable she'd put on the plate and started with the cold meat of the havling pig.

"Eew, what is this?" Jaelene spit out the purple vegetable.

Theron couldn't hold back his laughter. "That's a grapet. I use those to lure the wild havlings into my traps."

She frowned at him. "So you don't eat this then?"

He shook his head.

She cocked her head and gave him a slow smile. "At least it looks pretty."

"Yes, it does." He'd been afraid to insult her, but she'd taken her mistake in stride. Every interaction he had with her taught him something new. He was thoroughly enjoying her company. He would miss her when she reunited with her sister.

She shrugged one shoulder. "I told you I make no guarantees as to the flavors. Is there anything else on this plate I should avoid putting in my mouth?"

He grinned. "The small green balls."

She frowned. "Oh shoot, I thought they'd taste like peas. What are they?"

"They keep insects out of the food."

"You're joking."

He shook his head.

Her laughter rolled over him like a spring rain, refreshing and light. "I think you better give me cooking lessons before I poison us."

"I'd be happy to."

She pushed the green balls onto the pile of grapets and took another bite of the pig. When she finished chewing, she eyed him. "So where did you learn to cook?"

Having eaten all that was edible on the plate, he set it on the bed next to his hip. "In school. We all learn to cook."

"Really? In our schools we don't have to and a lot of us learn at home with our mom." She popped the last bite into her mouth.

"Here our mothers don't cook. My fathers took turns and they were all very good at it."

She picked up his plate and placed it on her own as she stood. "That's the second time you've mentioned having more than one father."

"I have three."

She plopped back down on the bed. "Three?"

The movement sent pain slicing up his leg and he couldn't hold back his grimace.

"Oh, I'm so sorry." She stood slowly. "I keep forgetting you're hurt. If I had a broken leg, and an arm that had been through a meat grinder, I'd be lying there moaning, but you are so fascinating and talkative that I forgot. Let me get these into water and then I'll be back and I'll splint your leg."

He didn't have a chance to reassure her as she strode from the room. She thought him fascinating? He liked that. He found her to be as well, especially the way she avoided looking at his cock.

He, Konala, and Rekah hadn't yet picked a woman from Earth before he left Loraleaf, so he hadn't had a chance to study women's behavior on Earth. He didn't remember Serena having a similar habit and her friend Toni definitely didn't. Could it be Jaelene was less experienced than the other two women?

Jaelene walked back into the room with two short and two long, rough cut chair legs. "Okay, so I hope you don't mind, but I took apart the second chair in the living room. I figured when you get better you can remake it."

"What are those for?"

She halted and gave him a frown. "We need to splint your leg whether you like it or not."

"Of course." He hid his smile at how impressed he was. It never occurred to him to use the wood from the furniture he made. She was definitely resourceful.

He glanced at her forgotten shirt still sitting on the floor, a dark red mound of his blood. She'd whipped that off quick enough to save his arm. He could have very well bled to death.

"You don't have to worry about me being squeamish with this." She carefully pulled the blanket, pillow and webbing away from the sides of his leg. "I've done this particular procedure to many an animal in my day."

He felt a certain amount of relief at that statement. "So you are a pet healer?"

She paused in her inspection of the chair legs. "No, I'm not a vet, but I used to bring home hurt and wounded animals all the time and our veterinarian showed me how to splint legs since I was racking up quite a bill for my parents to pay." She decided on the long logs and approached the bed.

"So you've never done this on a human?" His confidence in her waned.

"No, but it's the same principal." She glanced at him and his concern must have shown on his face. "You said in your filoz you have a man who helps animals, right?"

"Yes. Konala."

"Would you let him set your leg?"

"Of course, he—ah, I understand. Please." He motioned toward his leg with his hand.

She smiled then, her pleasure at his trust sending a pleasant feeling into his heart. He shouldn't be surprised he enjoyed her company so much. She was, after all, Serena's sister.

Jaelene went to work on his leg, and true to her word, she had it splinted expertly with minimal pain to him. He was impressed.

She finished tying the last of the webbing and stood. "There. Now just because you have a splint doesn't mean you can go about half-cocked. A splint isn't a cast and you could end up crippling yourself, so I suggest lots of rest. Do you have anything for the pain?"

He rolled his leg to test the splint and winced when he went too far. He sucked in his breath as the spike of pain came and went. "I do, but as long as I don't move either my arm or my leg I am comfortable enough."

"How about that fruit you gave me last night. Could that take the edge off?"

He hadn't heard that exact phrasing before, but he guessed at what she meant. "Yes, I think the kerasi would help."

"That's in the other storage room, right?" She had already turned to leave.

"Room? No, it's in the…" He was going to say the tunnels, but considering her curiosity, decided against it. "In the damp room, the middle door in the living area."

She nodded. "That's what I meant."

He glanced at the shiner hanging on the bedroom wall. Without it, she shouldn't notice that the "room" didn't end.

She returned with the fruit. "Here you go. I got one for myself to help me sleep. I'm not used to taking naps." She handed him the red-iridescent succulent.

He set it on the nearby chair.

"Aren't you going to eat it?"

He looked at it and then her. "Yes, but not until I'm ready to sleep."

"Uh-uh. You eat it now. You need extra sleep to heal. Your body can only concentrate on your injuries if you rest."

He gave her a hopeful smile. "I'd probably rest better if you were beside me." He patted the bed next to him.

Her eyes widened in surprise before she blushed. "I don't think so. I would bother you with my chatter. I'll just hang out in the living room for a while since I'm wide awake. You stay in here and don't move."

He squashed his disappointment. Of course she wouldn't join him. She only had before because she was exhausted after her escape from the boarox.

She pulled the shiner from the hook.

"Wait. When you bring that into the living area, hang it on the wall next to this door. That way a small amount of light will be present if I need to get up."

She gave him the kind of look his mom used to give him when she scolded him. "I don't want you getting out of that bed."

He smirked. "Then you better bring me that cup."

She frowned until his meaning dawned. "Oh." As her cheeks turned red, she held up her hand. "Wait, you'll need something to help you walk. You can't put any weight at all on that leg." She spun and disappeared into the living area, the light going with her.

He waited anxiously, impatient to see what her creative mind would come up with next. Grumbling came from the other room. She must be in the storage room, but he couldn't think what she'd find there.

A thump sounded through the rooms. "Shoot." Her voice revealed her frustration.

He thought of everything in his home and how it might help him, but nothing came to mind.

"Ah-ah! That will work." More grumbling followed and what he was sure were choice words then Jaelene's steps sounded across the living area.

No more noise floated to him. He tried to imagine what she

might devise. He listened intently but except for an occasional grunt, she didn't say another word.

The light in the other room moved and it was obvious she hung the shiner on the wall where he indicated. Her footsteps receded and he heard another thump, but no muttering followed it.

Finally, Jaelene poked her head around the doorway. "I have a present for you." Her sweet smile was present enough as far as he was concerned, but that wouldn't satisfy his curiosity.

"I like presents."

She stepped into the room and held out a post he'd used for his short shelf in the storage room.

He stifled the grimace at what might have happened to the shelving in there. She held the post horizontally and at one end was the small log he'd used for the arm of the chair she'd taken apart for his splint. It was tied perpendicular to the shelf post with infragile vine. He had no idea how that would help him. "What is it?"

Her smile faltered. "It's a crutch."

He shook his head. He understood a crutch was something that supported something else, usually in the building trades, but how it would help him was beyond his knowledge.

"You've never seen a crutch?"

He shook his head.

Undaunted, she let one end of the "crutch" fall to the floor and held it by the cross piece.

"Okay, here's how it works. You put this under your arm like this and you hold it down here and you use it instead of your other leg." She took a couple steps. "It is a bit too tall for me, so I imagine it will be a little short for you, but it's the only thing close to your height in this entire place."

His chest felt tight at the effort she'd gone through for him. A person she'd only met yesterday. "Thank you."

She worried her bottom lip before speaking. "Do you think it will work?"

He gave her a heartfelt smile. "I know it will. It's ingenious."

She shrugged one shoulder and looked away. "Not really. It's just the best I could do to imitate the ones we have in our country."

He continued to grin at her until she met his gaze again. "It's perfect." Her azure eyes fascinated him as much as her personality and he found himself staring into them longer than expected.

Jaelene cleared her throat and looked away. "I'll let you rest now. Be sure to eat the kerasi fruit."

Kerasi? Right, the fruit. "I will."

She'd regained her composure. "I'll just put this across the chair here so you can reach it when you need to get up." She laid the crutch beside the bed and stepped away. "Have a good night."

She closed the door behind her, leaving him in the dark, the shiner throwing a little light beneath and above the bedroom door.

He scanned the room in the darkness. What did Jaelene think of his home? He'd thought himself industrious to have established himself so quickly. It had only taken him three cycles of Selene to create a domicile.

He'd been excited to find the cave and was happy that it was closer to Haven than Loraleaf. There was less chance of running into Serena. He spent his days tracking the lawbreakers and keeping an eye out for any falsely accused in the jungle. That was where all the men in Haven had come from.

Last he heard from Lennix, only Wareson and Nassic, former leaders of Naralina and now the leaders of Haven, had an agapayto, but new filoz were forming as the men began to learn about each other.

Theron couldn't see himself joining a new filoz. The brothers of his heart were Konala and Rekah. But having Jaelene here, in his new home, made him long for companionship. He missed Loraleaf and the camaraderie there. Being alone was not only difficult socially, but physically, too.

What would he have done if he'd been hurt by the boarox and Jaelene wasn't here to help him? It brought home how truly vulnerable he was.

For the hundredth time, he thought about joining Haven. Maybe after Jaelene was safely with her sister. He glanced again at the room. It wasn't much, but he was loathe to leave it.

He picked up the kerasi and bit into it. Before he made any decisions, he had to heal. Then he would see Jaelene to Loraleaf. Only after that was accomplished would he determine what he would do.

~~*~~

Jaelene sat on the only chair now in the living room. There was no television or computer. She'd turned off her phone shortly after stepping through the portal when she couldn't find a signal. Maybe there was one here.

She pulled it out of her back pocket and waited for it to power up. Just her luck she found an interesting man living off the grid. For all she knew, in this country, there was no grid, but she couldn't picture her sister, pyrotechnic expert that she was, living without the luxury of running water. Though to be fair, Theron did have running water.

Her phone showed no signal. *Great.* She powered it off. Now what was she supposed to do? She was wide awake. There was no way she was crawling into bed with Theron with them both awake. He was far too handsome and naked for her to do that.

Why not?

She paused. He seemed to like her despite having spent more than twenty four hours with her. Then again, he didn't have much choice. But he really was nice on the inside as well as the outside.

No, she couldn't. First, it was probably that adrenaline rush of being in danger. She'd seen enough reality television shows to know that that kind of bonding didn't last. And second, the man lived in a cave in some backward country.

With new purpose, she rose and headed for the storage room. Something had to indicate what country it was made in. The lantern didn't illuminate the entire room, but what it did, didn't give her any clues. Not that she'd seen a single wrapped package in any of it earlier. Leaving that room, she opened the door to what Theron called the "damp" room. Though the room was closer to the lantern, it seemed darker. It had to be deeper. Checking what she could see for any manufacturing tags, she wasn't surprised that she couldn't find any.

She was in the middle of a jungle with no medical facilities with a man who wore no clothes. She hadn't even found paper earlier in the day when she went through the cabinet.

Maybe he hid something in the back of the damp room. She stepped out to grab the lantern when she remembered why it was hung on the wall near the bedroom. She could imagine Theron rising in the middle of the night to go pee and walking into the door because he couldn't see it, damaging his leg more.

She scanned the room. For a man who said he was good at making reflections, he didn't have a mirror anywhere. There weren't even any metal pans that she could use to reflect the light.

Challenged, but not daunted, she stepped back into the damp room. She felt her way a little farther into it. It turned dark fast. How far did it go? She moved farther along the wall until looking back she could barely see the open door.

Even if there was something hidden in here, there was no way for her to see it. This was stupid.

She was about to turn back when she had an idea. Pulling her phone from her pocket, she turned it on. "Yes." There was still more than half her battery left. Hitting the flashlight image, she pointed the light to the wall next to her.

The rock was a deep black, like coal and some of it was wet, but not from water running like in Theron's bathroom. It was almost as if the water beaded through the rock. She ran her finger across it and just like condensation, it pooled together and dripped downward.

"Okay, that's different."

She angled the light down and breathed a sigh of relief there wasn't any bat guano because after her experience in a bat cave in Costa Rica, she fully expected there would be bats. Just to make sure, she focused the light above her.

"Oh, wow." The ceiling was the same glossy black, but ahead it rose up at least three stories high. She must have come downhill. Either that or it was under a mountain.

She walked farther to put herself under the highest point of the ceiling then looked around her. "This could be dangerous." Four other tunnels fanned out from the central point. It would be easy to forget which tunnel she took.

The ground beneath her feet was like that in Theron's section of the cave, as hard as slate, just like the walls. That made it hard to draw an arrow. She checked her front pocket and found her lip balm, but that was far too small to point the way for her on the way back out.

She listened intently, trying to identify if anyone or anything was in the tunnels. Surely with the hard surfaced walls, noise would carry. It was dead silent. Happy about that, she whipped off her black tank and set it on the floor along the wall she'd entered from, angling it so it pointed back toward Theron's home.

Satisfied she'd find it again, she moved back under the dome and chose the tunnel to the far left. It couldn't hurt to stay to the farthest left. Then she would go right on the way back.

She checked her battery power. The last thing she needed was to run out of light. Still above the halfway mark, she continued her exploration.

Now she could tell she was going downhill, though not steeply, but the air grew cooler and moister. It would be a lot more fun if she wasn't walking around in just a bra, but she didn't plan to go too far.

She focused her light on the walls and floor ahead. The black started to show streaks of purple. At first she thought her eyes were playing tricks on her, but when she crouched down and illuminated a vein of the color with her light, it was definitely a deep purple distinct against the black.

Jaelene continued her exploration, enjoying the abstract

designs the purple rock veins made on the walls. It was like going to a museum of modern art, the way the purple cut through the black tinged with teal. "Teal?"

Shining the light back the way she'd come, she was able to pinpoint when the teal had begun. It seemed the deeper into the tunnel she walked, the more color she found…and the colder it grew. She checked her battery life again before walking farther.

The temperature dropped faster as she made a short steeper descent. The swirls of color in the black were punctuated with an orange dot here and there. She paused.

The orange appeared to pulse. She stood still. Was it her shivering causing it to look that way? One way to find out. She pressed the flashlight image on her phone again and her light went out.

"Oh my God."

CHAPTER FIVE

It glowed.

The small orange dots glowed with a light of their own and covered the tunnel she was in. The soft light reflected off the black, highlighting the teal and purple, making the whole area come alive. "This is beautiful."

Did Theron know about this? Was he hiding it? With the dim glow of the orange dots, she didn't need her phone and she moved deeper into the tunnel until it too opened up into another three-story dome with tunnels leading off all around, only this circular area glowed with charcoal sized orange lights and they all seemed to pulse at the same time.

If this wasn't a tourist trip, it needed to be. The sight was breathtaking. She put her phone down next to the wall just as it opened up to the dome then walked to the center and looked up.

The pulsation of the orange in the rock made it look like the purple and teal veins were moving up to the center, almost like an upside down waterfall. Was this natural or manmade? A hum she hadn't noticed before came to her attention as it pulsed in sync with the orange lights. The whole chamber vibrated, even the floor. It reminded her of a massage chair set to medium strength.

Too bad it wasn't warmer or it would make a great spa. But the air temperature had seriously dropped and she was too cold to explore any farther. Besides, she had nothing left to mark the way if she headed down one of the other tunnels.

Still, she could take a peek. Counting the number of openings as she went, she started around the room, peeking into the others, but each one looked like the one she'd come from. In fact, they were so alike that if it hadn't been for her phone, she would have missed her way back completely.

That risk, added to the cold, instigated her hasty retreat. Phone in hand, she made her way back up the tunnel. This time, she didn't turn on her flashlight right away. She stopped where the orange dots began. They seemed to occur in relationship to the purple and teal striations.

Then someone brushed by her.

Covering her chest with her arm, she quickly pushed the flashlight button and the passageway lit up.

No one was there. She flashed it down the tunnel, one way then the other, but there was nothing. She listened intently, but the fast pace of her heart was all she could hear.

There was no breeze so something must have gone by her in the dark. Maybe there *were* bats and by the feel of it, possibly really big ones. All the more reason to return to Theron's.

But first she wanted to find where the dots began. Nothing shone in the brightness of her phone. She switched off the light and immediately found the dots. She continued following them until she couldn't see them anymore, only the teal and purple.

She turned on her light and continued back until the teal faded away and even the purple disappeared. She located her tank top at the entrance to the first cavern she'd found and pulled it over her head. It actually felt warm against her cold, moist skin.

With more confidence, she continued up the passage toward Theron's. She switched off the flashlight on her phone as soon as she saw the glow from the living room. Did he know about the tunnels? What about the glowing rock?

She couldn't wait to talk to him about it. What if she discovered his country's biggest tourism opportunity? Maybe they'd name them after her. Jaelene's tunnels. Jaelene's Dome. No. The Dome of Jaelene. Oh, The Upton Dome. She liked that.

As she got to the door, she looked back down the tunnel. It was pitch black with no hint of the beauty it hid. She'd love to find a fabric with that pattern in it.

"Shoot. I'm an idiot. I didn't take a picture."

She looked back but the strange brush against her had her reconsidering any more exploration. Maybe another day. Theron would need time to recover and she could go back. Bending over, she plucked a kerasi from its basket and walked into the living room.

She closed the door behind her and sat in the remaining chair to eat her fruit. She was pretty tired anyway. The raw cold of the domes had caused her to tense up and now her muscles were tired.

When she finished the red fruit, she peeked into Theron's room. The man was still on his back, his face relaxed in sleep as his chest rose and fell steadily with his breathing. She checked the skin around his bandages in the dim light and it all looked healthy. At least no infection had set in, as far as she could tell.

She glanced at his leg and was pleased to see the splint firmly in place. Once again her gaze moved toward the place between his legs. His cock, relaxed now, lay among a nest of dark pubic hair. It was large and she could easily imagine what it would look like hard. The image was definitely enticing.

Her eyes strayed to his thighs, even in rest, the quads stood out from the jumble of muscle there. No wonder he could run with her on his back. It was a shame the beast had broken such a beautiful piece of male anatomy.

Which brought her back to her guilt. She pushed it away, not wanting to spend the night tossing and turning in Dante's ninth circle of hell. Quietly, she closed the door behind her as she stepped inside, leaving the lantern where Theron wanted it.

The light coming under and over the door acted like a nightlight which enabled her to move to the other side of the bed without bumping into anything and waking Theron.

She probably shouldn't sleep in her clothes again. She toed off her sneakers and slipped her jeans off. Then she unhooked her bra and pulled it out from under her tank. She left her socks on because she always slept in her socks.

Perfect. Comfortable, but not indecent.

She lowered herself onto the bed slowly, careful not to disturb Theron. Now that she had splinted his leg, she had her own pillow, so she had no excuse to curl up against him.

But she wanted to. Something about sleeping on his chest had been comforting. Despite his injuries she felt safe, which made no sense at all.

It was probably just that she was in a different country, all alone, with only a stranger to depend on. That had to be it.

Jaelene turned her back to Theron and pulled the light cover over her, leaving enough for him if he needed it in the night. At first, she couldn't stop thinking about the man beside her. The heat from his body warmed her back even though they didn't touch and his deep breathing was the only sound in the room.

She hadn't slept with enough men for sharing a bed to feel comfortable. In fact, she'd only spent the night with three.

On the bright side, she had no one waiting at home for her. She'd left a note for her parents that she was going with Serena and had already told her contractor she was unavailable for a few weeks. Her instinct about Serena hiding something had proven right.

Whatever country her sister lived in, it was nowhere near her apartment in Las Vegas or their parents' home in New Jersey. It was a strange place with naked tribal men and sneaky animals that tricked a woman into thinking they were hurt.

Angry tears started to flood her eyes and she took a deep breath. She wouldn't cry over the betrayal of an animal, a brute beast. Animals had landed her in hot water since the second she arrived in Theron's country. First, the porcupine and now the boarox. Then again, Talia had been a sweetie and had saved Theron.

She needed to look at the positive. Theron was the best part of the positive. He was brave, intelligent, strong, drop dead gorgeous, kind, caring, had great eyes, and he knew her sister. That he walked around naked was a bonus.

So why hadn't he made a move on her? She actually wanted him to. There was something calming about being around him. Maybe because his life was so simple.

She smiled in the darkness. What would he think of Cityside,

New Jersey? It would be like Tarzan going to England. And look how pathetically that turned out. No, Theron needed to stay here and she needed to go home after she discovered where Serena lived.

Maybe she could finagle a one night stand out of the trip. Something she could tell her friends about. Yes, she could do that. This time, instead of being the one surprised when no return call came, she could be in control.

He was still very hurt, so she had a couple weeks to plan. She was going to need that time. She'd never seduced a man in her life.

Rekah woke with a start, his body covered in sweat. The dream had been far too real. Theron and Konala had been exposed to rascide, the deadliest of plants. Immediately, he looked to his right at Theron's bed. It remained empty, his wish for it to be otherwise, unfulfilled yet again.

Turning his head to the left, he glanced at Konala's bed and stilled. It hadn't been slept in. Rekah's heart constricted. Quickly, he opened it to search out the brother of his heart, reaching for his anger of the past evening. Konala wasn't in the house, nor had he been. The clear glass ceiling showed barely a glimmer of Helios pushing back the night.

Throwing his legs over the side of the bed, Rekah leaned his elbows on his knees and let his head drop into his hands. Konala couldn't be *that* angry. Maybe he hurt too, but even as Rekah grasped at the thought, his heart told him he was wrong. Konala had come to terms with Theron's leaving.

Only *he* held onto to hope…and pain.

Shaking his head, he rose and strode down the hall that

curved around the tree trunk to the bath. Flipping one tiny lever of three, he stepped into the warm stream of water pre-programmed for him. His need was to wash away the sweat and the dream at the same time. As the soap mixed with the water, he washed his body, noticing a softening around his middle. When had that happened?

Last, he scrubbed his hair and beard, then stood still with his back toward the water and let the now pulsating hot water relax him. The water slowed, getting lighter and lighter until it was but a mist and Rekah stepped out.

Pulling a dryer cloth off a peg, he quickly rid himself of any wetness and hung it up. Standing in front of the sink, he stared at his reflection in the full wall reflector Theron had created for them. His stomach muscles were still clearly defined, but a strange softness had occurred along his sides. He would have to ask Jahl or Khaos about it, but with no disease on Eden, he wasn't too worried.

Lifting his gaze to his face, he let out an unexpected breath. He looked like an old discoverist he'd once met. His beard was much fuller and longer and his hair was almost to his ears. No wonder no one came for counseling anymore.

Turning from the sight, he strode farther around the tree and into the meal room to start the kafez. While he waited for the drink to brew, he walked to the front door and opened it. Loraleaf was quiet in the predawn light that barely sifted through the leaves.

All swinging vines remained still, the wooden walkways in the trees were empty, the lifts firmly camped on whatever level they had last been stopped. Rekah opened his heart and searched the settlement for Konala, but his own emotional state kept breaking his focus.

Turning on his heel, he returned to the meal room and poured his kafez. He took a sip and leaned against the wooden counter. It was best that not many asked his advice anymore. His heart was too preoccupied with Theron's departure.

At first he'd felt betrayed by Theron's decision to leave Loraleaf, but as the days turned to weeks, the pain of losing a brother of his heart had become the focus of his life. He looked out the window across the room, his gaze reflexively searching for Theron's return.

He sighed, taking another sip of kafez and bringing his thoughts back to the present situation. For a moment, he stared unseeing at Konala's chair. Konala didn't understand. He was ready to move on.

I've lost my filoz in three short turns of Selene. Maybe I need to search out another. Konala's words reverberated in Rckah's head.

"He wouldn't." He lowered his cup to the table.

He would.

The prospect of being without either Theron or Konala loomed before him. The vision was so startling, he rose from the table. "No." He fisted his hands as he let the pain of potential total loss flow through him. He allowed his heart the full experience, his knees almost buckling under the devastation.

By sheer force of will, he pushed the feelings aside and regained some semblance of normalcy. Being Kindred of Heart with a sense for others' emotions brought with it both strong abilities, and debilitating weaknesses, especially in his masculine society. He'd learned as a young man the extent he could go without being hurt.

And what he couldn't do was lose both brothers of his heart.

Picking up his kafez, he took another sip and brought it with him to the bath. He couldn't do anything to keep Theron home, but by the Crius, he wouldn't lose Konala as well!

If the man wanted to find a chosen one, then they would find one and solidify the link between them with a beloved. One who preferably didn't look anything like Serena.

As he proceeded to trim his hair, he grimaced. He hadn't been able to look at Serena without resentment since Theron left. In his gut he knew she'd done nothing to cause Theron to fall in love with her, but his own emotional state had refused to acknowledge that.

It was time to move on, as Konala had tried to tell him. He'd seen the excitement of the other men searching and finding their chosen ones. No others had been brought to Loraleaf yet, but soon there would be more women among them. Why not he and Konala?

And if Theron returned?

Rekah paused as he was about to tackle his unruly beard. What then? His heart skipped a beat.

He returned to his trim. He needed to give up that hope. It was what drove a wedge between him and Konala and it could well destroy any bonded relationship they might have with a woman.

Theron had made his own decision. They would all just have to live with it.

Theron covered Jaelene with his body, his cock sinking into her tight sheath. Her body, soft against his hard one, caused his need to escalate.

He leaned up, bracing his arms on either side of her to gaze into her eyes. They were the darkest of blues, almost black.

"Theron, you're teasing me. You know, two can play that game."

Her sheath contracted around him, squeezing him and letting go, causing pleasure to spread through his balls and up into his ass.

He took a steadying breath. "Not teasing, Khityki. Savoring. I want to always remember this. Your scent. Your voice. Your skin. Your wetness that tells me you are ready. I want to see the flush on your cheeks as passion takes you higher than the stars."

"Oh wow." She stopped squeezing him and her eyes-lids lowered a fraction. She nibbled at her bottom lip before she spoke. "No one has ever said something so wonderful to me."

Pride that he was the first to appreciate her mixed with anger that no one had treated her the way she deserved to be treated. A primal urge to claim her caught him off guard.

He could fight it, should fight it but for some reason he couldn't even remember why. So he didn't. She was his if she'd have him.

He lowered his head and kissed her as her arms looped over his neck. Then his hips started the instinctual motion that was born in all Edenists—to mate, to claim, to cherish.

His cock pulled from the heat of her sheath then drove back in, anxious to return. Jaelene's hands moved to his back and she broke their kiss. "Yes, Theron. More. So much more. Take me."

Lost to her wishes, he reclaimed her lips as he pumped into her, her moans and cries into his mouth building even as his own pleasure climbed. On the verge of exploding, he tilted his hips slightly, rubbing her tiny nub as his cock pushed in and out.

She broke their kiss again as her fingers dug into his back and a cry of pleasure issued from her throat. Her head tilted back and she imploded around him.

Her beauty as she came triggered the end of his control. He spilled his seed deep into her. The thought of a child being born of their union spread peace through him and he cradled his beloved against him.

She was asleep before he pulled out, her hands grasping onto him even in sleep. He gathered her close as his body relaxed and his mind cleared.

What about Serena?

Theron woke with Jaelene plastered to his side. The dream and reality blended making it hard for him to focus on why he was awake. That wasn't the only thing hard either.

Glancing down at Jaelene's dark hair, he looked at her closed eyes and forced himself to keep his breathing rhythmic.

"Don't get too close."

The voice, prophetic though it might be, came from outside and it was followed by a deep growl.

That's why he was awake. Talia was protecting her kill from yesterday and from the sounds of it, she was keeping it away from other Edenists.

His protective instincts roared to life as loudly as Talia. Between the dream and Jaelene's body cuddled against him, his need to keep her safe was no longer about his training or the fact she was Serena's sister. He didn't know exactly why, but he never fought his instincts.

Carefully disengaging himself from Jaelene, he slipped, literally, from the bed, landing quietly on the stone floor. If there were lawbreakers nearby, he didn't want to give away his location.

With his good arm, he hoisted himself to stand on one leg and pulled the "crutch" beneath his arm. Silently, he hobbled out of the bedroom and into the living area. Despite his concern, relief that he healed so quickly flooded him as he tested his arm by using it to brace against the wall as he made it to the door.

"We could use that meat." The leader of the lawbreakers was eyeing what was left of the boarox.

The short skinny man beside him consistently rocked back and forth from one leg to the other. "Let me hit the tigran. I can do it."

"Yeah, and destroy the meat as well." Sandale frowned at the little man.

Theron swallowed hard to keep from shouting out to Sandale. Knowing the man had turned lawbreaker didn't make it easier to see him as such. Sandale had been the gentlest of all men at Loraleaf. The calmest and the most wise.

The leader smirked as he looked at the little man. "I have a better idea. You attract the attention of the tigran and get it to chase you. Then you can turn whirlwind on it, but not until you are away from the meat and out of this clearing."

The little man frowned, but didn't stop moving. "I don't like it."

"You don't have to like it. Just do it."

Sandale gave the small man a piercing look. "The sooner the better. It's going to take a while to drag that big of a carcass back. If it is still out here in the mid-day sun, it will rot. You don't want that, do you?"

The little man shook his head vigorously.

"Go." The leader pointed.

Theron watched as the little man got Talia's attention and then ran, the big tigran followed. He wanted to yell at Talia to keep her from going. He had no idea what the little man would do to her and it worried him.

But Talia was fast. She could jump him before he could do whatever he did. The birthmark on his right elbow proclaimed him Kindred of Air. That would be no match for Talia's strength… he hoped.

Sandale and the leader moved in and tied the boarox carcass with infragile vine.

As they finished, Sandale paused. "There was someone here." He followed the torn bushes to the tree where Theron had been pinned by the beast. "There is Edenist blood here."

"How can you tell?"

"The color." Sandale pointed to the blood he looked at and then the blood on the ground near the boarox. "Edenist blood is redder than the purple of the beast."

"We should follow the trail." The leader dropped the boarox leg he'd been tying.

Sandale scanned the bushes and the ground nearby. "It doesn't go any farther than here. Whoever it was must have wrapped the wound and returned home."

"Still, we should search."

Sandale gave the leader a calculating look. "Which is more important? The food or the man?"

"Don't challenge me or you'll find yourself with no mind at all."

Sandale looked away.

Theron tensed. Scrat, the lawbreakers had changed Sandale through mind manipulation. He peered at the leader to find his birthmark, but couldn't see any from where he was.

The leader didn't let it rest. "Unless, of course, you would prefer to search for the lone woman and the disappearing man."

The sneer that followed proved the leader hadn't believed Sandale's story of his encounter with them which eased Theron's mind.

Sandale stalked back toward the leader. "Let's just get this boarox back."

The leader grinned, showing his rotting teeth. "Good idea."

The men hadn't gone far with the carcass before Theron started to review his options. As much as he didn't want to leave the safety of the cave, there was a good chance the lawbreakers would return. If they found him, he'd be in no shape to protect Jaelene.

"Theron?" As if on cue, her voice took him from his planning.

He wanted her to step up behind him, wrap her arms around his waist and lay her head against his back. That alone was warning enough that staying here with her could be dangerous to his heart.

He wasn't even Kindred of Heart. Why was he so susceptible to women? He turned to face Jaelene. "We are going to Haven."

"Why? We can't." She looked away before returning her gaze to him. "I mean, you can't walk. Your arm."

He studied her. It was as if she wanted to stay here with him, alone. No, he imagined it. It was the heady dream. That he could think such a thing just reinforced his decision to get her to Haven where she was safe. Even from him.

"My arm is almost healed." He raised it, smiling as pain shot through his biceps. "Just need to be careful of the stitches."

Jaelene frowned. "You better be careful of those. I don't stitch people up just to have them rip them apart the next day. I saw those gashes up close. There's no way they're healed that much."

He shrugged. "Edenists heal faster than humans. Either way, it doesn't—What?"

Jaelene's mouth had fallen open and her eyes were wide. "What do you mean Edenists and humans?"

By the Crius! He'd forgotten she didn't believe she was on another planet. She would find out anyway as soon as they made it to Haven. People there would expect her to know already and would quickly enlighten her. It was one thing to wait until Serena could tell her, but since they would be at Haven first, he wanted to be the one to explain.

He moved away from the door and sat in the only chair left. It would be less intimidating for her, or so Rekah had explained. "That portal you followed your sister through was not a way to move from one place on Earth to another. It was a way to move from Earth to Eden. I am an Edenist."

She backed up a step, never taking her gaze from him. "I think that boarox may have hit you too hard."

He pushed his loose hair out of his face. "Think about it, Jaelene. There are too many things that are different here. Talia, the boarox, the welchet."

She shook her head. "All easily explained by being in a different country. Different place, different animals."

He grinned. "And the naked men?"

"A tribe. Many tribes in Africa don't wear clothes."

He lost his smile. "And the eyllen as an energy source?"

She cocked her head. "The what?"

He pointed to the shiner still emitting light near the bedroom doorway.

She shook her head and backed up another step. "It's just another form of light bulb. Why are you trying to convince me I'm on another planet?" She worried her bottom lip before her shoulders relaxed. "My sister would have told me if she lived on another planet."

And Jaelene probably wouldn't have believed her either. Theron didn't want her afraid of him. He wanted her to trust him. He could prove himself later. "You're right. It's not important. What is important is that we get you to Haven safely."

"You didn't answer me about that. Why?" Though her attitude was confrontational, he could see her body had relaxed considerably. Maybe just planting the fact in her mind now may make it easier for her to believe later.

"The lawbreakers found the boarox and lured Talia away from here. They also noticed my blood on the ground. They plan to return to investigate. This cave isn't safe against them with my physical condition less than perfect. Haven has walls and is guarded and there are many men there who can protect you."

Her face softened. "And you."

He raised his brow. "Me?"

"Yes, while you heal you need protection. Will we leave after breakfast?" She moved to the cabinet, prepared to make him something to eat.

Theron's heart melted at her concern for him. One side of him wanted what was best for her while the other wanted to keep her hidden in his cave with him forever. Who would know?

But the lawbreakers were too close to discovering them. It had been three times now that they were near and Theron wasn't willing to risk Jaelene. "No, we will leave once Helios has descended. There will be less chance of discovery and it will give my leg more time to heal."

She looked doubtful. "Right. Okay, so how do I turn on this stove?"

As Theron instructed her in the use of the "heat top" and how to make the large eggs he stored in his "cold box," she focused her attention on her actions, shutting off the myriad of questions running through her mind.

But once he'd hobbled outside to look for Talia, her head filled with thoughts. Two vied for her attention: how could she seduce him if they left the cave and why he would want her to think she was on another planet? The first fueled her libido while the second fed her fear. By the time he returned, she was a bundle of nerves.

He must have sensed her unease. "Jaelene, please sit." He pointed to the chair he held for support.

Part of her wanted to run away and part of her wanted to run into his arms. It was crazy. Finally, she moved forward, not wanting him to question her actions. As she sat with her back to him, his hands came to rest on her shoulders. She tensed.

Immediately, he began to massage her shoulders. "You do not need to fear going to Haven. Though it is a new settlement, it is well built from what I have heard."

He caught her attention with that. "You've never been there?"

His hands didn't stop their work. "I have, but not inside. I lived in Loraleaf and as such had no need to enter Haven, but I have been contemplating joining them for a while."

She kept quiet though she wanted to know why he hadn't.

His thumbs rubbed along the base of her neck and she let her head fall forward.

"The leaders of Haven are Nassic and Wareson, who were

originally part of the Ruling Circle of Naralina. I don't know why they built Haven, but I'm guessing there was strong disagreement that caused a separation. They found their chosen one and brought her…home. I don't know her name."

Despite how relaxed her body felt, her brain ran at high speed and she couldn't keep quiet any longer. "What is a chosen one? Where was she? How far away is Naralina? Was she there?"

Theron chuckled behind her and his hands dropped away.

She turned in the chair. "You didn't have to stop."

He smiled. "No, but my leg needs rest if I'm to get you to Haven safely to satisfy your curiosity."

She couldn't believe how selfish she'd been. "You're right. Why don't you lie down and I'll bring you some cold ambrosia."

He nodded and used the crutch to make his way into the bedroom. His movements weren't awkward despite his injuries and her gaze fastened on his tight ass. Shoot. Even seriously injured, the man was way too sexy. Of course, being able to see every naked bulge of muscle and tan skin on him all the time kept reminding her of that. She really wanted him.

There hadn't been many men she'd really wanted, though when men made moves on her, she usually welcomed them, but she'd become used to the experience being a one-time thing.

Theron was different. He was not only built like a well-honed body builder, but he was sweet and kind and protective and caring and had far too many qualities for her to ignore.

What could it hurt? She'd probably never see him again once she returned home. She would be the one keeping it to a one-night-stand for a change.

She made up her mind. She could be in control for once and

there was no time like the present. Except, it would be a one-day-stand and she'd never had sex in the daytime before. Not that she would mind, but the atmosphere was so different.

Pulling out the ambrosia, she poured some into a glass mug. When she returned it to the mini-fridge, she paused. Closing the door, she pulled the appliance out of the cabinet. There was no cord or plug. She glanced at the lantern hanging from the center of the ceiling. How could a culture that seemed so primitive have such advanced methods of generating power?

Carefully, she returned the fridge to its normal spot and closed the cabinet. If she could understand how the lantern and fridge worked, she might be able to incorporate it into her designs.

She picked up the mug. One thing at a time. First, she had a gorgeous hunk to seduce.

CHAPTER SIX

Konala ran down the wooden walkway to the lift that would bring him to Khaos and Jahl's home, the note he'd taken off the rhybat clutched in his hand. If it was true, it could relieve them of a lot of danger in the jungle.

He stepped into the lift and threw the lever. As it rose, he looked down at his home. Former home. Last night he'd stayed in the sitki with the tamed animals. If Rekah didn't put Theron's departure into perspective soon, he would ask Jahl for a small room in the sitki since Jahl could build it in less than a morning's time.

He could stay there until he could find a filoz to join. He didn't like that idea much, but watching Rekah ignore life was far worse. He was ready to find a chosen one and reproduce. It was what they were meant to do.

The lift stopped on the top level where the leaders of Loraleaf lived with their agapayto.

He strode to the door of Khaos and Jahl's home and knocked loudly. He was anxious to see their reaction and discover what new rules they would put into place for the men of Loraleaf.

"I'll be right there. I just need to throw something on." The female voice on the other side of the door suddenly squealed with laughter before the door was thrown open and Jahl smiled at him. Just having Jahl smile was a new experience, so he hesitated. Jahl's close cropped hair and dark blue eyes made his visage stern. Rekah said it was due to Jahl's father's cruel treatment, but none of that sternness showed now.

"Come in." Jahl turned his head toward the living area. "It's just Konala. You can come out."

He stepped inside the luxurious home built around the largest and tallest tree in Loraleaf. The ceiling had been cleared and he could see up into the treetops. Theron had helped create the roofs that could darken or go clear with a switch.

Khaos appeared at the opening to the living area, a genuine welcome on his face. "Konala, please come in. Would you like some ambrosia?"

He followed Khaos to the bar in the living area, but didn't see Serena. "Yes, I would. We may have something to celebrate."

Jahl joined them. "Celebrate? Why? Do you have word from Toni?"

"Toni?" Serena joined them, her short black hair having grown just past her ears, and she was wrapped in a piece of cloth that hid her body from view.

It was considered rude on Eden to cover the body, but they all made allowances for women from Earth to get used to their culture. "Yes, I received this note." He opened his hand and carefully unfolded it then handed it to Jahl and Khaos.

Serena hopped up on a stool next to him and a slight whiff of vanilla filled his nostrils. It reminded him that his leaders had found the happiness he hoped he could have soon.

"What does it say?" Serena's excitement was obvious. "Is she doing okay? Did she find out something important? Does she like being in Naralina? I hope she hasn't punched anyone."

The last was said with a frown and Konala stifled a grin. He had liked Toni when she'd been in Loraleaf, especially when they had sex. She was a strong woman and could hold her own in many ways. She was also as open and free about nudity as their culture required, but she wasn't ready to choose just one filoz. So she'd offered to spy for them by joining a Pleasure Temple inside Naralina, a highly honored position for a woman not connected to a filoz.

Jahl put down the paper. "If this is true, our danger has been minimized."

"What did she say?" Serena grabbed the paper and scowled. "I can't read this."

Khaos, his long hair tied back in a leather thong, grinned as he walked over to her and wrapped his arms around her waist from behind. He and Theron had often been mistaken for brothers.

Khaos kissed Serena's temple. "We are using a code to protect Toni if a note goes awry." He looked at Jahl, a silent communication passing between them.

Jahl responded. "It says that the Naralina government suspended all work on the portal transport tracking system for openings outside of Naralina or other cities to focus on another project."

At Serena's confusion, Khaos gave her a squeeze. "Remember when we brought you to Eden and we had to transport into the middle of the jungle so no one could track us to Loraleaf?"

"Of course, that's when Sandale was mortally wounded."

They all remained quiet for a moment, the loss of the third of Loraleaf's leaders being the first for the settlement.

Though Konala could communicate with animals, even he could read the silence in the room. The three of them still mourned Sandale. They believed there was some indication that he lived, possibly being held by the lawbreakers, but he doubted it.

He'd made his own peace with Sandale's death. As with Theron, it did no good to stop life. It was too short, too uncertain.

Jahl finally continued the explanation. "What Toni is telling us is that the tracking system Naralina had been working on to find portal openings in the jungle has been halted. That means if any filoz in Loraleaf has a chosen one ready to come here from Earth, they can simply bring her directly here without fear of revealing Loraleaf's location to Naralina.

Serena's smile was wide as understanding dawned. "That means that if I want to visit Erin at Haven, I could do so through a portal."

Jahl scowled, his distrust of anyone involved with the Naralina Ruling Circle was well known. Unfortunately for Serena, Erin's agapaytos were former circle rulers.

Khaos turned her in his arms. "Yes, that is an example of what we can now do safely."

She looked at him with hope shining in her eyes. "Does that mean that Toni can come back here?" She raised her hand as Khaos opened his mouth to answer. "Of course," Serena held up one finger, "if she wants to." She held up another finger. "If she is done with your spying." She held up a third finger. "And if she is ready to settle down with a filoz."

Jahl answered. "She can come for a visit anytime, but she must stay in a Pleasure Temple or become part of a filoz for her own safety. And yes, she can come through a portal…at least until they decide to go back to developing the jungle tracking system."

Serena's shoulders slumped, but she still smiled. "So even if she has to stay there to keep track of that, she can still visit here."

Jahl nodded.

"That's awesome news!"

Konala smiled at the joy in her face, and the longing for a chosen one of his own burned in his gut.

A knock sounded on the door. Serena immediately left Khaos and opened it. "Rekah. Have you heard the news?"

Konala froze. Was Rekah there on purpose or was it simply coincidence? He waited for the brother of his heart to enter the living area.

Rekah nodded as Serena explained what had been discovered, his head bowed toward her but his body turned away. He'd cut his hair to its normal length and his beard was closely trimmed. When he finally looked up, he smiled. "Konala."

By the Crius, what was that? Rekah didn't smile anymore. Something had changed.

He simply nodded and returned his attention to Jahl and Khaos. "Do we need to confirm this information?"

Jahl nodded but Khaos shook his head, yet it was Serena who spoke. "Of course not. If Toni says they aren't working on that tracking device, then they aren't. She wouldn't tell us that unless she was absolutely positive. Did she say she heard this was true or did she simply say it was?"

Jahl glanced at the note again. "She's says they are no longer working on it due to another project."

Rekah stepped forward. "That begs the question, what are they working on that is more important?"

They all stared at him.

Jahl turned the note over as if the answer would be there. "That's a serious question. We need more information about what the other project is. Before I left Naralina, my father said the tracking device was their priority because they didn't want lawbreakers to have the Crius transport chips." He sneered. "He was determined to track any down and rip the chips from their bodies if necessary."

Serena immediately grasped Jahl's clenched hand in her two delicate ones. "I'm sure that was before you left Naralina."

Jahl snorted. "It was, but it wouldn't make a difference to my father."

Rekah touched Jahl's shoulder. "No, it wouldn't, which is why we must discover what new project he has the discoverists working on."

Jahl unclenched his fists, but he grasped Serena's hand in his. "We need Toni to stay a bit longer before she comes to visit." He looked down at his beloved.

The caring in Jahl's gaze made Konala's own yearning that much harder to bear. "I will send a short note by elseire bird. Toni's private room in the Pleasure Temple has a balcony."

Khaos raised an eyebrow. "And how do you know this?"

"You haven't gone into the city, have you?" Jahl scowled at him.

Rekah stood next to him. "I'm sure he hasn't."

He stared at Rekah for a moment, confused by his interest in any of their conversation. "No, I haven't. But Toni had to tell me which temple she was at and the configuration of the building so I could send the best animals for the purpose."

Khaos nodded. "Glad you thought of that." He placed another glass on the bar then filled them all with ambrosia. "We must celebrate." He lifted his glass. "To future safety and prosperity."

They raised their glasses, tapped them to their foreheads and drank. As Konala put his down, he found Rekah studying him. Why had the brother of his heart sought him out? He'd obviously used his ability to sense emotions to find him. "I will compose the note and have it on its way before night fall."

Jahl patted him on the back as he turned to leave. "Thank you for your help in this. If there is anything we can do for you, all you need do is ask."

He couldn't help glancing at Rekah before nodding to Jahl. "It is my pleasure to help all in Loraleaf." He turned and headed for the door when Serena grabbed his arm.

"Wait, I heard your henny hatched her eggs. Can I come by and see the babies?"

He felt Jahl's glower at Serena's innocent touch, so he turned to face her, disconnecting her hold. "Of course, but you will need to wait a few days. They have no feathers right now and need to stay warm beneath their mother."

"That makes sense." She smiled.

Again he turned to leave and made it to the door before sensing someone following him. He didn't stop. He walked out and headed toward the jump-off ledge. He grabbed a vine to swing across to the opposite side when Rekah's hand landed on his arm.

"Konala, wait."

He halted, but didn't turn around or let go of the vine.

"Come home tonight. I would like to talk about finding a chosen one."

Conflicting emotions spun inside him. Disbelief, hope, disappointment, but despite his confusion, he nodded once before swinging away.

Theron sensed Jaelene's intentions as she walked into his room. Her pheromones flooded his senses. Serena had never exuded them around him, but he'd caught them by accident when she was near Jahl.

A woman's pheromones were what the men of Eden craved, so much so that some filoz blocked their beloved's when traveling to another city. The male workers in the Pleasure Temples were often asked to do the same for the women residing there when they went into the city to acquire needed supplies. It was the only way they could venture out without too many men stopping them to converse.

With Jaelene's pheromones filling his bedroom, his cock twitched and every inch of his skin came alive with longing.

"Theron, are you asleep?" The disappointed tone of her voice forced him to open his eyes.

"No."

She sat on the bed next to him, her warm, nutty scent wafting over him, combining with her pheromones to knock out any control he had. He gritted his teeth to keep from touching her.

"I brought you some of the ambrosia." She held the mug up, but didn't move it toward him. "I love the taste of it. It's so refreshing. Would you mind if I took a sip first?"

He swallowed hard, his gaze riveted to her full lips then shook his head, not willing to loosen his jaw to speak.

Her mouth closed over the rim of the mug and the liquid flowed into it. The visual created a picture in his mind of his cock spilling its seed into her succulent mouth. His partially stifled groan broke the silence.

She pulled her mouth away from the cup and licked her lips.

He was wrong for wanting her, but his body ignored him, his balls tightening as he watched her pink tongue move across her full bottom lip. With his good arm, he pulled her against his chest.

Her eyes widened and then a small smile followed. She continued to hold the mug of ambrosia with one hand, but her other burrowed beneath his long hair and grasped the back of his neck.

Theron tried to ignore the feel of her breasts as they pushed against his chest. He thought of Konala and Rekah, reaching for the sadness that always came when remembering their friendship. He even thought of Serena and the pain of loving her despite the fact she was taken. What would she think of him if he took what Jaelene offered?

He clung to that thought as he forced his body to be still.

Jaelene's smile faltered. "Please, Theron. Won't you kiss me?"

He simply wasn't strong enough to resist her plea. What man could? But it was the self-doubt in her voice that gentled his need.

Using his wounded arm, he softly traced her cheek with his fingers, down to her chin where he tilted it up. He gazed into the depths of her blue eyes and discovered uncertainty and eagerness vying for supremacy.

A woman of her character and beauty should never feel so uncertain. With new determination, he lowered his face and kissed the corner of her mouth before nipping at the temptation of her full bottom lip.

Her breath caught and her mouth opened slightly.

It was an invitation he could not refuse. Covering her lips with his own, he moved his tongue to that enticing opening and pushed inside for a taste.

The tang of the ambrosia melded with a sweetness that was pure Jaelene, teasing his desire into full blown need.

She relaxed against him, as if relieved that he wanted her and she opened her mouth wider, inviting him to enjoy her as he would.

Her offering, her scent, her taste and her pheromones were a heady combination that far surpassed any drink he'd ever had at Libations. Every nuance of her being called for him to explore.

Her tongue hesitantly moved against his, wanting to taste him as well.

He let her take control but squeezed her tighter to encourage her even as he burrowed his other hand into the hair at the back of her head, supporting, but not directing.

Jaelene's tongue grew more demanding, her shyness finally giving way to her desire.

He could fulfill her wish in every way. Taking back control, he tilted her head and deepened the kiss, now sweeping his tongue through her mouth, claiming the new found territory as his.

Her hand left his neck and grabbed his hair. The pull sent pleasure racing to his groin. He moved his own from the back of her head to her shoulder and slipped the strap of her top down.

She broke away.

He clamped down on the moan that almost left his throat at her sudden retreat. Had he been wrong in what she wanted?

She pulled both hands down to the bottom of what she called a tank top. "I think I now understand one of the benefits of walking around nude. This is in the way."

Before he could follow her thoughts, she pulled her top over her head and threw it to the side. Then she reached behind her and released her breast binding and dropped that as well.

He couldn't help but stare at her pale round breasts. Each was no more than a handful with its corresponding nipple erect and waiting. "Holy Bendis, you're perfect."

She looked down. "Really? I think I'm kind of small."

Theron barely held himself back from grasping both round globes in his hands. She was created to be worshipped. He managed to shake his head. "No, they are the exact size they should be. I want to take them in my mouth and suck."

Her chest rose as she took a deep breath and he moved his gaze to her delicate face. Her own desire was reflected in her eyes, which had darkened to almost black. Her pheromones increased, their strength pulling at him.

"Do it."

At her words, Theron released his breath and leaned forward. He rested his hands on her waist and allowed his tongue a simple lick across one nipple. It wasn't enough, so he swiped the hard peak again then circled the entire areola with his tongue, wetting it to make the skin pucker.

Jaelene's hands grasped his head and tried to pull him against her, but he refused to rush such a wonderful experience. At his resistance, she gave up and just held on.

He returned his attention to the hard nub before him and took it gently between his teeth, biting carefully.

"Yes, Theron. More."

He couldn't help smiling at her acceptance of his attentions and holding the hard peak with his teeth, he tugged a little, just enough for her to feel the sensation it caused.

Her hips squirmed on the bed and the scent of her readiness rose, making his already stiff cock harder.

Determinedly, he ignored his own needs and stayed focused on the nipple in his mouth. He released it from his teeth only to follow with his mouth. Covering it and the areola, he lightly sucked.

"Yes, please, more." Jaelene's hands grasped at his hair even as she pressed her chest toward him.

He gave into her demand and sucked harder, pulling more of her breast into his mouth.

Her moan of delight released him to enjoy. He let go of her breast and nibbled on her nipple before sucking hard again, her vocal sighs of pleasure like the finest night music he'd ever heard. His soul felt whole.

He would love to create a reflection of them to watch her from all angles, but she wasn't ready for it yet. What would be even better would be to share her with Konala and Rekah. The longing inside him threatened to take him from his purpose and he ruthlessly buried his fantasy. Instead, he focused on giving her all the pleasure she could take.

When Jaelene's pants became near to breathless, he drew back, but kept her skin beneath his palms, stroking her waist to sooth her. Her eyes remained closed and her lips parted, her head tilted back just a little as if holding it upright was too much effort.

Finally, she took in a deep breath and released it, her eyes opening to look at him. "Wow, and that's just the beginning."

He laughed. "Yes, that's only the beginning." He smiled at her, pleased he could make her happy so easily.

She lifted her hands and ran them down over his chest and stomach. Every inch of skin quivered beneath her touch. She paused before going lower. "You're very large."

His cock jumped at her comment. "I would never hurt you." Doubt crept back into his consciousness. *What are you doing?*

Her gaze came up to meet his. "Oh, I wasn't worried. That was a compliment."

Jaelene grinned as Theron's eyes widened. He was such a sweet man. The somersaults her belly did told her he would give her the best sex of her life. He was a great tease when it came to foreplay, so it was only fair that she return the favor.

Moving her hands back up his rippled stomach, she marveled at the strength beneath her finger-tips. The man was a muscle machine. Living alone in the middle of the jungle probably did that.

She let her hands splay over the hard mounds of his chest, lightly brushing over his nipples before she followed the sinews across his shoulders. She didn't go any farther on his wounded arm, but she did give in to her need to grasp the large biceps of his good arm and finally the steel hard forearm.

He brought his hand up to brush strands of her hair back behind her ear.

How could he be so gentle with all this power just beneath the surface of his skin? Her stomach tightened as she lowered her hands to his thighs. She traced the grooves between muscles with her fingers, amazed by the hardness beneath them.

She moved her hands toward his groin, when he grabbed her wrists. She looked up at his face to find his dark brown eyes black and heavy lidded.

"No." His voice was gruff. "Your touch is too stimulating."

She frowned. "Is there such a thing?" It wasn't like she was an expert in pleasing a man. Her experience had shown that as long as a man could put his cock in her mouth or vagina, he was happy.

"Yes." Theron raised her hands to his face and kissed each palm before placing them in her lap. "It is important that I do not find pleasure before you do."

Was he for real? She was tempted to look over her shoulder for cameras. She felt she was being set up for a joke, but she was quite aware that the only people in the cave were the two of them. "How about if we find "pleasure" together?"

Theron shook his head, his face serious. "No. You come first. It is the way I was taught."

Taught? He was taught that a woman should come first? Oh, she loved whatever kind of schooling he had. "Okay, but I'm thinking for that to happen, I should probably get out of my jeans and onto the bed. I don't want you to hurt your leg." And she was anxious for him to lie back down. She would love to straddle him.

He didn't say anything, but he did nod, so she quickly slipped off the bed and dropped her jeans and panties. When she turned around she found him staring at her shaped pubic hair.

Zings of excitement went straight to the juncture of her thighs. If she hadn't been wet before, she definitely would have been from just his look. How could a man appear to both want to take her and worship her at the same time?

She crawled back up on the bed. In the hope he'd lie back, she straddled his thighs close to his groin, careful to avoid the break in his leg. By his surprised look, she had to guess he wasn't expecting her to climb on top of him. She really wanted to touch the hard cock sticking straight up in front of her, but before she could bring her hands to it, he'd caught them and pulled them behind her, neatly grasping them both in one of his.

The position pushed her breasts up. She smirked. "You really don't want me to touch you, do you?"

His face remained serious. "No."

"Fine, I promise not to touch."

He released her hands and brought his to her waist. Before she realized his intent, he'd rolled her off and onto her back. He lay on his side, his good leg beneath him.

She winked. "You do realize with your broken leg, eventually you will have to let me ride. There's no other way we can have sex with your leg in that condition."

"That may be true, but it is not my satisfaction I seek right now." He let his gaze leave her face and roam her entire body. "You truly are perfect."

Oh, he was good. "I think you need to get your eyes checked. My breasts are small and my hips too narrow. I've even been told—"

Theron's finger across her lips and the scowl on his face kept her from continuing. He took a deep breath before speaking. "I do not care who thinks such things about your body. To me it is beautiful." His eyebrows relaxed and a slight smirk curved his lips.

"I think you can tell exactly how beautiful I think you are." He pressed his cock against her hip.

Its hard silk sent her belly into performing flip flops again. She wanted to feel him inside her sooner rather than later, so she nodded.

"Good." He leaned over and kissed her nipple. The unexpected contact had her catching her breath. But when he began to suck, she forgot to breathe all together. It wasn't until he stopped to nibble on her peak that she remembered to take air into her lungs.

She burrowed her hand into his hair. Its length was almost as long as her own, but its silkiness felt very different. She vaguely wondered if he washed it with rainwater or the warm water from the cave. When he bit lightly at her hardened peak, all thoughts of rain dissipated.

His hand covered her mons had her brain split between the pings flowing from her nipple to her core and the anticipation of what he would do next.

He lifted his head from her breast and gazed into her eyes. Damn, but the man had the darkest eyes she'd ever seen.

"You taste good."

Her heart flipped over at the same time her sheath tightened. No one had ever said that before. If she wasn't careful, she'd get addicted to Theron.

His hand on her mons moved down even as his mouth sought her other nipple. One finger pressed against her clit as it slid into her wet pussy.

Theron's groan against her breast as his finger penetrated her sent more shots of pleasure down to her core. When he moved his finger out and in again at the same time he stopped sucking and started to nibble, she let out a moan of her own. She was so ready to have him fill her.

But Theron was in no hurry. His finger between her legs pulled out again, but this time he swirled her own moisture over her clit.

She pressed her hips upward, loving the excitement rifling through her as he played her hard nub for all it was worth. His mouth returned to her nipple to suck it inside and tongue it hard.

She tried to stay aware of what was happening, but the zings of pleasure from her clit combined with the spikes of elation from her breast to focus her attention on the building ecstasy waiting to explode. It would be faster to have his large cock inside her, but exhilaration swallowed her thought and spread throughout her body until it burst through her.

"Oh yes!" She cried out as her body splintered apart, every molecule jumping for joy. Aftershocks continued to ping inside her as Theron's fingers pressed against her sensitive clit. She finally lowered her hips, surprised to find she'd kept them pressed upward so long. Physical strength was not one of her strong points.

As she relaxed, she also let go of Theron's hair. Poor man. She was surprised she didn't pull it all out.

When he raised his head from her chest, she forced one hand to smooth his scalp, hoping she hadn't caused too much pain. His lovemaking was the exact opposite of what she'd experienced so far in her life.

The men she hooked up with didn't seem to think they needed to do anything special. A kiss, a fiddle with her nipples and they were ready to plunge in. It usually left her wanting more, but only two had seen her a second time and the sex had been equally unfulfilling. She'd found more enjoyment with her own toys.

Theron was gazing at her with smug triumph and she laughed at his expression. "Oh my, you have every right to be proud. I've never come like that with a man."

His smile faltered. "You have done so with a woman?"

She laughed again, unable to contain the joy she felt. "No. That doesn't interest me. Let's just say you're the best I've ever had."

Instead of preening, his gaze softened and he cupped her face with his hand. "You deserve that and more—every time." He lowered his face and kissed her tenderly.

Her heart flipped over. When he finished, she wanted to touch her lips because they felt like melted chocolate. "Wow, where did you learn to please a woman so well. Let me guess, you were the most popular guy in your school."

He shook his head, a small smile curving his lips. "No, we do not have women in our schools and I was not the most sought after."

"I see. You went to one of those private all-boys schools. This cave must be very different for you if you had that kind of life."

He started to shake his head again then stopped. "Yes, there were only males with me during my education."

She found her curiosity about him growing. "Then where did you learn about women?"

He shrugged. "Where everyone else did. At the Pleasure Temple. It's part of every man's education. Pleasing a woman in all ways is a strong value in our society."

A Pleasure Temple? His culture sounded a bit exotic. She'd heard of Geishas but this sounded even stranger. Maybe it was simply a different name for a whorehouse. "Did your father take you there?"

He grinned. "No, my fathers didn't need to go. I went with my friends, Konala and Rekah. We learned separately and then learned best how to pleasure a woman together." His eyes appeared less dark and definitely sad. "We were very good."

Okay, so he practiced having sex with his friends and one woman? Three women? Must have been three, but was it an orgy? Why the heck was she so curious? "That sounds like an interesting education. Don't get me wrong, I'm more than pleased you had it, but I don't think I'd want to be one of those women in a Pleasure Temple."

"No." His response was sharp and quick, his voice loud. "You would not be right for a Pleasure Temple. You need a filoz."

"I think I'm just fine with having you. At least until I go home." She'd only planned for this afternoon, but if they were both going to Haven then maybe they could make love even more. Then again, it would be nice if they finished this time first.

She smiled slyly and raised her hand to pull him down for another kiss, her body aching to feel him against her and inside her.

"No." He grabbed her wrist, the scowl on his face as serious as the one he gave her when he said the same thing about her not wanting to be in a Pleasure Temple.

"No, what?"

He put her hand down beside her then let go and rolled away to sit up on the other side of the bed, his good leg over the edge and his bad leg out straight. "I can't make love to you. I've already overstepped my bounds."

What the heck? Maybe she was wrong about him. Maybe

he'd leave her before they even finished. Her stomach tightened. It started to feel like it did when she'd called a man she'd slept with and only got his voice mail.

She hated that feeling of being not good enough beyond sex. "What are you talking about? I'm not married and I certainly don't have a boyfriend, so you are completely within bounds." She tried to relax. "Come back here so I can make *you* feel good." She was no expert, but she didn't have any complaints in that area. She couldn't imagine a man refusing oral sex.

Instead of reassuring him, her words seem to cause him to hurry more in his effort to get away from her. He stood, balancing on one leg as he reached for his crutch. "You don't understand. On this—" He paused as if picking his words carefully. "In our culture, there are only two places for a woman, either in a Pleasure Temple or with a filoz of two to five men.

He finally looked at her. "I can't give you that. I am alone."

Two to five—she shut down her curiosity and kept focused for once. Did his culture require marriage if they had sex? "Where I come from, I don't need any of that. We can just enjoy each other and then part ways. Though I have to say, I think you may ruin me for any other man at home." She winked, trying to bring the lightness back to their conversation.

But he wasn't interested. Not at all. "I can't. It goes against everything I was taught. It betrays my—it's wrong." He started to hobble out as if being in the same room with her was too much to bear.

She swallowed the lump in her throat, grabbed up her clothes, and covering herself with them, jumped off the bed. "Okay. If you don't want to have sex with me because of your upbringing, I can live with that. But you need to lie back down and get some rest. I want to go to Haven tonight and we can't do that if you're not able to."

He leaned against the doorway where he'd stopped. His face was anguished. She wasn't sure if it was from pain or his decision not to have sex with her…or the fact he'd started to.

Finally, he nodded and backed away from the door.

With her ego six feet under, she slipped by him and closed the door without slamming it, a feat for which she felt she deserved a gold medal. She jerked on her panties and jeans before slipping her tank top over her bare torso.

This was supposed to be a fun, sneaky trip to satisfy her curiosity regarding where her sister and her two husbands lived. It wasn't supposed to be a "crush Jaelene's self-esteem" experience.

That would teach her to try to seduce a man and walk away.

Heck, she'd been daydreaming about sleeping with Theron for the next few days when they hadn't even done the deed yet! She was pathetic. Obviously, she wasn't wired for casual sex, even if almost every guy she'd slept with thought of her that way.

She leaned back against the cave wall next to the door. A light vibration massaged her tense muscles. She needed to stay focused on why she was here, wherever "here" was.

First, she'd have someone other than Theron bring her to Serena's house. Then after explaining how hurt she was that Serena hadn't confided in her, she'd return home. She needed to keep it that simple and stop being taken off track by porcupines and tigrans and Theron.

Pushing away from the wall, she sat and put on her shoes and socks. That she'd become sidetracked by a well-muscled naked hunk really couldn't be all her fault, could it? That she'd let herself get rejected again was definitely her problem.

What was it about her that had men taking a taste then walking away? Did they think her breasts would magically grow when she took off her shirt? Did they expect her to not talk after sex and try to connect on more than a physical level? And could a cultural upbringing really have a man denying himself a no-strings-attached lay?

She finished tying her shoes and sat back. So what if she was an interior decorator who loved animals?It's not like she found the stock market, latest movie star sighting or new product development achievement breath-taking, but she listened and learned. Her conversation could be interesting, too.

Her eyes started to itch as she remembered dinner conversation at her parents' house. Once Serena moved away, her parents were thrilled to have her "brighten" their dinner. But whenever Serena came for a visit, it was as if what she had to say paled in comparison. How could blowing up walls be more interesting than decorating them to achieve the perfect atmosphere for someone to live in?

She rubbed her face. She was done being rejected. Screw the men who didn't want her. Actually, she wouldn't anymore. If they wanted to have sex, they damn well better hang around long enough to get to know her. She was done with hooking up unless it was it was on her terms, like her early twenties' fantasy of having two men enjoy her at the same time.

She glanced at the door to the bedroom. Theron did make her feel amazing plus listened to what she said. With a man like that, she'd never have to fantasize again.

She squared her shoulders. It didn't matter. He said he couldn't make love to her because he couldn't break his society's unwritten rules. Fine, then she would move on. Her stomach sank and her heart sighed, but her brain was in full control. She stood and looked over the living room.

As upset as she was that she'd been sidetracked, she had to admit the cave Theron lived in was fascinating. The vibrating walls, illusion entrance and the room full of glowing rocks would make for great stories. Now she had her own secret adventures that she could keep from her sister so she could show her how it felt to be left out.

Maybe a little more exploring was in order while Theron slept. She walked to the fridge. What she needed was a box of dark chocolates with orange filling. She stared inside the small appliance. "Looks like ambrosia it is."

Chapter Seven

Theron held Jaelene's hand as they slowly made their way to Haven. Her soft palm in his had him in a constant state of wanting and with their slow progress, it would take them all night. Selene was just a sliver in the sky and Bendis had not risen yet. A little light couldn't hurt.

Then again, that would show her exactly how he was feeling. At least he'd been able to leave the crutch behind and limp his way along.

The sooner they arrived at Haven, the better. He had no idea what kind of reception they would have, but at least he'd made friends of two men there. First, he would ask for sanctuary from their leaders, Nassic and Wareson. Then if those men needed confirmation that he wouldn't do harm, he'd call on Mykl and Lennix.

He didn't anticipate any problem, especially having Jaelene with him. He just hoped she didn't speak against him. She'd been unusually silent since he woke. He missed her usual chatter, but he didn't delve deeper as her body language made it clear she wanted to be left alone.

He'd hurt her when she'd inadvertently made him aware of the repercussion of enjoying her. Because he cared for her, more than he thought he could considering his feelings for her older sister, he couldn't limit her options. Jaelene would make a filoz very happy. His stomach tensed at the idea, but he would have to ignore it. It was the rules of—

The snap of a branch from a bush brought him to a halt. He felt more than saw Jaelene open her mouth and he squeezed her hand. He now appreciated the darkness as every fighting instinct woke up.

It could be a large animal or a lawbreaker, neither of which was welcome. He listened hard, attempting to hear breaths, but all was silent. If it was an Edenist, he could produce a reflection and draw the men away from them, but if it was an animal, his reflections would have no effect since the animals had different mechanisms for sight. Only when he combined his abilities with Konala's could his reflections work with animals.

He'd just convinced himself that it was nothing more than a rodent when a distinct stench wafted by. It was rancid, like that of a dead animal, but it moved. *Protect Jaelene.* His instincts took over.

He led her to the closest tree, and without a word hoisted her up to a branch above his head.

Her eyes were wide with fright as she put her fingers over her nose.

He silently let her know she had to stay where she was.

She pulled her legs up in front of her and nodded.

With her secure from most animals, he produced a reflection of himself where he stood, and hid behind her tree. Then he had his reflection walk away from them.

The smell appeared to stalk his other self, so he followed and watched.

Something that rancid shouldn't be able to move, let alone hunt. He kept the reflection walking, then had it turn its head back as if it checked to see if anything followed. What puzzled Theron was the lack of sound, the stench was the only sign there was anything there.

When he felt he was far enough from Jaelene, he stopped the reflection and had it sit down on a log and rub its foot, as if it were sore. Selene peaked out from behind a cloud, bathing the area in feeble silvery light. If anything wanted to attack, now would be the time.

He waited, unwilling to continue toward Haven until he knew what danger was in the jungle. Stealthily a shadow separated itself from the others. It had to be a lawbreaker, but one let out of the city long ago.

The Edenist was hunched over and filthy with a long knotted beard, but it looked as if the smell was purposeful. Handprints were on the man's skin where he'd smeared himself with the bowels of some large dead animal. He levitated off the ground by mere inches, almost as if he'd forgotten he did so.

That was why the man made no noise. The branch snap Theron heard must have been one that caught the man's arm. It hadn't been underfoot.

The lawbreaker slinked toward the reflection's back, a sharp rusted dagger in his hand. He raised it, spreading his lips wide, revealing razor sharp teeth. When he'd crept close enough to be within striking distance, he sniffed.

Theron watched, fascinated. The lawbreaker hesitated then

lowered his weapon. He stepped closer and slapped the back of the reflection's head, only his hand went right through it.

The old man spat on the ground, but still did not make a noise. Then he walked through the reflection, his fists clenched, the dagger swinging. Suddenly, he stopped and looked up into the trees.

Scrat. The lawbreaker was evidently smart enough to understand someone nearby had created the reflection. Theron dissipated his creation and waited.

When the man returned his attention to the log and saw there was nothing there any more, he stomped his feet, except they never touched the ground. Clearly angry now, his mouth worked as if he talked to himself, but no sound emerged.

Theron remained where he was until the lawbreaker moved off in search of other prey, the clouds covering what limited light there had been anyway.

As quickly as he could, he made his way back to Jaelene, who sat where he'd left her.

She opened her mouth, but he quickly shook his head and reached his arms up toward her to help her down. As her warm body fell into his arms, his heart began to race. She could have been hurt, even killed.

A shiver ran through his body, but Jaelene shook as well. He clasped her to him and held her close, soothing his hand over her back until she calmed. Finally, she tipped her head back and looked at him.

Again he wished for light. He wanted to know what she thought.

Whatever it was, ended too soon and she pulled away. Putting her finger to her lips, she raised her eyebrows.

He nodded before taking her hand in his and quietly continuing their journey. They walked throughout most of the night. His limp and her sleepiness slowed them considerably. He wanted to carry her, hating to see how tired she was, but his leg wasn't healed enough to hold her weight and it frustrated him.

When he came upon the savinstone in the middle of the small clearing not far from Haven, he stopped. The large gold monolith stood as a guide for him, letting him know he was very close. "We can stop here and rest."

She immediately plopped onto the ground, her legs stretched out in a V before her. "Oh, good. I feel like a walking zombie."

He wasn't sure what that was, but he guessed it wasn't a good thing. "We are very close now."

She looked up at him. "You better define close."

He sat on the ground across from her. "About five hundred strides."

She fell back, spreading her arms out. "If you want me to take a thousand more steps, we better stay here a while."

He didn't say anything. As long as it was safe, she could rest as long as she wished. Helios wouldn't arrive for some time yet.

"I don't see the big dipper. That must mean we're in the Southern hemisphere." She pointed at the sky. "That has to be the Milky Way. Look at the cloud of stars."

He tensed as he gazed at the Dickinson constellation. The large grouping of stars, made it look like a night cloud in the universe and it had been named after the high poetess of Eden over two hundred years ago. He'd completely forgotten that his stars were different from Jaelene's on Earth. Would she come to the right conclusion?

She remained quiet while she studied the sky.

He watched her face in the darkness, her curiosity showing as her eyes darted from one end of the sky to the other. It had been a long time since he'd conversed with someone who had the same level of curiosity as he had. He would miss being with her.

For the elevendieth time, he went over his reasons for bringing her to Haven and why it was best for her, but it still hurt to know that eventually she'd go to Loraleaf without him.

"Oh wow, look at that." Jaelene sat up and pointed at the savinstone.

The very top of the gold boulder glowed with a pinkish light. Theron looked behind him on the horizon and groaned. Bendis was rising. He glanced to the north and Selene's sliver was still prominent in the sky, shining brighter with her brother's appearance. He watched Jaelene's face as the second moon's light reflected on Eden.

She still watched the savinstone. "How come that rock is glowing like that?"

"It's gold and the rising moon's light reflecting off it causes it to glow."

"Gold?" She stared harder at the rock before her gaze swept up to the sky. It quickly lowered as she caught sight of Bendis not halfway over the horizon, its large round shape appearing to be touchable.

Jaelene jumped up. "It's a meteor! I think it's going to hit!"

He rose and grabbed her hand, afraid she would run off into the jungle, the fear on her face as real as when they'd encountered the old lawbreaker. "It's not a meteor. It is Bendis rising. That's our second moon."

Jaelene's panicked gaze left Bendis and shifted to Selene. Back and forth it went until Bendis had cleared the horizon.

He wanted to comfort her, but didn't know what to do. She was always curious, so he tried explaining. "Selene's orbit is much more circular, but Bendis has an oval orbit, so half the time it is in the sky it is too far away to distinguish as a moon and the other times, it is very close, making it impossible to miss."

Jaelene continued to stare open-mouthed at the rising moon.

He squeezed her hand. "As I tried to tell you before. You are on the planet Eden. This is where your sister lives."

At the mention of her sister, Jaelene's gaze locked with his.

She refused to freak out in front of this gorgeous man. No. She *would* remain calm. She wasn't going to die a horrific fiery death because a meteor was about to hit the Earth. No, she was simply on another planet with two moons where her sister lived.

Her sister lived on another planet? *She* was on another planet? Maybe the meteor idea was better. At least it would all be over in a few seconds.

She stared at Theron, trying to accept the unacceptable. She almost had sex with an alien! Her sister's husbands were aliens!

Freaking out was becoming more appealing by the second. She had alien brothers-in-law and had let an alien touch her between her legs and suck on her nipples.

Her knees collapsed beneath her and she sat on the ground abruptly.

"Jaelene!" Theron's voice was anxious but not loud.

That's right, they had to hide from the criminals. Criminal aliens.

The clearing started to spin and the corners of her sight turned dark.

Theron's arms were around her, comforting her. Her vision cleared and the world stopped spinning, or rather the scene before her did. She forced herself to look into the face of the "Edenist" that held her.

He cradled her in his arms as he stared at her with furrowed brow, his eyes worried.

"I'm on another planet."

He nodded. "Yes. This is planet Eden." He smoothed her hair away from her face with a gentle touch.

"You are the same species as my sister's husbands Jahl and Khaos?"

"Yes. I lived in Loraleaf with them. They still live there."

She looked away. Okay, if her sister was having sex with the same kind of men, then she could probably relax about that. "So it was the portal. It really transported us through space?"

"It is an advanced technology left to us by the Crius."

She wasn't going to ask what the Crius was. She wasn't sure she wanted to know right now. "And I can go home through this portal?"

He hesitated. "Yes."

She sat up, breaking out of his hold. "What aren't you telling me? I can go home through the portal but what?"

"Jahl and Khaos will have to decide that."

She could feel panic rising. "Decide? It's my choice. Why would they have to decide anything? I want to go home. Keeping me here is kidnapping." Oh wow, what did aliens care about kidnapping?

"You're the ones who abduct humans and operate on them and erase their memories aren't you?" She crawled backwards, her fear taking over her common sense. "All those people we thought were crazy were telling the truth."

Theron didn't come after her. He simply sat there naked, on the ground, shaking his head. "No, we don't 'operate' on people. We come to Earth to find our beloved."

The sadness in his voice cut through her panic and knocked on her curiosity.

"Why can't you find them here?"

"No females are born on Eden. Only males. To keep our race alive, we must go to Earth and find someone who believes in life on other planets, who will love us in return, and who will come to Eden."

She got stuck on the first requirement. "But I didn't believe in life on other planets except in theory. That's more Serena—oh."

Theron rose and held his hand out toward her. "I'm not very good at this. Rekah was the one Konala and I were depending on to help our beloved adjust, but since I am no longer with them and am destined not to have a beloved, I need to get you to Haven. There is a woman who has transitioned to Eden from Earth. She will be able to better explain."

His acceptance that he would never have a woman to love triggered a buried fear of her own. She pushed it aside. Now was not the time to bemoan her failure in finding someone special. She looked askance at Theron. "In this Haven there is one woman? And how many men?"

He shrugged. "I do not know. It is a newer settlement. Maybe a hundred."

She stood, but didn't get any closer. "I'm not sure I like those odds." Before the man with blonde hair had come after her, she may have been fine with more men than women, but not anymore.

Theron sighed. "Have I let any harm come to you since I found you?"

He had helped her get away from the blond man by carrying her. And he was hurt because he'd saved her from the boarox. And he'd protected her from the lawbreaker he found on the way here. "So you are saying that you will be my bodyguard around all the men at Haven?"

"Bodyguard?" His gaze roamed over her from hair to feet.

Her traitorous belly flip flopped at his look and she scowled. "It means you protect me against all threats."

"Then yes. I will be your bodyguard."

She should feel better about that, but she was still a bundle of nerves.

"If I am to protect you, I need to get you behind the walls of Haven before dawn."

She looked up at the sky to find the big moon much higher and the very beginnings of light from the sun edging the horizon. Walls sounded good to her. So did talking to a woman who actually came from Earth and now lived here.

She dug deep, remembering all the ways in which Theron was nice to her. He'd never been angry, even when she'd done something stupid. And really, what choice did she have in the middle of a jungle on another planet? Shoot. She *had* to trust him.

Hesitantly, she walked toward him and finally grasped his hand.

His smile was kind and reassuring.

Still in shock, her mind wanted to go in a million different directions, but she was in no emotional state to follow, so she focused on walking. After all, it was only a thousand more steps.

Konala ran up the steps inside the tree trunk that led to the entry platform of Loraleaf not far ahead of his patrol partner. Today, he and Rekah were heading to Earth. They'd decided to focus on women interested in unidentified flying object sightings. A woman who already believed that aliens came to her planet should be able to adapt well.

But first he needed to report on the tracks he found. He'd just stepped into the lift when Rekah opened the door of their home. "Did you find something?"

The brother of his heart must have been waiting, as anxious as he was to explore the women of Earth. That was a reassuring sign. Though it appeared Rekah wanted to move forward yesterday, Konala hadn't been completely convinced. "I did find something. I need to report it to Jahl or Khaos."

Rekah strode to the lift. "I'll come with you. Khaos is mediating an argument, so it will have to be Jahl."

He waited until his friend was on board and moved the lever. As they rose toward the third level of walkways, Saphr swung by and nodded before landing on the second level.

"We may need Saphr's help on this."

"What did you find? Is it another lawbreaker mess?" Rekah scowled, having seen the last site they had left behind with an uneaten and unburied feroon carcass with crossed out circles written in blood on the trees.

"No, and glad I am of that. I'll explain when we get there."

The lift stopped on the third level and they walked side by side, stride matching stride until they reached their leaders' home. They had been together so long they often knew each other's minds.

Rekah stepped back and Konala knocked.

Khaos opened the door. "Something isn't right. Come in. Tell me."

They stepped inside the entry way and Konala's gut tightened. Khaos could often sense the future. "What have you seen?"

Khaos didn't meet his gaze. "It is unclear as of yet, but it involves the lawbreakers and one of our own."

He shook his head. "I don't think what I found has a connection, but I could be wrong. I found the tracks of a boarox and it was headed toward Naralina."

Khaos and Rekah both stared at him in surprise. Rekah spoke first. "A boarox? Are you sure?"

Khaos jumped in. "They don't come this close to the equator."

That's exactly why he was concerned. "I know. I have never seen one before, but the tracks I found can only be that of a boarox. I haven't seen anything else like it."

"Neither have I, but we all learned about them in school. They prefer weather that fluctuates more." Rekah appeared more curious than concerned. "What do you think could cause them to come this far?"

He'd been thinking about that since he'd seen the tracks. "It could be a lack of food source, but for that to be the case, there would have to be a widespread killing off of their prey. Or it could be lawbreakers trying to corral them for meat. Or it could be a water source issue."

Khaos raised an eyebrow. "Could it be a temperature change?"

"No. They do prefer it a little cooler, but if it was warming away from the equator, they would still stay with their food source and their fur would simply come in lighter with the next shedding."

"Keep an eye on this. If it's lawbreakers causing them to move, I'll want to know. If it is something larger, it may be something too big for us to handle on our own."

Rekah spoke. "Do you mean joining forces with Haven?"

"I didn't say that." Khaos shook his head. "Let's just keep a watch."

Konala agreed. "I will let the other patrols know what to look for."

"Thank you."

He nodded at Khaos and looked at Rekah, who opened the door.

Khaos turned toward his living area and they left. As soon as they were in the lift, Rekah turned to him. "Do you think it is lawbreakers?"

He shrugged. "I don't know what it is, but I don't think it is a positive development."

They strode to their house together. Their connection was back. He could feel it. If the boarox moving this close was a bad sign, it would be nice to have a son to carry on and the only way to do that was to find a beloved on Earth.

Once inside, Rekah faced him. "I know you still have doubts about my willingness to move forward with choosing an agapayto, but I *am* ready."

For the first time in three months, Konala felt the tension in his shoulders release. "Good, then let's see what we can find."

He moved next to Rekah, leaving a space between them that

two men could walk through and pressed the chip beneath his skin under his left arm. Rekah did the same and the portal opened between them.

They stepped in front of it to view.

"Where on Earth did you choose?" Rekah studied the brown scenery.

Konala focused on a house below that looked like every other house in the neighborhood, including the pool in the backyard. "This is Nevada. Shortly, this house will be the site of a gathering of people anxious to learn about unidentified flying objects or UFOs, as they call it in America."

Rekah grinned. "This is a good place to start. I suggest we hover above and watch and if we see any potential women, we can further investigate."

They moved the portal to inside the home where a couple was busy setting food about the house. It didn't take long for their friends to arrive. Konala ignored the men and studied the women carefully.

He didn't have any particular type in mind. He simply waited for what he hoped would be some kind of recognition in his heart that a particular female was his mate. After everyone had entered and gathered food and drink to a resting place, he still hadn't found any particular connection. He raised an eyebrow at Rekah.

"That one." Rekah pointed to a woman of maybe thirty years old who gazed at the host with awe. The man spoke of having an encounter with a short, skinny, big-eyed alien who wanted him to leave with him.

Konala watched her reactions. It was obvious she was excited that someone had actually seen an alien. Though she sat very straight, her whole torso leaned forward, her wavy red hair just brushing her shoulders.

He looked at Rekah. "She does seem fascinated."

They continued to observe her and as soon as the host was done telling his story, the red-headed woman spoke up. "So do you think they could be watching us right now?"

Konala smiled and shared a knowing glance with Rekah.

The host looked up. "I know they are."

She looked up as if she could see the portal and her eyes grew wide. They were a brilliant green and alive with wonder.

"Let's find out more about her." Rekah moved the portal closer to view her profile. They waited until the people stood and dispersed, forming small groups to talk about what they'd learned. When the red-headed girl walked outside to talk with the host and his wife, they followed.

The three people stood next to the pool and she immediately peppered the host with questions. "How do you think they are watching us? Is it from space or do you think they are invisible? Why do you think they watch us? What do they want to know?"

The host laughed. "Star, you want me to tell you what an alien thinks? I have no idea."

At her disappointed expression, the host continued. "But if you come back next month, I have a guest coming who has actually gone with them and come back."

"Really? Who is it?"

He shook his head. "I can't tell you. You know we have to keep some of this to ourselves. People don't believe us and I don't want this woman to be subjected to ridicule."

Star took a deep breath. "Of course, I understand."

The host put his hand on her shoulder. "Now if you will excuse me, I should make the rounds."

The man and his wife walked back into the house, leaving Star to stare up at the sky.

"If you're up there, I really want to meet you. I don't believe you mean us harm. If you're watching, I want you to know that I'd like to talk to you."

Konala looked at Rekah.

His friend was grinning. "I believe she just invited us down." Rekah stepped toward the portal.

Konala barred his way with his arm. "She doesn't expect us to actually come down there. She's just hoping."

"I can feel her hope. It is like a beacon of light."

"That may be, but we need to know more about her before we make contact."

Rekah stepped back and frowned. "Are you saying you want to watch her for years to be sure she is right for us?"

He shook his head. "No, not for years, but a lot longer than one visit."

Rekah's frown disappeared. "You don't feel anything for her."

From the tone of voice, it was clear Rekah had reached out with his ability to sense emotion and discovered Konala's lack of connection.

"No, but that doesn't mean I won't."

Rekah nodded. "I feel—"

"Aacckk!"

At Star's yell, both of them turned.

She'd fallen into the pool and was floundering to stay afloat.

"Scrat. She can't swim." Rekah jumped through the portal before Konala could stop him.

~~*~~

Theron refused to let go of Jaelene's hand as the night guards walked them to a two story dwelling made of wood. Light could be seen coming from a few windows in the small town as men started to rise for the coming day.

He tried to look at the settlement as his new home, but its position on the ground instead of in the trees would take getting used to. It was hard enough adjusting from tree life to his cave, but this was like a rudimentary version of Naralina, and he'd left Naralina's civilized ways for a reason.

He could sense Jaelene's tension and squeezed her hand to reassure her. Not only was she on a strange planet, but now she was in a town of men and her uneasiness with nakedness probably didn't help her comfort level.

They were let into a surprisingly comfortable living area with two large couches and a number of padded chairs. He led her to one. "Please, sit down. I know you are tired."

"I am."

As she sat, he held her hand. Not sure why, but his gut told him it was best that he did.

The guard left and immediately sounds could be heard above them. Low voices muffled by the floor kept him from hearing what was said.

Then a pair of bare feet came down the stairs.

"Another woman! I thought I heard them say that." A woman with shoulder length, straight platinum blonde hair, and a cloth wrapped around her body, ran down the rest of the steps and across the room, stopping in front of Jaelene. "Hi, my name is Erin."

Jaelene started to get up, but he put his hand on her shoulder, knowing how tired her feet were.

She glanced at him in relief and held out her other hand. "Hi, I'm Jaelene."

Erin smiled as she shook. "Welcome." She looked up at him. "And you are?"

"Theron."

"Oh, you're a friend of Mykl. Welcome. Thank you for bringing me another woman to talk to. It's been a long time since I had that chance. I think almost four months since I saw Toni."

A breeze blew his hair back and he glanced up to find the leaders of Haven standing at the bottom of the stairs, a frown on one face and a scowl on the other. Not exactly the welcome he'd hoped for.

The one with the scowl had short wavy brown hair and was clearly Kindred of Mind, his spiral tattoo prominent on his left arm, which meant the one who frowned and had long black hair much straighter than his own was Kindred of Air and the one responsible for the sudden breeze in the room.

Despite their confrontational stance, he chose a more diplomatic route. He gave a slight bow to each man. "I apologize for the early morning disturbance. We have travelled all night to gain the safety of Haven."

The woman, Erin, obviously the beloved, or agapayto of the two leaders, walked over to them. "Nase, I hope you two aren't going to treat these poor, tired visitors like you did Jahl."

The man of the Mind Kindred flushed. "He broke into our bedroom. He deserved to be distrusted."

Theron had not heard *that* story and couldn't help the quirk of his lips.

The other man lost his frown and stepped forward. "I am Wareson. I'm guessing from your reaction to Nase's comment that you find Jahl's entrance amusing."

He could lie, but why? "I do, only because that sounds like Jahl. He is a bit like a bullish feroon at times, which is why it is good that he still has Khaos to temper him." In actuality, he believed it was Serena who had softened Jahl's edges.

Wareson looked down at Jaelene. "I understand you wish to rest."

The man's smile was friendly, but Theron didn't like the way his tone made it sound as if she were *his* responsibility. Before she could reply, Theron did. "Yes, we are both weary. Jaelene is not used to walking so far and I was wounded by a boarox so I could not carry her."

Nase grunted as he moved forward. "A boarox? Did you walk from the pole?"

The man's disbelief was palpable. Something about him reminded Theron of Jahl. No wonder they didn't like each other. "I know it sounds impossible that a boarox would wander here, but I'm positive that's what it was."

Both men looked skeptical. He couldn't blame him. When he saw the animal so close to Jaelene, pictures from his school days flashed through his mind. It was the only reason he recognized it.

Jaelene nodded below him. "It was a boarox. At least if an animal that's as big as a bison, with a scrawny short tail, flat ugly face with a floppy upper lip and a mouth of multiple rows of teeth, which I saw up close and personal, is a boarox, then that's what it was."

The two leaders looked at each other, no expression, but

Theron could tell a decision had been made. The same thing used to pass between him and Konala and Rekah.

Erin, who'd stood aside while her agapaytos talked to them, stepped between the four of them and faced her men. "I think this talk of boarox and anything else important can wait until these two have slept. This man has been injured and Jaelene is falling asleep sitting up." She turned and focused on Jaelene. "Would you like your own room, or would you like Theron with you?"

He tensed. He could not contradict what Jaelene decided.

Nase laid a hand on Erin's shoulder. "He cannot stay with her if she is not his beloved." Nase faced him and raised an eyebrow, clearly asking her status.

He couldn't claim her, but he could not let her go either.

Jaelene stood and kept her gaze fixed on Erin. "I would like my own room, but would it be possible for Theron to be in a room next to mine?"

Erin's smile was gentle. "Of course. I know how it feels to be in a strange place." She looked over her shoulder and frowned at her men. "They forget how hard it can be for a woman to adjust to being here."

Nase smirked. "Adjust? I don't know what that is. You still cover your body in front of strangers."

Erin turned back to Jaelene. "See. Clueless."

Theron was pleased to see Jaelene give a small smile. "Thank you. I'm ready to fall asleep right here."

Erin hooked her arm around Jaelene's then looked at him. "Come with me. I'll show you where you can rest. When you wake, I'll have Jerumbala take a look at you. He's our healer."

He'd heard they had a healer at Haven, and was honored to be treated by him. "Thank you."

Erin smiled and led them from the room. Nase started to follow them only to have Wareson step behind them instead. It appeared Wareson was aware of exactly how confrontational Nase could be. Perhaps Wareson was the one he should speak to first about staying in Haven.

CHAPTER EIGHT

Rekah gritted his teeth against the cold water in the pool and quickly swam to the surface. He wrapped his arm around the flailing woman to help her float. "I have you. Relax."

Star grasped his arm and twisted to grab onto his shoulder. "Don't let me drown! Oh, please don't let me drown."

"Don't worry, I won't." He kicked them to the side of the pool where Konala waited. As he lifted her up, Konala pulled her onto the patio.

She shivered, her clothes completely soaked.

Even a good swimmer would have been taxed with all that weight. Just another good reason not to wear clothes. Rekah pulled himself up to sit on the edge of the pool. He glanced at Konala, who crouched beside her and shook his head.

He was well aware it was too soon to meet a woman. They hadn't even decided if Star was their chosen one or not. But he couldn't have let her drown when he had the capability of saving her. He shrugged in reply which just caused Konala to smirk. It was good to see his friend back to his usual easy-going self.

Konala patted her back gently. "You will be fine." His voice was kind, the same one he used with frightened animals.

Star threw her arms around him. "Thank you. I was so scared."

"I know. It was Rekah who saved you."

The woman immediately drew back to look at him in confusion.

Konala gestured toward him. When she turned and saw him, she threw herself against him, her arms grasping him tight. "Thank you."

He gave her a hesitant squeeze, not sure how to deal with a grateful, wet woman in clothes. "You are welcome."

She pulled away and looked at his face. "I will always remember this."

Konala grimaced behind her.

Rekah kept his face neutral. "Why did you jump in the pool if you can't swim?" Her logic concerned him.

She shook her head, her red hair plastered to her head stayed in place. It was much darker now that it was wet. "I didn't jump in. I was looking up at the sky and took a step back and lost my balance. The next thing I know, I'm in the pool."

She looked back at Konala. "I'm so glad you two heard—Oh my. You're naked." She turned back to face him. "Why is he naked?"

Her voice bordered on panic. He let his heart connect with her emotions and found he was right. He tried to think of a believable reason why he and his friend would be near the host's backyard pool without clothes.

"We're nudists." Konala's answer relieved him.

She looked down at him and scooted back. "I didn't know people still did that these days."

He nodded, having nothing else to add since he had no idea if there were still nudists in America.

Konala rose, his cock now at the level of the poor woman's face. "We need to be going. We didn't know our neighbor had company. We'll come back later."

The woman stared at Konala's cock, but didn't respond.

Rekah rose, happy that Nevada was so warm, quickly dispelling the chill of the pool. "Yes, we should go."

Star moved her gaze to his cock and spoke to it. "Does that mean Mr. Daniels is a nudist?"

He looked at Konala, who was smirking again then tipped the woman's face up. "You'd best ask him yourself. Maybe you want to go inside and get dried off now?"

Her brows lowered in puzzlement before her green eyes widened and she shook her head as he dropped his hand. "Oh no. I can't walk in there looking like a drowned rat." She scrambled to her feet. "They'd laugh at me. I've had too many people laugh at me already. I'd prefer it if this group didn't know how clumsy I was."

She looked at Konala and then him. "You won't tell Mr. Daniels or the others, will you?"

Ah, here was their assurance. "We won't tell him if you don't tell him you saw us here in his backyard while he had guests. He wouldn't be very happy with us."

She smiled and held out her hand. "It's a deal."

He shook her hand, her skin soft, her hand small in his.

She turned to shake with Konala. "It will be our secret."

He shook her hand solemnly, but Rekah could tell he was barely keeping back a laugh.

Star nodded to him one more time, then stepped around

Konala and strode down the side yard toward the street in the front.

Voices inside the house coming close to the backdoor eliminated any opportunity for immediate conversation. Instead, he and Konala ducked to the other side of the house and stood side by side leaving space between them and pressed their Crius chips. With the portal open, they ducked back through.

As he looked back, his stomach tensed. Scrat.

Standing on the front sidewalk, looking down the space between house and fence was Star, her eyes wide, her hand over her mouth.

Jaelene held up her index finger. "Let me see if I have this right. This planet was 'seeded' by 'the Crius' with humans from earth during early civilization and it was your favorite poet and the women taken from Earth, who civilized it?"

"Yes." Erin swung her arm wide. "And the men developed special abilities as they evolved with the planet."

Jaelene took another sip of kafez, the hot brew not exactly the drink she needed to handle what she was learning. A shot of Scotch would come in nicely right about now, but she didn't want to broach that subject quite yet. "So what are your husband's abilities?"

"Nase, or Nassic as he was named, is Kindred of Mind and he can make you tell the truth."

Jaelene swallowed, her concern for Theron growing. He was being interrogated by Erin's husbands. Not that he had anything to hide, but he was still recovering from his wounds. She was astounded that he could walk without a crutch in under twenty-four hours. It must be his planet.

Erin continued. "And Ware, or Wareson, is Kindred of Air. He can push air with his sight. He can be so forceful as to knock down over a dozen men, as he did with your sister's husbands, or he can be very gentle and creative." Erin blushed and took another sip of her ambrosia.

Okay, so obviously having two husbands agreed with the woman. Jaelene couldn't imagine having one, though she wanted one, desperately. Two seemed almost greedy, but since no women were born on Eden, as she'd learned, it did make sense in a way.

Erin interrupted her thoughts. "What is Theron's ability?"

She frowned, trying to remember what he'd said. *This symbol marks me as part of the Kindred of Light.* "Oh, I know. He says he can make reflections."

"He says he can? Haven't you seen any?"

She shook her head. "No, I don't think so. When he told me that I thought he meant mirrors and found it strange that he didn't have any in his home." She snorted. "I had no idea I was on another planet or I would have—wait, I do think I've seen what he can do. He made the entrance to his cave look like it wasn't there. When we walked in, it was as if I walked through solid rock."

"And you didn't think that was odd?"

"Of course I did, but I figured it was an optical illusion made by the rock, not by Theron."

Erin's gaze turned crafty. "So what do you think of Theron? I know my husbands are giving him the third degree, but they are careful of any Edenist who comes here. They will give me the over-protective male version. What's your take on him?"

That was a good question. "He's incredibly kind and sweet. There's a sadness about him that I can't quite figure out. I think it has to do with being away from his 'filoz.' He's very protective as well and has saved me three times in the few days I've been here."

"Sounds like it's a good thing you found him."

She nodded. "Very good." Erin opened her mouth to ask another question, but Jaelene wanted answers too. "How did you meet Nase and Ware?"

"Ah, now that's a story." Erin smiled. "I went on a nude cruise with a friend, and no, I didn't go nude, so I stood out like a sore thumb. But they both were so hot and sweet, I fell for them."

She cocked her head. "Really, just like that?"

"Yes, though there was a bit of a hiccup. We got through it. Luckily, the men of Eden will do anything for their women."

As a thud was heard below them, Jaelene had an idea. "Anything?"

"Yes." Erin wiggled her brow.

"Great, let's go downstairs."

The other woman slowly smiled, a gleam in her eye. "Good idea."

As she and Erin walked down the stairs into the living room, they found Nase shaking his hand out.

"By the Crius, I was sure that was him."

Erin frowned. "Did you just punch Theron?"

Ware grinned. "No, he punched the wall because what he thought was Theron was a reflection."

"Wow, he must be very good at that." Erin walked to Nase and kissed his knuckles.

The always aggressive man melted before her eyes. Wow, to have a man do that for her would be heaven. "So where is Theron?"

Erin frowned. "Good question."

Jaelene looked to her right to find Erin standing next to her, but when she looked back at Nase, Erin was still there, her mouth opened in astonishment.

"Nase." Ware pointed toward the second Erin. "Just think what we could do with two Erins." He wiggled his brow for emphasis.

Jaelene blushed at the obvious sexual innuendo, but was too curious not to focus on the image of the woman beside her. She moved her hand to the reflection's shoulder and it went right through. "Oh wow." She made as if to hug the woman and her arms caught only air. "This is wild."

"I'm glad you enjoy it." Theron stood behind Ware, surprising the man enough to make him push air across the room in defense.

"Where in the universe did you come from?" Ware scowled.

Jaelene bit her tongue to keep from laughing out loud.

"Actually, I was here next to your beloved."

Nase turned and threw his fist at Theron.

Jaelene sucked in her breath before the man's fist went right through the image. She couldn't help laughing this time.

Ware walked across the room to the other Theron and passed right through him. "By the Crius, this would completely frustrate an enemy." His smile reappeared.

"It does come in useful on occasion." Theron's voice next to her had her turning her head. Somehow she knew that was the real Theron.

"Or it could cause the enemy to lose all logic." Nase headed for Theron.

She stepped in front of him. "I don't think so. You've done enough for one day."

Nase stopped short of touching her, his scowl leaving as he raised one eyebrow. "I have?"

She pointed at him. "Yes, you have. Now if you will excuse us, we're going out for a walk." She looked back at Theron to find his gaze on her, his lips curved in a small smile.

He took her hand in his. "If you will excuse us?"

Erin laughed as they exited the room.

Theron felt his heart grow two sizes the instant Jaelene stepped forward to protect him. His connection to her was growing and it surprised him. His heart belonged to Serena. Didn't it?

"I'm sorry." Jaelene lifted her chin as they walked. "I was tired of Nase and his bully tactics. That man needs to chill."

He squeezed her hand. "I'm glad you wanted to come out here. I've never been inside the walls of Haven. I find it interesting to see how it is organized. It is only about two years old while Loraleaf is almost five."

They walked hand and hand down the center of the walled town. Various homes and work areas scattered about with no apparent plan.

"You aren't limping. Does your leg feel that much better or are you just trying to be macho around all these men?" Jaelene glanced to the side at the men working on a new building.

It was actually a little of both. "My leg feels much better. We heal very fast here."

She shook her head. "I find that absolutely amazing. You have a phenomenal body. Wish mine could heal so fast."

He found her body to be perfect, so he didn't respond, but he couldn't ignore the fact that she thought his body impressive.

"Haven reminds me of an old west town I've seen in movies, only the buildings look more solid." Jaelene looked at him. "The biggest difference here is that all the men are naked. It's strange for me."

He brought them to a halt, unable any longer to resist touching her face. He brushed his knuckles along her jaw bone. Her skin's softness never failed to surprise him. "I know it is difficult to adjust to our ways, but it is possible. Look at Erin. She seems very happy."

Jaelene's blue eyes searched his face. "And very much in love."

He felt his head lowering. He wanted to kiss her again. His heart demanded more connections.

"Theron! I just heard you were here." The sound of Lennix's voice broke the moment and he turned his head to greet his friend.

"We came last night. This is Jaelene."

Lennix smiled widely, showing perfect teeth. His hazel eyes twinkled with pleasure. "You have a beauty to rival Selene."

Jaelen cocked her head. "Who is Selene?"

Lennix widened his eyes in pretend shock, his hand coming over his heart. "I cannot believe that Theron has yet to introduce you to Selene. I would be happy to do so tonight."

Theron held Jaelene's hand harder. "That's not necessary. She has already seen our small moon and Bendis as well."

"Oh, yes. I like Selene. Bendis, not so much." She smiled coyly and Theron felt his gut twist.

He wanted Lennix's attention off Jaelene. "Where is your home? Is your filoz brother about? I would like to meet him."

Lennix still didn't take his gaze from Jaelene though he spoke to Theron. "My home is on the other side of the front entrance.

Stori is out on patrol, but if you come by after Selene has risen, I will be happy to introduce you."

Jaelene blushed, finally seeing Lennix's interest in her.

There was no possibility of him bringing her to Lennix's home at night. "Last I spoke to you, you had found a woman as your chosen one. Have you made contact yet?"

That snapped Lennix's attention away from Jaelene. "Yes, we have found her, but we are still watching her. We want to be sure she will fit in here. Erin has been very helpful in helping us decide on how to make first contact." He turned to Jaelene. "She said we should wear clothes." He scrunched up his face in disgust.

Jaelene laughed. "Oh I hope so, especially if you meet her where she lives. Walking around without clothes can get you arrested and thrown in jail." She shook her head. "Not a pleasant experience."

Lennix nodded. "So I had read."

Theron squeezed Jaelene's hand. "We will continue our tour of Haven."

Lennix finally understood. "Of course. We do not have a Libations like you do in Loraleaf, but we do have our baths which you may want to try." He winked at them and went back the way he had come.

"Baths?" She faced him, her blue eyes sparkling with curiosity. "What did he mean by that?"

If they were even somewhat similar to Naralina's, he was sure she would like them. "I have not seen the baths here either. Should we go explore?"

"You think?" She rolled her eyes. "Of course we should explore. This town is fascinating."

If she thought Haven was interesting, what would she think

of Loraleaf? A need to watch her reaction to his home burned hot in his gut.

Since he still held her hand in his, he resumed their stroll. "Loraleaf is older than Haven and it is behind solid walls as well, but they are see-through and they reflect the outside, so no one can tell where it is."

She stopped scanning the compound and looked at him. "But it can be found by walking into one of those walls, right? Have you had animals bump into it?"

He chuckled, pleased at the way her mind worked. Very practical and very animal focused. Konala would definitely enjoy her company.

What if Konala and Rekah wanted Jaelene as their beloved? He sucked in his breath. Part of him would be happy for them, but the idea of being left out of such a beautiful union left a sour taste in his mouth.

"Theron? That wasn't a trick question." She grinned saucily at him, taking the sting from her remark.

"No, animals don't bump into the walls because Loraleaf is a town in the trees. There is one staircase in a large tree trunk to gain access. The lowest level is higher than any animal known to Eden, so the walls are actually far above the ground."

He held up his hand as she opened her mouth. "And no, birds do not fly into our walls. This is because I worked with Paxon to make the walls, not Konala. Animals can see through my reflections unless I work with Konala to create them."

Jaelene stopped, her eyes moving with a myriad of thoughts. "So that's why Talia could see me watching her. She knew someone was home in the cave and wanted a petting session."

He smiled at how quickly she understood. "Yes. Konala can communicate with animals, so with his ability and mine, we can create reflections like fences to keep animals from straying or a reflection of an animal that preys on one of ours to teach them not to ignore the fence."

"You scare your animals?"

"Only if necessary. We don't have many. The jungle animals have been wild since Eden evolved and there are very few that have been tamed. Luckily, not many jungle animals are dangerous to Edenists."

Her shoulders slumped. "Like a boarox."

He nodded. "Yes, but they are rarely this close to the equator. Something must have caused that animal to wander so far."

She placed her other hand gently on his wounded arm. "I'm sorry I didn't stay in the cave. I'm such a sucker for an animal that's hurting."

"You have a big heart. That is not something to be sorry for."

"I didn't know an animal could fake being hurt. That's scary." She shuddered, emphasizing her fear.

He let go of her hand and held her by her waist. "That is how a boarox catches its prey. Its body shape makes it too slow to hunt, so it pretends to be wounded so smaller animals will think it will be an easy kill. It is simply Eden's way."

Her blue eyes lit with understanding. "That makes sense. Is the tigran the only predator it has?"

"No, but most of its predators live closer to the poles. I think this one may have been kicked out of its territory by a bigger one."

"They grow bigger than that?"

"Yes, but I have never seen one before." And that concerned

him. If he was home, he'd ask Konala about it. He would send a message to him through the patrols.

Jaelene's hand came to rest on his cheek. "There's that look again."

He refocused on her. "What look?"

"That sad, wistful look. If you're hurting, why don't you do something about it?"

He would if he could. "Do not worry about me. It will go away." Someday. "Shall we see if we can find the baths?"

She pointed to her right. "We already have. At least I think we have if that sign means water."

Theron glanced at the sign with the Kindred of Water sign on it. "They must have an Edenist with water abilities. Shall we go in?"

She pulled out of his arms, causing a momentary disappointment until she took his hand and pulled him toward the door. He grinned at how comfortable she was with him now.

As they stepped through the arched entry and opened the wooden doors, air much more humid than the jungle greeted them. He scanned the area in a second and smiled. Now this was a bath.

"Wow." Jaelene let go of Theron and stepped into the large round stone room with two halls leading away from it. "This looks like a real Roman bath, not like one of the fake ones I've helped create in a couple million dollar homes."

She walked to the edge of a large pool with steam rising from its surface. It wasn't very deep, at least not at her end. Stone steps to her right led into it and there were only three. The walls looked like stucco plaster of some sort but had a maroon color to them with a light pattern of leaves and swirls. She could envision it in a bedroom in a new home.

Theron walked along the side, his stride showing a slight limp now. She'd completely forgotten his leg had been broken not forty-eight hours earlier. Actually, according to Erin, Eden's days were only twenty-two hours long, so that meant Theron's leg was broken only forty-four hours ago.

Theron was staring at the pool, a look of longing on his face. She stepped up to him and put her hand on his good arm. "Did you want to go in?"

He started as if he'd forgotten where he was. "I do. Would you like to?"

It did look heavenly. "I'd love to but I don't have a bathing suit."

He smiled kindly. "We don't wear bathing suits when we bathe. Do you?"

She gulped at the warm look he gave her. "But anyone could come in."

He turned around and walked to the door. Using the length of vine hanging next to the door, he looped it around a hook made for the purpose. "Now they won't."

She looked at the pool again. It *would* feel good.

Theron stepped behind her and whispered in her ear. "What are you afraid of, Khityki?"

You. I like you too much. I depend on you too much and you aren't interested. She wasn't about to tell him her fears. "What does that word mean? You said it to me once before."

He placed his hands on her shoulders. "You are changing the subject. Why do you not want to disrobe and enjoy the warm waters of the bath?"

Oh, he meant getting in the water. That was easy. "You've seen me. It's not like I'm Miss America or anything."

Theron lifted one hand from her shoulder and pointed across the water. "You are a special person, Jaelene."

On the other side of the pool floated a reflection of herself, but it was so beautiful she couldn't believe it was her. She studied every feature and each was exactly the same on her. Her small naked breasts, her narrow hips, her big lower lip, yet a silver inner light showed through and her blue eyes sparkled like the sun hitting the blue waters of the sea.

Her eyes watered and her heart swelled. She looked up at Theron. "Is that how you see me?"

His dark eyes grew almost black. "No. It is how everyone sees you. This is you."

Hurt she'd thought she buried exploded within her, the tiny pieces disappearing into thin air as she stared into Theron's eyes.

She needed him in her life.

Turning toward him, she hooked her hand around his neck and lifted up on her toes to kiss him.

He lowered his head, his lips brushing hers in a soft kiss.

She relaxed her hold on him, hoping for more, but he straightened, his face unreadable.

"Will you bathe with me?" His voice had lowered to a husky base that sent tingles all over her body.

She nodded, her throat too tight to speak.

Gently, he lifted the top of her tank over her head. Then he unclasped her bra hook and pulled the straps off her shoulders and down. His gaze on her bare breasts caused her nipples to harden.

Toeing off her shoes, she quickly unbuttoned her jeans and he stepped back to give her room to shimmy out of them. She pulled off her socks and before she lost her nerve, she pushed her panties down. As she stepped out of them, she glanced at Theron.

His eyes were that black color that she now associated with him having strong feelings. She just hoped it was because he liked what he saw.

"Come." He held out his hand and she took it.

He walked toward the steps. It felt strange to be walking naked, hand in hand, with a man. It made her wonder. "If I were to live here with you, would it be normal for us to walk like this down the center of Haven?"

Stopping them at the steps, he faced her, clearly looking for the right words to explain. It was one of his characteristics that she liked. He was always careful with his words, as if he didn't want to hurt anyone.

"If you were to live on Eden with your filoz then it would be natural for you to walk naked anywhere with your beloved."

After talking with Erin, she now understood better the whole filoz thing and why he shied away from saying she would be walking with him. "So if I was part of you and Konala and Rekah's filoz, I would be expected to walk around naked, right?"

His intake of breath told her she'd hit a sore spot, but she wanted to know, not only about naked walking but about him and his best friends.

"Yes." His one word answer came out on a breath as if he had held it for a moment too long.

"Wouldn't that bother all of you? I mean, to have the other men see me without clothes? Would they try to take me away from you?"

Theron seemed to pull himself together and he moved them down the steps, still holding her hand.

The warm water was relaxing. "Oh wow, this is perfect."

"I had hoped you would enjoy it." He led her to deeper water so she could stand but her breasts were still exposed, floating on the surface.

She liked that he kept her hand in his. She could swim just fine, but his constant attention filled a hole inside her she didn't realize was there.

She was also aware of the fact he hadn't answered her questions. "You didn't tell me how you and Konala and Rekah would react if other men saw me naked."

He stiffened slightly. "We would be proud to show you off. Other men would remain respectful as they would sense you were taken once you were bonded to a filoz."

She'd forgotten about the bonding. Erin said it was an amazing experience, but didn't go into detail. "I don't think I could walk around naked in public."

He smiled. "You could, even if it was just to see how others reacted."

"You're right. " She laughed. "I'd probably do it once to see what really happened."

He winked. "Maybe you would get used to it."

As his gaze wandered toward her breasts, she purposefully lowered herself in the water until just her head showed. "I don't think I would. I'd be like Erin."

He lowered himself as well, and she pouted. She enjoyed looking at his body, but fair was fair.

"Erin doesn't always wrap herself." He smirked. "It is only because we are here and she isn't used to us yet."

"Holy heck, does my sister walk around naked?" The sudden thought was too hard to contemplate.

Theron's face lost all expression. "I do not know." He let go of her hand and ducked under the water, swimming toward the deeper part of the pool.

Okay, so talking about her sister walking around naked upset him. Why? Was it that she was at Loraleaf and he wasn't? Jaelene couldn't resist the need to make him feel better and she dove under the water to find him.

She wasn't under two seconds before she noticed a small school of shiny tiny fish. How could that be in a pool and why didn't her eyes sting from chlorine? She popped back up. "Did you know there are fish in this pool?"

"Yes." Theron spoke from behind her, back in the shallow section. "They keep it clean by ingesting the bacteria."

She spun around treading water. "Do they need to be fed?"

He shook his head. "The bacteria is their food, so as long as people use the bath on a regular basis, they will thrive."

She swam toward him. The sadness she sensed about him on occasion was back. It had to be Loraleaf and his friends. "You miss Loraleaf, don't you?"

He barely nodded.

She'd thought she wanted someone else to bring her to her sister, all because he tried to tell her she was on another planet. That and because of his unwillingness to make love to her. But that was before he showed her the image of what he thought she looked like. Now, she wanted to be with him every moment. What woman wouldn't? "Will you take me to Loraleaf to visit my sister?"

Theron felt his heart lurch. Go to Loraleaf? See Serena again? What would Konala and Rekah think? Would they speak to him? Did they understand? Had they found a chosen one yet?

He couldn't. He gazed at Jaelene. Her hopeful expression dug into his chest. Maybe Mykl or another could take her. He pictured her walking away from Haven with two men he didn't know. His stomach tightened. He didn't want another man around her. No one knew her like he did.

She was special.

"Theron, please?" She cocked her head, her eyes pleading with him to say yes.

The blue depths of her gaze claimed him. "I will."

Jaelene's face lit with joy. Jumping up out of the water she wrapped her arms around his neck and kissed him. The moment her lips touched his, he pulled her tight against him. Her breasts crushed against his chest and her belly pillowed his cock.

She leaned her head back, her eyes alight with glee. "Thank you."

He didn't say a word, just studied the unique woman in his arms. Her pert nose, soft skin and sharp mind were made for Eden.

Her face lost its smile and she nibbled at her bottom lip as she glanced down at his mouth.

Kiss her. The silent thought repeated over and over.

After many moments, she titled her face up, her eyes full of entreaty. "Theron?"

She may have said his name but he heard "Take me" beneath it. He couldn't deny her any longer.

He cupped the back of her head with one hand and lowered his lips to hers. She opened her mouth and he claimed it as his own, sweeping his tongue inside to meld their tastes together.

She buried her hand in his hair, her grip telling him she wanted him. He stroked his tongue along hers, over her teeth and finally gave in to his need to nibble her lower lip.

"Ah." Her breathy response fired him.

He trailed tiny sucking kisses along her jaw to the side of her neck and finally to her collar bone.

Her hips pressed against his hardened cock as she arched back, offering him her breasts.

He couldn't have resisted if he tried and he lowered his mouth to one full globe and sucked it into his mouth.

Jaelene moaned, her grip on his hair hard as she pulled his head closer.

He let his suction go suddenly and immediately bit at the hard nub in his mouth.

"Oh, yes!" She rocked her hips upward, instinctively seeking his cock.

He pulled at her nipple then let it go, his total focus on giving her the pleasure she deserved.

She opened her eyes. "I want you inside me."

Need shot to his groin and his balls tightened. "Wrap your legs around me."

Her legs floated up and she pressed her pelvis tight against him.

Even in the warm water, he could feel the slickness that was her. Walking to the steps, he sat down. "Take your pleasure as you will."

Her eyelids lowered and her look became sultry. "I will." She lifted herself above him and let the tip of his cock touch her opening.

His hands rested on her waist, but he didn't push her down, though he craved that more than air.

Her fingers gripped his shoulders, showing her purposeful delayed fulfillment was as much sensual torture for her as it was for him. She moved her hips in tiny circles, brushing against his cockhead, but not moving lower.

Suddenly she stopped. "Oh shoot."

Chapter Nine

Theron tensed. "What is it?"

"We need a condom, unless you've been tested." Jaelene rested her ass on his lap, her entry no longer tantalizing him.

"Tested?" He didn't remember anything about testing around sex in his training about Earth. Was this something else that would keep them apart?

"Yes." She dropped her hands from his shoulders. "For sexually transmitted diseases?"

He breathed easier. "We have no diseases on Eden."

Her eyes rounded. "No diseases at all? No cancer? No Multiple Sclerosis? No Chicken Pox?"

He chuckled at her switch in attention. Only Jaelene could go from making love to thirty questions in less than a second. "No. No diseases, no infections, no sickness."

She stared at him as she digested this new information. Then both eyebrows rose as she nodded. "I really, really like your planet."

He laughed, the joy and pleasure he felt in her too much to contain. Holy Bendis, it was good to laugh again. He couldn't remember the last time he had.

She smiled at him. "I really, really like your laugh, too."

His heart filled and in that moment he knew he could never let her go. "I'm glad. And I would really, really like to be deep inside you."

"Whoa." She breathed the word out as her smile left and her eyes darkened to a color a man could drown in. "Let me see what I can do to grant your wish." Without taking her gaze from him, she gripped his shoulders again and floated above his cock. Keeping her gaze on his face, she lowered herself over the top of his cockhead.

He groaned as her slickness encompassed him. She was tight, but she stretched, grasping him hard.

She moved herself halfway down and the sensations ran rampant through his groin and up his spine. Every nerve in his body waited in anticipation for the next part of her glide.

"You're big." Jaelene's whispered words caught him by surprise.

She'd seen his size before, even said she liked it. Was she nervous? "You are in control, take what you want."

"I want you." She lowered her head and captured his lips. As her tongue swung inside his mouth, she lowered herself, agonizingly slowly, down to his lap until she was fully impaled on his cock.

Reactively, his hands tightened on her waist, though he did not push his hips upward as he wanted to. He pulled away from her lips, the only way he could control his raging need.

Jaelene's eyes were closed and she didn't move an inch.

He took deep, heart-slowing breaths to remain completely still and let her determine their next move toward fulfillment.

Jaelene was sure she'd died and gone to heaven. Nothing she'd experienced in her life so far had ever felt as good as Theron inside her. It wasn't just his sexy body and how fully he filled her.

It was *him*.

He made her feel precious. Smart, too. And he didn't get bored with her questions or ignore her interests. He was everything she wanted in a man, including his hard physique and gentle touch.

As much as she tried to enjoy the moment, let it imprint on her memory, her body had other ideas. Her sheath tightened and she moved her hips in small circles as if she could push farther against Theron's lap and take him deeper.

"Khityki." Theron's quiet voice had her opening her eyes.

As soon as she did, he lifted his hips, tilting his position. She gasped as he slid deeper inside her. "Oh my God, Theron." She pushed down and moved her hips forward and back, her own juices giving her a gliding spot against him despite the water surrounding them.

"Come for me. Find your ecstasy." Theron's eyes were so dark, they appeared bottomless.

Somewhere inside her she found the strength to talk. "Come with me." She wanted him with her.

His eyes seemed to reflect some kind of inner light, but before she could question it, he'd pulled her lips to his and speared his tongue into her mouth like his cock had speared her body.

She wrapped her arms around his neck and welcomed his invasion both in her mouth and in her sheath. She continued to swivel her hips back and forth as Theron's hands on her waist encouraged her movements.

Her muscles tightened of their own accord as sharp jabs of pleasure pulsed from her clit to her core and surrounded the cock inside her. Each move sent new excitement through her, spiraling around her sheath and flowing through her.

One of Theron's hands moved up to grasp her head, tilting it to allow him to more fully ravage her mouth. The other left her waist and clasped one ass cheek, pressing her body tighter against him.

The extra pressure increased the intensity of her pleasure and she came to the edge of orgasm. Her sheath tightened hard. At Theron's groan, joy, simple and pure, burst through her.

Her body rocked as his come filled her. She felt as if a million shooting stars flew through her, sending her into outer space. She floated on a cloud as comets whizzed about, creating spurts of happiness inside her.

As she came to her senses, she opened her eyes to find Theron gazing at her with such sweet caring, her throat closed. But when she noticed the sparkles of light in his dark eyes that truly looked like stars, she found her voice. "Your eyes."

He looked away.

She caught his chin in her hand and turned his head to face her, but still he looked down. "Theron, look at me."

When he lifted his gaze, the stars were gone although his eyes remained the pitch black she now associated with his passion. "There were stars in your eyes."

He studied her carefully. "I know. Do you find that disturbing?"

She'd seen him sad and afraid for her life and even bristly around Lennix, but she hadn't seen this look of uncertainty on him until now. Had someone told him his eyes were scary? "No, not really. They were definitely startling, but I didn't find them disturbing. Of course, I didn't have much chance to really look at them."

He lowered his gaze as his hand stroked her back.

When it was clear he wasn't going to elaborate, she asked. "So how come you have stars in your eyes?"

His gaze snapped back to her, his lips twitching. "It is part of my reflection abilities."

Did that mean he saw stars when they made love? She opened her mouth to ask, then shut it. She didn't want him to say no. For once, she was happy with her own conclusion.

His lips turned into a full smile. "No other questions?"

She raised her index finger. "Not about that, but I'm sure I'll have more before the day is through."

He chuckled and pulled her against him in a comfortable hug. "Ah, Jaelene, you are a very special woman."

She was glad her head was over his shoulder so he couldn't see how much his words meant to her. It just figured that she'd meet such an amazing man on another planet instead of on Earth. She planned to enjoy everything about him until she went home.

She sat back, suddenly aware that they were still connected. "And you are a very special man." She kissed him on the cheek then pulled herself off him. "Oh." The sudden emptiness she felt surprised her. How could those men who slept with her have disconnected so easily? She liked Theron inside her too much.

Shaking off the uncomfortable feeling, she turned and swam toward the other end.

Theron swam next to her, almost as if he were protecting her.

She stopped and found it too deep to stand, the memory of the boarox suddenly coming to the fore. "There's nothing else besides those bacteria fish in here, is there?"

Theron stood, his head above the water, and offered her his arm. "No. This is a place to bathe safely. If we were in a watering hole, then you would need to be watchful."

She took his offered arm, the image of an alligator filling her mind. She really needed to get a handle on what to be afraid of on this planet and what not, especially since they still needed to make their way to Loraleaf. "So you aren't necessarily protecting me in this pool. You're just keeping me company?"

He opened his mouth but she held up her index finger. "I mean besides our lovemaking." She felt the heat rise in her cheeks at saying it out loud. "I only ask because you have that protective look on your face again. You know, the one where you stare at me then glance over the area. It makes me a little nervous."

Theron chuckled. "You are far more observant than most. You are right. I am watching out for you, but only because even in a bath a person could drown."

Oh wow. She was a good swimmer but he didn't know that so he was right there. "I'm actually a pretty good swimmer. Want to see?"

He nodded and she let go of his arm. She swam all the way to the deepest end of the pool and then back past him to the shallow end and finally back to him.

Theron's smile was wide. "You are a very good swimmer, but you are also out of breath."

She held his arm again. "I guess I'm a little out of shape."

"I think you are the perfect shape." His eyes darkened and instead of feeling self-conscious, she felt beautiful.

How did he do that? How did he make her feel so cherished? He should give lessons to men back home. And she should remember that their time together was limited. "If this is a bath, shouldn't we be soaping up?"

"Of course." He walked toward the shallows again with her on his arm. She loved floating along beside him, the water more buoyant than at home.

He stopped on one side of the pool where a stone statue that looked like an octopus with the face of a horse hung slightly over the water.

He lifted a flap at the end of one tentacle and thick white liquid came out in his hand. He brought it to his nose and sniffed. Shaking his head, he rinsed off his hand in the pool and tried another tentacle. He repeated the process four more times before he smiled. "This one. These all have soap, but this one fits you."

Curious, she moved toward the dispenser and lifted the flap and let a little soap fall into her hand. She sniffed. "Oh, that smells so much like the almond soap I use at home."

He nodded as if he could possibly know what she used. She cocked her head and raised one eyebrow. "So which one will you use?"

He studied her for a moment then gave her a sly smile. "I'll let you choose."

She lifted her chin. "Okay." Turning back to the statue, she started from the beginning. There was a citrusy soap, a vanilla scented soap, a fresh linen scent, one that reminded her of suntan lotion, another that made her think of Christmas and the almond one that she liked. There were only two left. The next one reminded her of rosemary or thyme or some such spice. It was pleasant, but didn't fit Theron.

Squirting the last one into her plan she inhaled. Hmm, cocoa. "This is it. You should use this one." She held her palm up toward his face. He took her wrist and sniffed. His smile grew wide. "Good choice."

She beamed with her success. It felt like she'd passed a test with flying colors.

Theron placed Jaelene's hand with the soap on his chest over his heart. She'd chosen his scent. Edenists had a better sense of smell than humans from Earth. Her choice proved her senses had attuned to him. Their connection was strong.

Relief and worry battled for dominance. Her feelings were real but he needed Konala and Rekah or another Edenist in order to claim her.

"Theron? Are you okay?"

He looked down to find he still held her palm to his skin, a sensation he thoroughly enjoyed. He smiled. "I'm better than 'okay.' I feel as though my soul is healing beneath your touch."

Her brows knitted in confusion.

Quickly, he released her hand. "The bath is a great place to find peace and tranquility."

She smiled coyly at him. "That's not the only thing we found here."

He laughed, her wit pleasing him once again. "You are right, but I imagine we better bathe and get back or I have no doubt Ware and Nase will be sending men out to find us."

He glanced at the windows set in the ceiling. He wouldn't tell Jaelene that an Edenist with levitation abilities could easily look in and see they were inside.

She looked up as well. "You're right. It looks like the sun is already setting. Your days here are short."

"Just shorter than yours."

"Good point." Jaelene began to wash herself and he turned away to allow her some privacy. Though he ached to rub the nut-scented soap so close to her own aroma all over her body, he resisted, aware that to push their closeness too quickly might scare her away.

If Konala and Rekah had already met her and loved her, he wouldn't be so careful, but she could easily be claimed by a filoz and he could not fight that. All the more reason to return to Loraleaf immediately.

He smiled inside at that thought. Just a few days ago, he was anxious to avoid going home. How quickly his life had changed.

After they finished in the bath, he walked her back to their rooms inside the house of Haven's leaders. As soon as they entered, Erin commanded that they keep her company while her agapaytos cooked dinner. He was happy to let the women talk, observing Jaelene's mannerisms and interests while learning more about her background.

He stored that information in his head to use when needed to convince his filoz that she was their chosen one. He'd never heard of one man choosing for the rest, but then again, Jaelene wasn't supposed to be here.

He was very glad she was.

At dinner everyone relaxed and enjoyed themselves, but as he soon learned, that was only a breather.

The next morning began like the last with Ware and Nase trying to get information from him while Jaelene learned more about Eden from Erin.

Erin had set up a lesson plan and was testing it on Jaelene. The only problem he saw with it was that Jaelene still expected to go home to her old life. She had no idea that she wouldn't be allowed to, but no one told her that. He didn't have the right to tell her that. Not yet.

The hardest part of the morning was when Nase asked him direct questions. The man's ability to force a person to tell the truth was impossible to resist.

He'd been able to answer the questions as he wished by projecting a steady reflection of himself over him, which is what Nase concentrated on, making it possible for him to avoid revealing too much about Loraleaf. His own leader, Jahl, had made it clear, he was not ready to share much with the newer settlement.

Since he was a guest at Haven, he continued to be polite. The time spent in the settlement gave Jaelene time to learn more about his planet and the afternoons were sweet pleasure as the two of them spent their time enjoying the town while he told her about the two brothers of his heart.

But he would not make love to her again. She needed to connect with Konala and Rekah, and it was that question, whether she would or not, that caused him to delay their leaving. He was selfish, extracting every moment of joy with her he could in case he lost her.

Even as the thought appeared, his gut twisted and his heart froze. He couldn't lose her.

~~*~~

Konala sat at Khaos and Jahl's kitchen table. Rekah and Serena were there as well. He and the brother of his heart had been called to meet since they were the next filoz in leadership.

Konala thought back to Star. He and Rekah had watched her two more times over the last week and he still felt no connection. She was a nice woman and would probably adjust to Eden quickly, but she wasn't for him. He hadn't broached the subject with Rekah yet. If Rekah used his ability at all, then he was already aware of it.

Khaos leaned against the counter, but Jahl stood straight, his bearing that of a man who wasn't happy with what he needed to do. "I've decided to send a patrol to Haven to let them know about Naralina's switch in focus away from a detector for portal openings in the jungle."

Rekah nodded. "That is the right thing to do. I know it was difficult for you to come to that conclusion."

"Difficult doesn't begin to describe it." Jahl grimaced.

"Jahl never was good at sharing." Khaos winked at Serena.

She smiled innocently. "I think he shares very nicely with us."

At her remark, even serious Jahl's lip quirked upward.

"I'm guessing you've asked us here because you want one or both of us to go." Rekah looked at him. "I will unless you would like to."

Before he could speak, Khaos did. "We would like Konala to go."

"I am happy to, but why me specifically?"

Jahl looked at him. "Because we want you to communicate with any animals they have. Find out if they have had any contact with Naralina."

He shook his head. "They would not know that. The best they would know is if any strangers came to the settlement."

"That's good enough for me." Jahl crossed his arms. "Strangers could be from Naralina or lawbreakers or new men joining them. I want to know about any of the above."

Serena sighed. "I thought you and Wareson had buried the hatchet."

Rekah stared at Jahl for a moment then spoke. "He has, but his distrust of Naralina leaders runs too deep for a single visit to erase it."

"Rekah." Jahl's voice was stern. "This isn't about me. It's about the safety of Loraleaf."

"Very true." Rekah shrugged. "But you are a part of that equation."

Konala could see that Rekah wasn't going to back down, so he stood. "I can portal through now. That should get their attention."

Khaos shook his head. "That wouldn't go well. Use the portal to get next to the settlement and request entrance. None of us want any surprises. Think of how we would react."

The man made a very good point. "I will do as you suggest." He was excited to go. It would be interesting to see what was behind the high cyndistone walls, their teal color making it seem as if they were just part of the jungle.

"Good." Khaos moved to stand next to Jahl but left a space between them. "If you are not back by this time tomorrow, we will retrieve you."

"I will give them the news and find out all I can in that time."

Jahl and Khaos touched the chips benteath their arms and the portal opened. Jahl pointed to the jungle scene before them. "This is only fifty strides from Haven. Good luck."

He gave his leaders a quick nod, made eye contact with Rekah and stepped through. The portal closed behind him.

He recognized the area from other times he'd come by to confer with Haven's patrols. Now instead of patrols, they could watch the ground through portals, eliminating most of the threat of the lawbreakers *if* Naralina continued to be focused on some other project.

He started toward the settlement when the lack of noise caught his attention. He listened, but all was silent, not even the chirp of a bird or the shuffle of a welchet. That meant a man was nearby. A Haven patrol? A lawbreaker?

He reached out with his mind and found a rhybat huddled in his hole, petrified of going above ground. It didn't take long to confirm what he had guessed. A man stood above. The last thing he wanted to do was lead someone to Haven if it wasn't a patrol.

He tried to communicate with the rhybat again but it had burrowed deeper into the ground, a clear sign that it was truly scared. The problem was that rhybats were afraid of their own shadows, so it didn't help him judge the level of the threat, if there was any.

Better to assume the worst. He checked one more time for animals, particularly for birds, but none were within his range. Whoever it was, was not liked by Eden's creatures. That had to mean it wasn't a patrol.

He moved behind a very large tree, similar to the one that held his home aloft, and waited. As he watched, he continued to search for an animal. Stymied, he was about to find a tree to climb when a light breeze blew through, rustling the leaves and bringing with it a distinct stench.

Konala's skin tingled at the smell of dead animal and his

muscles quivered with revulsion. He picked a wide leaf from the pander bush brushing his hip and held it over his nose.

The stench grew stronger and his eyes started to burn. How could something smell like that and still be alive? He crouched where he was, hoping to get some relief, but it reeked everywhere.

Every fiber of his being cringed at the essence of putrefied dead animal. He had to move away from it. Rising, he quietly walked in the direction he had come from. He counted fifteen strides before he was hit from behind and slammed to the ground.

He rolled, coming up into a crouch, but couldn't find what had hit him. He'd lost his leaf and his stomach rolled as the smell traveled into his lungs. He scanned the area and his watery gaze found his attacker.

It had to be a long time lawbreaker. The old man hovered near another tree, his mouth moving as if he was talking to himself, but no sound came out. The stench definitely came from him, his beard a scraggly mess and his naked hunched body covered in dried blood and membranes.

Konala's senses rebelled but he pitied the Edenist. He rose again and faced the man. "What do you want?"

The old man didn't acknowledge him, just continued to look at him and move his lips. Then his eyes widened and he flew at Konala.

Something flashed in the sunlight and Konala grabbed the man's wrist to keep the sharp blade from connecting with his body. The lawbreaker twisted to get free and he let him go.

The old man was insane, but his insanity did not give him strength.

Konala looked at the man, levitating only inches from the ground then turned and ran back the way he'd come.

No sound followed him, but when he looked back, the lawbreaker was behind him. He continued his run through the bush, parallel to where Haven was, not wanting to lead the old man there. Finally, he sensed a grendal ahead. He ran for the animal while communicating his wishes.

He leapt into a shallow river and the old man jumped on him. Once again, he grabbed the man's skinny wrist to keep the blade from connecting, so the wiry creature slammed its head into his.

He lost his balance and went under for a moment. The flash of blade through the water had him ducking. He kicked out and caught the man in the stomach.

As the lawbreaker doubled over, he wrested the sharp blade from his hand and threw it downstream. The old man scrambled after it, his hand still curled as if he still clasped it.

Konala jumped from the water and ran again. He hoped the old man would stay in the river, but even as he sensed the grendals gathering ahead, he looked back to find he was still pursued.

Finally, he broke through the clearing the grendal had told him about and he ran into the middle of the herd. When the old man saw the big black animals with large tusks facing him, he stopped.

Grendals were not aggressive animals by nature, but when threatened, they were deadly. His hope was that the old man would recognize the danger and run. He was wrong.

The old man's lips curled up in what must have once been a smile and he attacked the first grendal he came to.

The squeal of the herd was deafening. He leapt on the old

man and pulled him away from the animal before he could do any damage, but now the herd was angry and wanted him.

Scrat. What in Selene's name was he supposed to do now?

It was the fifth day when the healer finally pronounced Theron completely well. To him, the diagnosis was two days later than it needed to be. It was obvious Nase had made Jerumbala wait.

Once the healer left, Nase and Ware stared at him, as if expecting him to continue to accept their interrogation, but he was finished. He'd been polite, told them of the ability of Sandale, though he didn't mention Sandale by name, and he'd given them all he had learned while living in the cave. It was enough. "Jaelene, are you ready to see your sister?"

Her eyes lit with excitement. "Absolutely."

"But I haven't finished her lessons yet." Erin moved toward her men, obviously ready to have them make her happy by keeping them there.

He grasped Jaelene's hand. "I'm sure she'll learn everything she needs to know when we get to Loraleaf."

Nase stepped forward. "That may be, but—"

Mykl ran into the house. "We need you at the gate." His look encompassed Ware and Nase.

The two leaders immediately strode from the house and the rest of them followed.

Theron had every intention of using the distraction to leave Haven, but when he saw what had caused the alarm, he stilled.

Standing just inside the walls of Haven was the brother of his heart with the lawbreaker who had almost caught him and Jaelene. Both of them were dripping with water.

Others gathered, making the opportunity to leave better, but he had to know what had happened.

"Theron, what is it? What are you thinking?"

He squeezed Jaelene's hand. "That is Konala."

She tried to see over the heads of the gathering men. "I'm too short."

He looked down at her. "No, you are just right. Come." He ushered her toward the front, the men parting for her.

Ware pushed air on Konala and the old lawbreaker as they approached. "Lennix, take the old man and put him in the storage building with some food and place a guard there."

Lennix and Mykl grabbed a hold of the struggling man and walked him away.

"You stink." Nase backed up a step as if the smell was contagious.

Konala grimaced. "This is nothing compared to how he smelled before I got him in the river. It was the only way I could breathe, tie him up, and keep him safe from the grendals."

"How did you—" Ware stopped. "That can wait. I think we would all appreciate it if you would make use of our bath house immediately. We can talk when you have cleaned up."

Konala smiled. "I would appreciate that."

Ware stepped aside and motioned with his hand to point the way.

Theron waited for recognition, hoping against hope the brother of his heart would be pleased to see him, but before Konala's gaze could land on him, Jaelene caught his attention.

CHAPTER TEN

Jaelene focused on the man with bright blue eyes, far lighter than her own. This was Konala? Her heartbeat raced at the speed of light as he stared at her. While Theron was obviously a bit older than her, Konala looked exactly her age. And she was such a sucker for blond hair.

As she looked at him, his lips lifted in a heart-stopping smile that brought her breathing to a halt. Oh shoot. Talk about instant attraction. His smile made her hot and happy all at once. She wanted to take him to her room and…

Theron squeezed her hand and her breathing started again. She needed to calm down. This was Theron's moment. Konala was part of *his* family. She looked at Theron who continued to stare at Konala.

She glanced back at Konala to find him striding toward them, his face unreadable.

He stopped in front of Theron and his lips lifted in that amazing smile. "I am glad to see you are alive."

Theron just stared, but his hand around hers squeezed tighter and tighter.

"Ow."

He looked down at her and relaxed his hand. "Sorry."

"Are you going to give him a hug hello or what?" She raised her eyebrow in expectation.

He grinned and looked back at Konala. Theron let go of her hand and pulled his friend in for a man hug.

Her eyes teared up, thrilled that the reunion appeared to be a happy one. Maybe now some of Theron's sadness would go away. It might be silly, but she wanted him to be happy. Maybe Konala could convince him to go home for good.

Theron stepped back. "Nase is right, you do stink."

She grimaced. "Now so do you."

He chuckled. "I suggest we get ourselves to the bath house." Theron wrapped his arm around Konala's shoulders.

"I'm looking forward to seeing it." Konala's grin remained. "I've heard about it but this is my first time within Haven's walls."

"Then let's go." As Theron faced his friend in the right direction, he reached back and grabbed her hand.

Her heart warmed that he would want her with him at such an important moment.

But they did stink. She used her other hand to hold her nose. She wasn't the only one either. As they strode down the center of Haven, the men who didn't know of the commotion at the gate, were giving them a wide berth.

Konala leaned his head forward to look at her. "Are you going to introduce me?"

Theron looked at her, his smile wide. "Of course. Jaelene, this is Konala. Konala, this is—"

"Jaelene?" Konala stopped, making all of them halt. He

slipped out from under Theron's arm and stepped in front of them to look at her. "You're Serena's sister."

"I am." She cocked her head. "Is that a good thing or a bad thing?"

Again he gave her that smile that made her knees feel like putty. He glanced at Theron before returning his gaze to her. "You love animals."

"Yes, I do." She nodded enthusiastically. "I'm so thrilled that Serena talked about me." A little of the hurt from her sister not sharing her secret planet went away.

Konala crossed his arms. "She told me when I gave her a welchet to take care of that she couldn't tell you because you loved animals and were the one who kept bringing them home."

She swallowed hard as jealousy rode hard inside her. It was wrong because she loved her sister. She should be happy Serena had a pet…but she wasn't.

She was the one who always brought the animals home, but never got to keep them. The only animal that stayed was Bumble, but she'd brought him to her parents after she and Serena had left home.

Now Serena had a pet welchet? That was the porcupine creature she'd seen in the jungle. It was cute. She couldn't stifle her longing. "I am a little jealous. I always wanted a pet I could keep as my own."

"Then I will give you one."

"You will?" The surge of happiness inside her was over the top for such a simple act of kindness, but she reveled in it anyway.

Konala nodded. "Absolutely. Any kind of animal you would like."

Her mind raced with possibilities, but she had no idea if they were on Eden. The only animals she'd seen so far were—"Even a boarox?" She winked to let him know she was joking, but at Konala's widening eyes, she quickly retracted her request. "No, I'm kidding. Can I think about it?"

Konala looked to Theron. "How does she know about a boarox?"

Before Theron could reply, she answered. "I got a little too up close and personal with one before Theron rescued me."

Konala dropped his arms. "I knew I was right. I saw boarox prints near Loraleaf."

Theron squeezed her hand. "If there was only one then we don't have to worry about it."

She nodded. "Nope, Talia rescued Theron like he rescued me."

"Talia?" Konala looked at Theron.

He flushed. "I named a tigran that found me."

Konala laughed. "Necessity makes strange bed fellows."

Obviously it was some private joke between the two men. "Let me guess. Theron usually doesn't name animals."

"You are correct. In fact…" Konala shook his head. "Let's just say that 'Talia' is a big improvement."

Oh, there was definitely a story behind that.

"Come, I can't stand my own stench." Theron tugged on her hand and pointed to Konala. "Never mind yours."

The other man laughed and fell into step on the other side of her. She immediately pinched her nose closed. Konala smelled far worse than Theron.

When they reached the bath house, Theron opened the door and let her enter first. She loved the soothing color of the place as well as the warm steam rising from the pool.

There were two men on the pool deck drying off. She felt like she'd walked into a men's locker room by accident, but they grinned when they saw her.

One was Lennix, but she didn't know the other man. Lennix smiled at her and winked. He was such a flirt.

Then his nose wrinkled and he looked at Theron and Konala. Recognition was clear in his eyes. "I think you two need the bath house more than we do." He glanced at her. "It's all yours. Enjoy." He wiggled his brows, before he clapped the man next to him on the back and exited through the door they had entered.

Konala didn't hesitate. He walked down the steps, his thigh muscles obvious beneath his skin as he took each step. "Now this is living well."

Theron approached her. "You will join us."

The statement was not a question and she looked to Konala. Her voice barely made a whisper. "I can't."

Theron's brow knit. "Why? You did two days ago when we came to bathe."

Konala swam to the deep end, his tight ass breaking the surface of the water in addition to his feet and arms.

"I did in front of you. I don't know him."

Theron's puzzlement was obvious. "But he is the brother of my heart. There is no difference. He would enjoy you, too."

A vision of the two of them making love to her almost buckled her knees.

"Please. For me." Theron's eyes were dark and for a man who never asked anything of her, she would be heartless to deny him.

She glanced at Konala who was now standing next to the

soap dispenser. He'd gone under water so his short blond hair was wet and looked like amber. She returned her gaze to Theron and nodded.

He reached out to take her hand and she snatched it away. "I'll go in, but you need to wash first." She wrinkled her nose at him. "You stink."

"Very well." He looked serious, but light danced in his eyes. The man was trying not to laugh at her.

He could laugh all he wanted as long as he kept Konala busy. She watched as Theron moved down the steps, his body no less ripped than Konala's, though he was probably an inch or two taller. He wasn't as darkly tanned either. Maybe living on his own meant he stayed within the safety of the cave walls and not outside.

Heck, she forgot to tell him about her discovery in the tunnels. She'd do that after they all were clean. It was hard to concentrate as it was with that smell. Right now she had a different discovery to explore, skinny dipping with two out of this world hunks.

She couldn't believe her courage at being willing to get naked and join them. She'd been titillated by the idea, but when Theron asked so nicely, she had to give in.

Watching them constantly, she toed off her shoes and pulled off her socks. Both men took turns glancing in her direction. She wished they would just focus on catching up, but they weren't even talking, just washing their strong bodies which didn't help her concentration.

She'd got down to her bra and panties when Theron glanced over again.

"Could you two just turn your backs for a minute?" Her voice sounded frustrated, probably because she was. She had a plan and they weren't cooperating.

Theron raised one eye brow then turned away. Konala already had his back to her and stayed that way. Neither man moved. Konala didn't even wash the soap from his body. Great.

Quickly, she unhooked her bra, pulled off her panties and dove into the deep end of the pool.

Her body was barely submerged before two hulking men swam toward her under the water.

She scrambled up and to the side just as Theron and Konala rose on either side of her. "Holy guacamole, you scared me. Give a girl some room to breathe."

Konala grinned. "You can breathe near me now. I'm clean."

No kidding. She could smell the orangey citrus scent of him even though only his head was above the water.

"As am I." Theron, on her other side, smiled, his long black hair plastered back away from his face, making his cheek bones appear even stronger than they usually did.

Breathing was actually a little difficult with two such good looking men gazing at her as if they wanted to eat her up. "You two may be clean, but I'm not. I still need to wash."

Theron shook his head. "No. We need to wash you."

Her grip on the side of the pool slipped as the muscles in her entire body turned to mush.

"Stass, don't try to slip away now." Konala grabbed her arm to hold her afloat.

She gazed into his light blue eyes that reminded her of the Caribbean Sea. "Who is Stass?"

"It's not a who. It is an expression." He looked at Theron for help.

Theron remained silent for a moment then he nodded. "It is like your American expression 'whoa' or 'hold on.'"

She liked how Theron thought about what he would say before speaking. Not something she was good at. "I wasn't trying to slip away, I just lost my grip for a moment."

Konala pulled her away from the wall by hooking her arm around his neck. "Let's get you to the shallow end so we don't lose you."

She really was a good swimmer, but these two were definitely nervous about her being in water over her head. It was so sweet, she really didn't mind. Besides, with her body touching Konala's as he swam them across the pool, she wasn't sure she wouldn't drown if she let go. His physique was as hard as hers was soft.

When they reached what she considered about three feet, she pulled away. She'd just met the man and here she was swimming naked with him. Besides the fact he was drop dead gorgeous, she didn't know anything about him.

Actually, that wasn't true. She knew he could communicate with animals, which was the most awesome ability she could imagine having. Anyone who could talk to animals had to be decent.

"Are you ready to be washed?" Theron stood beside her.

She jerked her head up. She kept her body beneath the water, her knees bent so she could be somewhat hidden.

Konala moved up next to Theron and stood, rising out of the water like a golden Neptune. Side by side, she could see the height difference clearly, but while opposite in looks from facial structure to coloring, both men sported serious biceps, muscular shoulders, ripped abdominals and well defined pectorals.

She worried her lower lip. They were the sweetest eye candy and they were interested in *her*. She had to be dreaming.

"Come, Khityki." Theron held out his hand to her, his endearment, whatever it meant, always made her feel precious.

What did she have to lose? Her instinct told her Theron would never let Konala say anything bad about her body. To have two handsome hunks wash her was a dream. Why not live it?

Pulling her courage out from its hiding place, she slowly rose to stand, the water now only covering her to her hips as droplets fell from her shoulders and nipples and ran down her tummy and into the water.

She watched Konala closely for any sign of disappointment.

He sucked in his breath, his stomach ripples hardening. "By the Crius, you are beautiful."

She flushed and looked at Theron just to be sure he was okay with this. The look of pride on his face was unmistakable. Holy heck, the men on Eden really did like to share their women! No wonder her sister lived here.

Theron took her hand and walked her to the edge of the pool where the soap statue was. Konala stepped to the wall of the pool and opened his arms.

She had no idea what that was supposed to mean. She looked at Theron.

"Turn around and back up against Konala."

Her heart started to beat double-time. Put her back against that hard, heavenly chest? He didn't have to tell her twice.

The minute she did as Theron requested, Konala linked his hands with hers and whispered in her ear. "Relax and enjoy."

His low voice along with his words sent a shiver of anticipation down to her toes.

Theron flipped the flap on her favorite scent and lathered his hands. Then he brought them to her neck, slowly massaging her skin, moving toward her ears up along her hairline and finally to her forehead where he made small circles until he started down her nose.

She closed her eyes and did as Konala suggested. She leaned back against him and let Theron clean her face and neck. When he finished that part, his hands left her.

"Keep your eyes and mouth closed and hold your breath."

She did as told and he sluiced warm water over her head. It was an incredible feeling.

Konala let go of her hands and she wiped at her eyes even as Theron's hands held her waist and pulled her forward a couple steps. The next thing she felt was a tug on her hair and she looked over her shoulder to find Konala washing her hair from the bottom strands up.

She turned back to Theron. His gaze was tender, as if washing her was all he ever wanted to do with his life. It was addictive, but she reminded herself that she would have to leave all this pampering soon. She'd have to go back to work or her bills wouldn't—

Konala's hands reached her scalp and leisurely massaged it. She closed her eyes again, tilting her head back a little to give the man full access to her head as she reveled in the sensations.

He also scooped water over her head, over and over again until her hair was rinsed thoroughly.

Again she wiped the water from her eyes. This time she found Theron's eyes had darkened.

Konala's hands on her shoulders surprised her, but as he massaged her back with the scented soap, she relaxed again, secure in the knowledge that Theron had her. Konala only went down to her lower back before working his way back up and down her arms all the way to between her fingers.

She would be the cleanest person in Haven by time he was done. Again he rinsed where he'd cleaned. When his hands replaced Theron's on her waist, she assumed that Theron would take over. She tingled in anticipation of Theron's touch on her breasts.

But Konala's hands didn't stay on her waist. They moved across her tummy, swirling the soap. Her anticipation grew, but she looked to Theron.

He took both her hands and held them out to the side. "Relax and enjoy."

His repetition of Konala's words made it clear that these two men were one. What Theron could do then so could Konala.

She caught her breath as Konala's hands moved up to cup her breasts. That's when she felt his light kiss on her neck.

"So perfect."

Theron had uttered similar words just a few days earlier. These two men were obviously in tune. She lost her train of thought as Konala flicked a finger across each hard nipple.

When his thumbs joined his index fingers and squeezed, lightning, hot and white, struck down to her core. She moaned even as she moistened inside.

"Do you like that Jae? How about this?" He rolled her nipple between his thumb and finger.

"Yes." She let her head fall back against him, her hands still firmly grasped by Theron who watched Konala play with her.

He pulled her nipples gently then let go to take both her breasts in his large hands and massage them.

When he was done washing her front, he rinsed her off again.

Theron lowered her arms. "Now lean back."

She knew without looking that Konala was right behind her so she did. He caught her against his chest.

Theron cupped soap in one hand. "Lift your leg."

She did as requested, and Theron held her entire leg out of the water as Konala supported her. Thereon started with her thigh at the juncture of her legs and massaged the soap all the way down to between her toes. After repeating the process on the other leg, once again without touching her sex, he let her leg float to the bottom of the pool.

"This is all we can do in the water." Theron pointed to the edge. "We need you to sit up there."

Her tummy started its somersaults at the idea of these men, one of whom she'd just met today, washing her most private areas. Before she could make a decision whether to allow such an intimate event, Konala picked her up and sat her on the side of the pool.

If she didn't want this to happen, now was the time to make it known. "Wait."

Both men froze, Konala's hands on her thighs and Theron's hand beneath the soap statue.

"What is it Khityki? Would you like something else?"

Their complete willingness to give her whatever she wanted was overwhelming in its own right. "What if I wanted to wash myself?"

Konala stepped back, his hands sliding from her thighs. "You may do whatever you like." He winked. "You can even wash us if you like."

She shook her head and bit down on her lips to keep from smiling. She already had a sense of Konala's fun personality and it didn't surprise her that he'd offered. "And if I just wanted to get dressed and leave?"

Theron's face tightened, his eyes losing the luster they had when they made love. "If that is your wish, we would respect that, but we would try to convince you otherwise. As I told you before, you are special and we want you to feel that way."

Konala studied her as if he tried to read her mind.

Her earthly morality, or what was left of it, tried to get her to leave while she could, but her heart craved the way these men made her feel. There was no Serena to distract them and take their focus. It was just her.

The two of them watched her, completely still as if they were afraid to frighten her away. If she allowed this to continue, her heart would hurt a lot more when she returned home to her job, her parents, her life. It all seemed so boring compared to what she'd experienced since coming to Eden. She liked these men more than she should.

Should she stop before she got hurt and focus on going home or should she enjoy the pleasure of a relationship with them and then go home heartbroken? She didn't like either option.

She let her gaze wander over the bath, so much like the pictures she'd seen of them in ancient Rome, a place she hoped to visit one day. It was doubtful there were any baths like this still in use. Should she follow the saying, when in Rome do as the Romans do? While on Eden do as the Edenists do?

She made eye contact with Theron, her first Edenist lover, his brown eyes chocolatey right now, like his scent. Then she looked into Konala's light blue eyes that reminded her of the sky on a warm summer's day, his citrusy scent fresh and inviting. She was here, now, experiencing things she'd never done before or even could do at home. And she had two men who really liked *her*.

Her heart rejoiced as she made her decision. "I just need you two to know that I've never experienced anything like this. I'm not talking about the planet, because well, of course that is totally new and a complete surprise and no one on Earth would have had this experience except my sister and Erin and I imagine there are other—"

"Jaelene." Theron's lips curved slightly as his eyebrow rose.

Oh heck, she was rambling again. "Sorry, I got off track a bit. It's just that I'm nervous because I've never had two men interested in me like you are. I fantasized about it, sure, but I couldn't even get one man interested in me for more than a night or two back home. So I don't have a clue how to do this three-way relationship thing."

She had to stop to breathe and noticed an odd look on Theron's face as his gaze finally left her and he looked at Konala.

Konala looked at him and nodded before he turned to her. "Four-way."

She frowned. Four-way? Four-way what? Four-way relationship? Oh. They wanted to share her with Rekah.

"Um." This was crazy. She hadn't even met the man. "Um, let's just focus on the here and now, okay?"

Theron's eyes darkened. "I think that is a wise idea."

"Not me." Konala turned his head and gave her a mischievous smile. "I'm only focusing on you." His gaze ran from the top of her head to her feet dangling beneath the water. When it rose again and stopped at her lap, she felt her cheeks heat.

Theron moved through the water, the soap a small puddle in his big hand. "I know what *you* want." He shouldered Konala out of the way. "Allow me to wash her first, then you can taste."

Jaelene swallowed hard. Taste? Wash? Her cooled body heated fast with those words.

Konala gave her a seductive grin before he hopped up on the edge next to her and stood, his package even with her gaze. This close, she could see the veins in his cock as it stood straight out from his body, hard as the surface she sat on.

He turned and walked away causing her to twist around to watch him. His ass was as muscular as Theron's. Was there a law or something against being overweight?

Theron's hand on her thigh had her turning back toward the pool.

He nodded at her. "Spread your legs so I can wash you."

Her heart thudded hard against her chest as her sheath tightened. He really wanted to clean her *there*. She looked down at the triangle of dark hair she kept shaved neatly. It was a bit less neat than usual because she hadn't found a razor since arriving on the planet.

"Don't be afraid." Theron's eyes were dark again, but his voice could sooth a wild tiger. "I will be gentle."

She had no doubts about that, but she'd never had anyone do something so intimate. Then again, she'd made her decision. *Come on, Jaelene, just open your legs.*

"Here. You can lie back now." Konala crouched behind her and placed a fluffy pillow on the deck.

That would make it easier. Slowly, she lay back and Konala adjusted the pillow for her.

Theron gently nudged her legs apart, but she stared up at Konala who remained crouched behind her. He soothed her hair back and Theron's hand touched her mound.

His hand traveled down to her pussy and he carefully massaged the area between her thighs and her outside labia before brushing over her opening and inner lips. His large fingers moved upward to her clit and softly washed it.

She could feel her own wetness seep from inside her. Did he see it? She stared at Konala in an effort to not make any noise, but as Theron poured warm water over her clit, she moaned.

Konala's eyes darkened almost to cobalt. "The water may feel good now, but wait until you feel my tongue."

Her sheath tightened and her core ached at his husky words, anxious for his mouth. Holy heck, when had she become such a nympho? Then again, what woman wouldn't be with these two men?

Theron bent her legs, placing each foot on the edge of the pool. "Lift your hips for me, Khityki."

She did as he asked, too lost in the moment to ask why. Konala had started to trace lazy circles around her areolas, making her nipples hard even though he had yet to actually touch them. When she felt Theron's finger at her anal hole, she pulled her hips upward.

Konala chuckled, but Theron's large hand splayed over her abdomen. "If you want Konala's attentions, you must let me finish."

Theron sounded as if he scolded her, so she lifted her head a little higher to look at his face. She relaxed when she saw the slight curve of his lips. They must think her so strange compared to other women they had who were used to Eden.

Even as the thought formed, she frowned. She didn't like the idea of anyone else having these two men. As illogical as it was, it was how she felt. Determinedly, she made herself relax her hips back to where Theron wanted them. She could enjoy this as well as any other woman.

Konala chuckled before distracting her with the brush of his lips against hers. Then Theron's finger glided between her ass checks and she focused on staying pliant. He cupped his hands over her butt and massaged her. It relaxed her and excited her at the same time.

Konala kissed the tip of her nose and then each cheek, his feather-light touches making her feel cherished. What did she ever do to deserve this? Was it all those animals she saved?

Warm water gliding over her ass and onto the deck beneath her told her her bath was done. Now this was an experience she doubted she'd share with Serena. It wasn't like they had to tell each other *everything.*

Oh, is that what Serena thought?

Was she wrong to resent her sister for not telling her about Eden? It wasn't something intimate like this. She didn't want to know what Serena did with Jahl and Khaos. If it was anything like this, she really didn't want the details.

Theron grasped her hands and pulled her to a sitting position, her legs dangling in the warm water once more. He kept their hands linked as Konala jumped into the pool next to him. "I want you to know that you have changed my life."

"You've changed mine as well." She smiled saucily. "Trust me, it will never be the same."

He didn't shake his head, but she could tell he didn't mean it the way she took it. Something about her had helped him. Already she could see the sadness fading from him and she was inordinately pleased with herself, though she was sure most of it was because he'd reunited with his best friend after months of being alone.

To show him she understood, she wiggled her hands from his and grasped his face. She couldn't put it in words, but she gave him a sweet, caring kiss, something she hadn't done before.

When they broke apart, his eyes sparkled, literally, reflecting shards of the sun that filtered in through the small high windows.

Konala jokingly pushed Theron aside. "Time to share. You need to give me the chance to earn a kiss like that."

Theron smiled smugly. "You have to work hard for that."

"I plan to." He winked at her and she could feel herself heat.

Theron patted her thigh before boosting his hips up on the edge of the pool and moving behind her. "Konala wants to inspect my work."

"You don't mind, do you?" Konala's boyish grin made it hard to deny him anything. He was just too damn handsome. Still, she hesitated. She'd had men do oral sex with her, but she'd never been satisfied. They always thought they were more skilled than they were.

Theron sat behind her, his legs on each side of hers, his chest against her back as he wrapped his arms around her. "Anytime you want to stop, we will."

We? Now what did that mean?

Konala grasped her waist and kissed her belly button. She giggled. "Don't. I'm ticklish there."

"No, you can't deny me that spot of all spots." He sighed, loudly and dramatically. "Now I must be content with other more hidden places."

It just made her giggle again. It had to be her nerves. All this new sexual—"Oh."

Theron's hands had moved up to cup her breasts and his fingers played with her nipples, squeezing and twirling them like Konala had done when he washed them.

Konala's hands smoothed their way down her thighs. Then he kissed her waist, her abdomen, her mons. He continued to the inside of her thigh and she spread her legs a little wider. When she didn't go far enough to make him happy, he nudged her leg with his nose.

She giggled again as it was something a dog would do, though not to her thigh. Bumble always nudged her hand looking for a treat. A brief spear of homesickness hit, but it disappeared as Theron leaned her head back and kissed her.

Konala kissed her as well, but his kiss landed on her clit.

She opened her mouth in surprise and Theron's tongue entered her mouth. She leaned into him, letting him have his way with her as Konala's tongue began to explore her folds.

Heat built low in her belly at the dual sensations created by two different men. The teasing had gone on too long and she wanted satisfaction soon. Grasping Theron's neck, she tangled her tongue with his, seeking for his passion.

Konala must have sensed her need because he moved his tongue to her opening and slowly pushed it inside. She arched her hips against his mouth, silently asking for more.

Theron, didn't let her mouth go as he pinched her nipples lightly. Every squeeze sent fiery heat to her sheath where Konala's tongue invaded her. Theron broke their kiss as he pulled his legs from around her and knelt with her head in his lap.

She could feel his hard cock against her head and she wanted to taste, but he had other plans. He leaned over and latched his teeth on her right nipple just as Konala moved his mouth over her clit and licked.

Her body burst into flame. It was too much stimulation and yet not enough. Her sheath clenched, weeping that it was empty but the excitement continued to build inside her.

Theron paid homage to her breasts with his mouth and fingers while Konala continued to work her clit, licking, scraping with his teeth and finally sucking it into his mouth.

Her tension hit its pinnacle and she bowed as her orgasm flashed through her, burning her up inside and out until she felt like ashes floating to the pool deck. Every nerve ending pinged as her body relaxed and her heartrate slowed.

She couldn't open her eyes for what seemed like an hour, but was probably no more than minutes. When she did, it was to see Konala in all his naked glory, a light towel in his hands.

"Now I need to dry you."

A shiver raced over her at the prospect, but though her body was ready, her brain was reticent. A girl could only take so much on her first date with *two* men. "Thank you, but I can handle that myself."

"Very well." He handed her the towel.

Theron helped her to stand and luckily, kept his arms nearby for support as she stood on wobbly legs and held on to him while she dried each one.

When she was finished, she quickly dressed even though Konala frowned at her and Theron seemed resigned that she wouldn't stay naked. As far as she was concerned, Erin had been on Eden almost a year now and she covered up, so the last thing she would feel guilty about was wearing clothes.

CHAPTER ELEVEN

Theron locked his teeth together to keep from laughing at Konala's pained expression when Jaelene began to dress. The brother of his heart was all about living in the moment. He couldn't understand Jaelene's need to hold on to her earthly ways.

That was another reason Theron hadn't been sure about his own reception. When he and Konala and Rekah left Naralina with Jahl, Khaos, and Sandale to build Loraleaf, Konala never planned to return. He said his goodbyes to his family that night and never looked back. Theron expected Konala to have easily moved on without him.

It had to be Jaelene. Otherwise Konala would have looked at him like a distant relative, but even Theron could see the instant connection between Konala and their chosen one.

Chosen one. How had he gone from being in love with another filoz's beloved to having his own chosen one? That moment when he looked at Konala in the bath and silently asked if Jaelene was the one, he had hoped, though he thought it could never be. Konala's nod of agreement meant there was a chance.

Now they just had to convince Rekah and Jaelene. Of the two,

Rekah would be easier. When he left the city, he mourned the loss of his family, or rather his fathers for a long time. Rekah may be still missing him. But Jaelene did not expect to stay on Eden for long. Luckily, he now had an ally in his quest.

"By the Crius, we have company."

Konala's words had him spinning around to find Ware and Nase blocking the exit.

Nase stepped forward and faced Konala. "We want to know why you are here, and why alone."

Scrat, he'd completely missed that fact. All patrols were run with two men from different filoz. Konala was alone. Did that mean his companion was killed by the old lawbreaker? Loraleaf couldn't afford to lose another man.

Konala grinned. "No need to use your truth forcing ability on me. I bring good news." He opened his arms wide.

"You do?" Nase's brow knit in puzzlement.

"Yes, I do." Konala looked at Theron then back to Nase. "Naralina is no longer working on a way to track portal openings outside city walls. They gave that up."

Ware and Nase stood silent for a moment, probably thinking exactly what Theron thought—all the possibilities that were now open if it were true. Filoz could safely bring their chosen ones to Eden to bond. They could travel between the two settlements without worrying about lawbreakers. They could even use the portals to watch their enemies.

He could show Jahl and Khaos that Sandale was alive.

"This is life changing news." Ware's voice was low, his mind obviously still processing the information. "Come back to our home. We need to discuss this."

Konala shrugged, but Theron turned to Jaelene.

She looked at him in confusion. "Why is this good news?"

He explained as they headed to the largest home in Haven. "We do not want Naralina to know about these two settlements, Haven and Loraleaf. This is because either we left there for a reason, which is why Loraleaf was built, or in the case of Haven, men were falsely accused of crimes they didn't commit."

"Why did you leave—"

He shook his head at her and looked at the two leaders who walked behind them.

"Okay, so you don't want the city to know where you are and…" Jaelene's eyes lit with understanding. "You knew the city was working on tracking portal openings, so you couldn't open a portal too close to a settlement, but now you can. Heck, now even we can take a portal to go straight to my sister's."

Konala opened the door for Jaelene as they all entered. "At least we can for now. They are working on another project and from what I understand, the discoverists are spending every waking moment on it."

Ware closed the door. "What is this other project?"

"Oh, you're back." Erin came down the stairs to join them. "What's the project?"

Konala shrugged. "We don't know yet. We had only asked Toni to find out about the portal tracking. Now that we know there is some other project, we have asked her to find out what it is."

Nase looked at Ware. "I don't like it."

Jaelene raised her hands to the side. "What's not to like?" She held up her index finger. "You can now travel without worrying about lawbreakers and even visit each other easily."

Nase smiled at her. Theron hadn't seen the man smile at anyone but Erin and he didn't like it.

"No, I *do* like that we can travel safely. What I don't like is the 'other project.'" Nase looked at Ware. "If Grandall is involved, it can't be good."

Ware nodded. "I agree. We need to confer with Jahl and Khaos."

"Not both of us. I'll go." Nase gave them all a hard look as if he expected them to deny him.

As far as Theron was concerned, Nase wouldn't be stepping one foot in Loraleaf. He glanced at Konala who stood on the other side of Jaelene. The man's jaw was tense. Obviously, he agreed.

"No, I will go." Ware's tone brooked no argument, yet Nase opened his mouth, but didn't get to speak.

Erin stepped in front of Ware. "Let me come with you. I can see how they do their surveillance. Maybe I can help them. Your abilities here make my skills worthless."

Ware shook his head.

"Really?" Erin wouldn't give up. "I think it's important for me to meet with their agapayto and compare notes. I could learn something."

Ware shook his head again.

"Please. It would be so nice to talk with another woman who has been here awhile. Adjusting to Eden isn't as easy as you think."

Ware's face softened but still he shook his head. "I cannot let you come. I need to see this place and be sure it is safe. You stay here with Nase."

Theron bit back his angry defense of Loraleaf. They'd existed years before Haven. If Ware thought they had a rudimentary settlement, he was mistaken.

The coaxing and arguing continued a few more minutes. He and Konala grinned but didn't say anything. They didn't want Nase in Loraleaf either and preferred that Erin stay behind as well. Jaelene actually rolled her beautiful eyes at one point.

"Enough. My reasons are sound. I will go with Konala and Theron." Ware frowned at his beloved.

Jaelene stepped closer to Theron. "And me."

Ware looked about to speak, but Theron refused to have the man command anything from them. He was not their leader and was lucky that they would allow him to come to Loraleaf with them. "Of course you are coming with us." Though he spoke to Jaelene, he kept eye contact with Ware.

Ware finally nodded agreement. He probably realized they could easily leave him behind and he'd never find Loraleaf.

Theron wouldn't be willing for Ware to come if he didn't think it was important that he meet with Jahl and Khaos about new portal openings. Some kind of protocol needed to be set up. Before Ware could further make demands, he looked at Konala. "Open the portal."

He and Konala separated and he pulled Jaelene to the side. Then he pressed the chip under his left arm as Konala did the same and the portal opened inside Loraleaf, just outside his old home.

Just seeing it again caused his throat to close. He'd never expected to be there again.

He looked at Jaelene, who had stepped in front him to see. Her blue eyes were wide with awe, her head slightly cocked as she gazed at his home.

Konala grinned at him before taking her hand. "Are you ready to see your sister?"

She looked at Konala and then at him. "Please."

He wanted to take her hand, but motioned Ware forward. "Welcome to Loraleaf."

Jaelene stared at the place they called Loraleaf. It was amazing.

Wooden walkways ran between the largest trees she'd ever seen. They made the Redwood forest look like saplings.

Scattered among the branches were homes built around the massive tree trunks. They appeared to be at three levels with the first level where they stood and even that one was at least two stories off the ground.

Vines hung from strategic branches and some of the naked men used them to go from one walkway to another, while others used what appeared to be open-basket elevators.

She looked at Konala who still held her hand. He watched her with a smile on his face.

"This is your home?"

He nodded. "It is. Do you like it?"

She looked around her and her gaze caught Theron's. "I love it." In private, she needed to ask him how he could ever have left such a wonderful place.

Konala squeezed her hand. "That's where I live." He pointed to the closest round building on that level. "Rekah, Theron and I are second in command and live the closest to the entry from the ground." He pointed to a square trap door on its own platform off the main walkway.

"There are stairs in an old tree trunk that allow us to reach the ground unobserved."

Ware appeared as awestruck as she was, but he found his voice at that. "What do you mean 'unobserved.' Though you are high in the trees, your activities can be seen a long way into the jungle."

Theron grinned. "Actually you can't see any of this." He spread his arm wide. "I combined my reflection ability with another's air abilities and we fuel them with eyllen to create thick walls to protect our home. What men see outside is merely a reflection of the area. Loraleaf starts at this level, so men could walk right under us and not know we were here. Plus, it's impenetrable."

As Ware's eyes widened, Jaelene felt a sense of pride in Theron. It wasn't that she had anything against Erin's husband, but she could tell that he didn't expect Loraleaf to be so advanced. If she *were* to pick a town to live in, she would choose Loraleaf.

Like her sister did.

Hurt and pride swirled inside her. It must have taken a lot of courage to choose to live on another planet, but she still wished her older sister had confided in her. Even if she didn't believe a place like Loraleaf existed…until now.

She squeezed Konala's hand to get his attention. The whole hand-holding habit had quite a few perks.

He took his gaze from Theron and Ware and focused on her. The light blue of his eyes always calmed her, except when they turned bright with his passion.

She blushed, but didn't look away. "Could I see my sister?" She said it quietly. She told herself it was because she didn't want to interrupt Theron and Ware's conversation, but the truth was, she was both excited and afraid to see her sister. She would definitely get an earful.

"Of course." He squeezed her hand in return as if he could sense her unease. Did all these men have a sixth sense or something?

"Theron, Jaelene would like to see Serena."

Theron's gaze snapped to Konala and then to her. "Are you sure you're ready?"

She swallowed hard. "Yes. No use delaying the inevitable." She grimaced and tried to focus on the hug she was sure to receive… eventually.

"True. Konala, take Ware with you. I'm going to search out Rekah."

She looked askance at Konala. His face didn't change, but she got the distinct impression that he tensed. Did he expect problems between Theron and Rekah? If Rekah was the one who could sense emotions, he would probably be happy to see Theron. There was no doubt that Theron would be happy to see him.

Her chest tightened as she envisioned their reunion to be like his and Konala's. Of course, she had no idea why Theron had left. He'd always avoided the question, but his pained look told her he'd been hurting. Maybe he needed to make peace with Rekah.

Just like she needed to smooth things over with Serena. "I'm ready when you are." She glanced at Ware and he nodded.

"This way." Konala led them to the closest elevator and moved the lever.

She caught site of Theron entering his home before the smooth ride of the basket elevator had her full attention. "It feels like we're riding on air."

Konala smiled. "You are, partially."

Ware was quiet, but she could see him thinking, taking in everything he saw and liking it. Bet he would institute new ideas when he got home.

When the elevator stopped, they were on the third level. She thought that was all the levels there were, but farther down the center of the tree grove, she could see a couple other elevators that went higher.

Konala walked them over a short private walkway to a huge round building set apart from any others. He knocked on the door.

Khaos opened it. "Konala, you're back." It took him a second before he looked past her and frowned at Ware. Then his gaze snapped back to her. "Jaelene!"

She smiled because what else was she to do? "I came for a visit, brother-in-law."

"Ah, so that is what I sensed. I thought Serena would be going home for an unexpected reason. I saw you and she together. Now I know why."

She wasn't sure if he meant he really saw the future or was just covering up his surprise. She had no idea what "abilities" her sister's husbands had. It's not like Serena told her.

Resentment burned in her gut again and she attempted to snuff it out. "Is Serena here?" She tried to look around the big man.

"She is." He looked over her head at Ware. "Follow me."

They filed into the living room. Wow, her sister lived the high life, literally as well as figuratively. There was a large bar in one part of the living room and outside the floor to ceiling windows she could see a cage. That's right, Konala said Serena had a pet.

"Khaos, who do we have for—" Serena stopped as she came around the corner. Her eyes widened and she froze for a moment.

Unfortunately, she found her voice. "Shit Jaelene, what are you doing here?"

"Nice to see you too, sis." She lifted her chin, the hurt at being left in the dark surfacing. "Maybe if you'd told me you lived on another planet, I wouldn't have had to follow you and gotten lost and needed to be saved like a gazillion times."

Serena's scowl disappeared. "How could I tell you? You wouldn't have believed me anyway."

"Then that would have been my problem, but you didn't even give me a chance. We always told each other everything." She sounded like a five year-old but she didn't care, her hurt grew as she was able to finally confront her sister.

"Everything? I don't think we've told each other *everything,* and this," she spread her arms wide, "is a secret. I had to keep it from you, for Loraleaf and for Eden."

"Why? And don't give me that 'I was protecting you' crap that mom used to give us. Heck, she even said that when she told us there was no Santa and that's why she'd lied about him for so long. I never did understand how letting us believe in Santa was protecting us."

Serena's lips quirked up. "I didn't get that either. But keeping Eden a secret from you was so you wouldn't know about the planet. There are strict rules here and very few choices for women. I wanted you to have all the choices in the world."

Jaelene cocked her head. "But you had choices from out of this world."

Serena opened her mouth then shut it. She looked at each man in the room and her face softened. "To tell you the truth, I'm glad you know. It was *so* hard to keep all this from you. I'm sorry."

The hurt inside her lost its edge and tears welled in her eyes to match those in her sister's.

"Oh my God, come here." Serena opened her arms.

She ran to Serena and finally got the hug she'd been wanting since she first found herself lost on Eden.

"It *is* good to see you." Serena pulled away but kept her hands on her shoulders. She frowned and lowered her voice. "But you have no idea what this means."

She didn't like the sound of that. She looked behind her at the three men watching them. Konala stepped forward. "Do not be concerned. She is our chosen one."

"What?" Serena shook her head. "How?"

Konala grinned crookedly. "Theron."

"Theron? He's here?"

Khaos's gaze shifted to Serena's and an odd look passed between them. Jaelene didn't like it. Was it Theron or that she was—"Wait, what do you mean *your chosen one*. I never agreed to be that and don't think I don't know what that is because Erin told me all about this *chosen one* thing. If I'm chosen, I think I need to have a choice in the matter. Right? Isn't that what the chosen thing is all about? I mean—"

Konala turned her away from Serena and held her shoulders. "Look at me, Jae."

Her heart beat a mile a minute as panic took root in her stomach.

"Jae." Konala's pleading voice got through and she lifted her gaze to his.

His eyes held her own as he rubbed her shoulders, calming her panic. "A chosen one is not a beloved. You have the choice to deny us if you wish, but I ask you to consider the possibility."

Why did this feel like a proposal from one man for two? She looked at her brother-in-law whose face was devoid of any emotion. Then she glanced at Ware who grinned. What was *he* so happy about?

Serena pulled her away. "I think I need to talk to my little sister and sort this out."

"Sort what out?" The voice that came from the entry way was barely a step above a growl.

"Hi, Jahl." Her other brother-in-law was scowling at Ware, but when she spoke, his jaw went slack.

He shook his head. "Jaelene?"

Theron walked into his old home. Nothing had changed. All the furniture was in the same place, at least in the living space. It was as if he'd never left. He took a deep breath. Yes, this was home. He was proud of what he'd done in the cave, but the boarox proved to him how dangerous it was to live alone in the jungle.

He strode through the kitchen and into the bedroom. It had to be a good sign that Rekah and Konala hadn't eliminated his bed, though it surprised him because that would have been Konala's way. Hopefully, that meant that Rekah still wished he was there.

The front door opening had him turning on his heel. He strode toward the living area surprised he heard no more footsteps. As he came in view of the door, he found Rekah standing just inside.

"What are you doing here?"

At Rekah's greeting, he stopped. "I've returned. I hoped you would welcome me home."

The brother of his heart sneered. "How can you live here when you are still in love with Serena?"

He didn't answer at once. This was not a side of Rekah he'd ever seen before. "I am no longer in love with Serena."

Rekah slammed the door shut behind him. "You lie. I know what you feel and you are in love."

"I am in love, but with Jaelene." He waited, letting his friend think about it. Last he had heard from Mykl, Rekah had asked about him, wanting to know that he was alive and well. He'd thought that meant Rekah was concerned, but now he wasn't sure.

"So you have formed another filoz." Rekah strode by him and dropped the bread he carried on the table in the meal room.

Theron followed him in. "No, I haven't formed another filoz. I couldn't. You and Konala are the brothers of my heart. You know that."

Rekah spun. "You left us. Avoiding Serena was far more important than staying with your family. You made your choice."

Guilt threatened to close his throat, but he pushed it away. He couldn't undo what he'd done. "Yes, I did, but I missed my family. Every day I thought of you and Konala. I wanted to be here. I am sorry."

Rekah studied him, obviously reading his emotion. Then Rekah nodded and turned back to the cabinets. He took out a large bowl and opened the cold box as if their conversation was done.

Theron's home may not have changed, but one brother of his heart certainly had. Rekah was no longer the man he used to be. He was cold. What if he met Jaelene? What would he say? Theron's instinct told him it wouldn't be good. He needed to talk to Konala.

His first loyalty was now to Jaelene. "I am also sorry to see the man you have become. I had hoped for something else. I will find somewhere else to stay."

Rekah shrugged, but didn't turn around. "I am who I am based on my experiences. If you don't like it, you are welcome to leave…again."

Still unable to reconcile the man he spoke to with the one he'd left behind, he finally turned and left.

As he stepped outside into the sunshine, his heart ached. His actions had caused far more damage than he'd imagined. Somehow he had to fix it. There was more at stake now than there had ever been.

He strode to the lift and pushed the lever. As he rose, he contemplated his options. One thing he was sure of. He wouldn't be leaving again.

When he reached the home of Loraleaf's leaders, he wasn't surprised to hear that Serena had taken Jaelene on a tour of Loraleaf. He secretly hoped that would influence her more toward staying with him and Konala.

He watched as Jahl and Khaos quizzed Ware, finding it humorous now that Ware was in the opposite position he'd been in at Haven. The man took it all in stride though, sitting back on the long couch, relaxed, while Jahl paced in front of the bar and Khaos stood leaning against the wall.

Konala and he sat in the two chairs in the living area. Once they'd discussed the news regarding Naralina and the portals, Theron had to interrupt.

"I have more news that I haven't told anyone, but Jaelene may be telling Serena even as we speak, so you need to know."

Jahl frowned. "Then tell us instead of talking around it."

"Sandale is alive." He probably could have eased into it, but sometimes Jahl's gruff manners, irritated him. Still, the man was a good leader.

Khaos actually smiled at Jahl. "I told you."

Jahl shook his head. "We'd hoped, but…"

Konala recovered first. "How do you know?"

"I saw him at least three times when I lived alone. He is alive, but he is with the lawbreakers and he is not himself."

"What do you mean?" Jahl gripped the back of the bar stool he stood next to.

"He purposefully dropped an unconscious man and he attacked Jaelene."

"What?" Jahl's fist came down on the bar. "Then it's not Sandale."

Theron didn't need Rekah's ability to read emotions to understand why Jahl refused to believe it. No man in Loraleaf would ever hurt a woman and Sandale had been one of their leaders and the most compassionate of men. He chose his words carefully. "It is Sandale and yet it isn't."

Jahl rubbed his hands over his face. "Will you please make some sense?"

"I am. The man I've seen is Sandale, but I believe that a Kindred of Mind is among the lawbreakers and they have altered him somehow. He has his abilities, but he is cruel. If I hadn't distracted him with my reflection, he would have taken Jaelene against her will."

"No!" Khaos surprised them all with his outburst. "He would not have, but you are right, he isn't what he was."

For once he was happy that Khaos had a sense of the future and could collaborate what he'd seen.

"I sensed Sandale but also another presence, an immoral one. It feels like there is a constant struggle for dominance. We need to help him."

"I agree." He looked at Konala. "If one of my filoz was taken, I would do whatever was necessary." He moved his gaze to Jahl. "And in this case, what is necessary may be difficult."

"Once again you are one step ahead of us, Theron." Jahl frowned. "Speak."

He looked from Jahl to Ware, who had been silent, listening. "We need to capture Sandale but his ability to cause mass unconsciousness is formidable." He moved his gaze back to Jahl. "We will need Ware's help."

The man scowled. "I don't think—"

"What did you have in mind?" Khaos sat on the bar stool Jahl still gripped.

"We need to enclose Sandale without getting close to him. If we build an invisible box that will keep his ability from affecting us then I could use reflections of people he wants to get to and lure him inside. Once the prison is sealed behind him, we can transport him and take time to figure out how to help him be Sandale again."

"Why can't you build the box with Paxon like you did the walls around Loraleaf? Then you wouldn't need him." Jahl pointed at Ware who continued to remain silent.

That bothered Theron. Was Ware thinking it was their citizen, and therefore their problem? "The walls around Loraleaf allow our abilities to be used through them. This box would have to be sealed which means that we would need a way to keep air flowing and provide food and water without breaking the seal.

Ware is Kindred of air and his ability to move air is exactly what we need."

Jahl's face didn't relax. In fact, it was obvious he tried to find another reason not to include Ware.

Khaos broke the silence. "You have not said anything, Wareson. It appears we could use your help. Would you be willing?"

Ware stood. "Yes, because the control over this man is wrong and dangerous to all of us. But I do request a favor in return."

Theron tensed as did every other person in the room. "What?"

Ware didn't look at him. Instead he spoke to Jahl. "I would like to see Loraleaf."

No one spoke as the two men stared at each other. Finally, Jahl nodded his head once. "I will show you what we have built."

Ware smiled. "And I will help in any way I can."

Theron's tension didn't abate at the agreement. Instead, he was anxious to get to work on the trap. He was ready to show Jaelene what he could do when he combined his abilities with others.

"This is happy news and calls for celebration." Khaos rose and went behind the bar.

As they all moved to receive their drink, Theron whispered in Konala's ear. "I saw Rekah."

Konala simply lifted an eye brow in question.

He shook his head. "We need to make a decision."

They broke apart as Khaos handed a glass to Konala then he stepped up and received his own.

"To Sandale." Jahl raised his glass. "And bringing him home safely."

They all lifted their glasses, tapped them against their foreheads, and took a drink.

As soon as they finished their ambrosia and agreed to let all of Loraleaf know the exact nature of the quest to capture Sandale, they parted ways—Jahl to fulfill his obligation to Ware, Khaos to search out Serena and himself to find Paxon.

As he and Konala left, instead of taking a vine below, he nodded toward the lift. Once inside, he set it in motion and lowered his voice. "Rekah has no use for me. I do not know what he will do when he meets Jaelene. I think you should be the one to introduce her. If he rejects her, you and I will need to make a decision."

Konala nodded solemnly, but didn't say anything about which way his loyalty would go.

Theron didn't envy him his position. He'd only met Jaelene that morning and soon he might be forced to choose between her and the brother of his heart.

The lift came to the first level and Theron exited. He closed the half door behind him. "I will not lose her."

Konala met his gaze but with no expression on his face, pulled the lever and the lift rose.

Theron watched it until it stopped, then he turned and strode toward the lab where Paxon could usually be found. His heart was heavy in his chest, but as he walked past his home, Paxon called his name, a smile on his face and joy in his eyes.

Theron smiled back and picked up his pace. This was where he belonged.

CHAPTER TWELVE

Konala found Jaelene in Libations and it appeared he was just in time. She, Serena and Khaos were about to leave. He smiled, an easy thing to do when around her.

Their connection was exactly what he thought love would feel like. On Earth, they called it "love at first sight," but it was far more than that. It was an invisible thread that connected them as if it had been torn asunder when they were born and now it was finally repaired, making them whole.

Was Rekah part of the same thread?

He shook off the question. He'd find out soon enough. Instead, he focused on his chosen one. Even as he thought the words, his chest swelled with happiness and pride. "There is someone I would like you to meet."

She met his smile with her own. "Is it Rekah?"

"Yes."

She turned to her sister who appeared about to argue. "It's okay. Now that I understand how this whole *chosen one* versus *beloved* works, I'm fine. I get it. I'm engaged without being asked, therefore I'm *chosen*, but I don't have to go through with the wedding if I don't want to and become a *beloved* or *agapayto*. Right?"

Serena nodded. "Yes, but remember what I said about sex and bonding."

Jaelene blushed, making her pale white skin rosy with a healthy hue. She looked beyond beautiful to him.

"I've got it. I'm good. Now go home. I'll see you later." She waved at her sister as if that would make her leave faster.

Serena frowned. "You're sleeping in our guest room, not at Konala's."

Jaelene rolled her eyes. "Yes, mom."

Konala laughed before Serena started to scold and he grabbed Jaelene's hand. "We'll be back after dark, sis."

He pulled Jaelene out of the establishment before Serena recovered from her shock at being referred to as his sister.

Jaelene giggled. "That was great. It's not often I've seen my sister at a loss for words. Even when she found me in her living room, she was able to speak. You're good."

He winked. "I'd be happy to show you how good I am."

She looked away, but the flush in her face told him she wasn't insulted. Good. What he wanted to do was show her his animals and the beauties of Loraleaf, but he had to first introduce her to Rekah.

He couldn't see how Rekah could resist her.

As they strolled along the walkway, the men of Loraleaf did not avoid staring and smiling, something he found he didn't appreciate. After the fifth man passed and Jaelene's gaze remained looking at the branches, he stopped and pulled her around to face him.

"Are you uncomfortable?"

"A little." She cocked her head. "It's weird for me to see men walking around without clothes. In Haven, the walking area was so broad, it was easy to resist looking at, well, you know, the manly parts. But here, with these walkways only two people wide, it's up close and personal, if you know what I mean."

He leaned back against the railing, leaving space between them. "Do you feel uncomfortable looking at my 'manly parts'?"

Her gazed moved down and his cock reacted. Holy Bendis, even in the pleasure temples as a young man, he didn't respond that fast.

She looked up at him beneath her lashes. "I will admit to liking your parts a lot."

He hardened even more, which begged the question, why was he torturing himself like this. His voice lowered of its own accord. "I would like very much to feel myself inside you."

This time, that rosy hue he enjoyed so much spread over her face and down her neck. She didn't say anything, but she did nod.

He chuckled and pulled her gently against him. "Jae, you make my body hard and my heart swell."

She smiled. "Your body is already hard and if your heart keeps swelling, you should probably see one of those healers."

Konala threw back his head and laughed.

Then he kissed her.

She responded hesitantly at first, despite how intimate they'd been that morning, but as his tongue swept through her mouth, tasting every surface, she started to reciprocate.

When a tiny moan issued from the back of her throat, he forced his lips away and took deep breaths. An Edenist strode by and grinned.

Scrat, he wanted her right now, but he had to take her to Rekah.

"What's wrong?" She looked up at him, her blue eyes, the color of caball feathers, were confused.

"I want to take you right now, here on the walkway, but I have a feeling you wouldn't want everyone to see us."

"Oh." She looked around. "I almost forgot where we were, but you're right. I guess we shouldn't kiss unless we are somewhere private because around you, I go up like a match thrown on gasoline."

"And I," he pushed his stiff cock against her stomach, "turn to stone when you kiss me."

She instinctively pressed back against him. "Heck, you really are stone."

"Maybe we should go see Rekah," he grinned. "Before we block the walkway."

She pulled away and looked at his cock. If she kept that up, he'd never go down.

He took her hand again and directed her to a jump-off ledge. "Wrap your arms around my neck."

She looked over the short rail. "Why?"

He pulled the vine wrapped around the hook that held it there. The infragile vine had been cut from its mother plant and fused to the tree high above them by Jahl since he was of the Eden Kindred and could manipulate anything not alive. "We are going to swing down to the first level. It will be faster."

She looked above where the vine connected to the tree. "I don't know about that. It's one thing for one person, but with two people, it might break."

"It won't. It's infragile vine. Trust me. I would never let anything harm you." He dropped his smile and stared at her, silently willing her to trust him.

She looked over the edge one more time then scanned his body before meeting his gaze again. "Okay."

Though he wanted to yell his joy at her trust, he kept it inside, well aware that she still wasn't completely convinced, but would take the risk with him. "Wrap your arms around my neck and if you want you can wrap your legs around my waist."

She gave him a sly smile. "Anything to get me against that cock of yours, huh?"

He swallowed hard as that part of his anatomy reacted to her mentioning it. "Ah, yes."

"I thought so." She held him tightly around the neck and then *did* jump up to encompass his waist with her legs. "I'm only doing this so you have two hands to hold our weight."

"Of course." He could easily take both their weights with one arm, but he wouldn't tell her that. Stepping up to the edge, he grabbed the vine and swung across to the second level.

She jumped off once he had two feet on the landing. "Wow, that was a rush."

"You liked it?"

"I did. We have to do it again, right? Because your house is over there and that's probably where Rekah is."

"Correct. But we need to grab a vine that will go in that direction." He took her hand and walked her to another jump off ledge. This time, she hopped onto his body like they had swung a hundred times already.

"Okay, I'm ready. Let's go."

He chuckled silently, but grasped the vine and swung them across again but down one level. "That's it."

She slid off him and he stifled a groan of pleasure.

"I could get used to that." She watched him as he looped the vine around a hook.

When he finished, she took his hand and started for his house. Surprised, he let her lead, too pleased that she'd initiated their contact. Whether she realized it or not, she was already strengthening the thread between him. This was the ready acceptance he'd been hoping for.

"So what do I need to know about Rekah? I know he reads emotions, so is that a constant thing or is it only when he wants to. I imagine you only communicate with animals when you wish to and I know Theron only projects reflections when he decides he wants one, but sensing emotions could be like telepathy. Not that I believed in that before now, but I've read books where the people can't keep others thoughts out of their minds and they go insane. I can see where if Rekah was constantly bombarded by—"

"Jae." He slowed them down, her stride having become as fast as her conversation. "You don't have to be afraid of Rekah. He is a good man. He can choose to read an emotion or not. He is the one that men come to when they are conflicted, or miss their homes, or are trying to choose a potential beloved."

She worried her bottom lip as she pondered his statement. "So he's like the local psychiatrist?"

"Yes."

"And he's a good man like you and Theron?"

He liked her way of thinking. "Yes."

"Is he attractive?"

He raised his eyebrow. "I don't know."

She brought them to a halt just steps away from the house. "You don't know if he's attractive?"

He shrugged. "It's not something I think about. My only concern is women, and in particular, you."

She held up her index finger. "What does Rekah look like?"

"He's blond like me, but his hair is a little longer. He wears a trim beard and he is taller and broader than I am."

Her eyes widened. "You mean like Jahl?"

He shook his head. "No, Rekah is bigger than Jahl."

She contemplated that. "I guess he's the gentle giant. That's how I'll think of him."

Konala wasn't sure how Rekah would react to that idea if he knew. He'd probably be happy with it if he liked Jaelene. But Rekah wasn't one to get attached quickly and his mother's lack of love for his fathers, who doted on her, made him careful.

They'd been watching Star every day now and there was no discussion about making a decision yet. For that he was grateful because he was not interested in Star, even before he met Jaelene.

"Okay, I'm ready." She smiled at him, but through it, he could tell she was nervous.

He squeezed her hand. Rekah would know she was nervous as well and that was good. "Then please, come in." He opened the door as the smell of a spicy sauce wafted through the air.

"He's cooking our evening meal. Let's see what he has." He led her through the living area and into the meal room. "Rekah, I've brought company for dinner."

The moment the door opened to the house, Rekah sensed

Konala's unease and a woman's nervousness. It had become a habit to sense the emotions of those who entered as it helped him keep everyone calm.

As the two walked in, he also felt the connection, Konala's stronger but the woman's was growing. *This* was Theron's chosen one.

Betrayal sliced hard into Rekah's gut. First Konala demanded that he choose to move on with life, and now he expected him to agree to the woman he brought with him. He'd rather be dragged across the Samuvian desert.

As they entered the kitchen, two more strong impressions came to him, the woman's scent was nutty, like his favorite treat, and she was afraid to meet him. He'd never had anyone fear him. It bothered him.

He turned around to find Konala smiling and the woman staring at him, her eyes wide.

"So tell me, is he attractive?" Konala spoke to the woman, a lopsided grin on his face.

She blinked, finally bringing her gaze to his. "Oh wow, I love your eyes. I mean, I've never seen that color green before." She turned back to Konala. "The answer is yes. And you were right, he is bigger than Jahl. A lot bigger."

"*He*, is actually Rekah, and you are?" Rekah didn't step closer as he usually would to make a person feel at home. His own emotions were too mixed to be the sympathetic listener.

He found the woman's dark hair and pale skin attractive, but her emotions moved in different directions so quickly, it was difficult to follow and yet fascinating at the same time.

"Hi, I'm Jaelene. I'm Serena's sister." She held out her hand.

Serena's sister? No. His resentment toward Serena which had faded with his acceptance of Theron's departure, resurfaced hard.

"You are visiting her here?" He shook her hand loosely, indifferently.

She glanced at Konala. "Yes, but I got lost. And then a man came after me and Theron saved me. He even saved me from —"

"Jae, relax, he won't bite." Konala grinned at her.

She squinched up her nose at Konala. "I hope not because there'd be nothing left of me." She turned back to face him. "That's what I was about to tell you before I was interrupted. Theron saved me from a boarox. Now *that* would be a big bite. Have you seen the teeth on those things? I did and it was far too close for comfort."

"You saw a boarox and his teeth up close?" Rekah's protective instincts rushed through him and he had to force himself to stay where he was.

"I did, but then Talia, that's Theron's tigran, bounded out of the trees and tackled the boarox while I helped Theron back into the cave. He was a mess, a broken leg, his arm scratched to ribbons by those teeth. I had to put so many stitches in his arm that I lost count. Not that I wanted to count because it was hard enough sticking the needle into his arm without actually counting how many times I did it. Talia took care of that boarox and probably kept the lawbreakers from the meat, but I'll be perfectly happy if I never see another boarox again. Luckily, Theron healed quickly while I investigated the tunnels and you wouldn't believe what I—"

Konala tipped her chin up and kissed her, silencing her effectively.

Rekah's heart, concerned by her tale, suddenly raced ahead as he witnessed their kiss, wanting to be a part of their intimacy.

He forced his heart to slow. They were studying Star. How could Konala do this?

Konala lifted his head away and wrapped his arm around Jaelene's waist, keeping her close to his side. "You'll have to excuse her. She's been through a lot since she arrived on Eden."

"That's what it sounds like." He redirected his thoughts like he did with those who were too upset to talk right away. "This boarox encounter is concerning."

"It is. I saw the scars on Theron. The beast appears to be everything we learned about in school." Konala gave Jaelene a worried expression. "I can't believe she and Theron lived to tell the tale."

Though Rekah's heart twisted at the thought of Theron's pain and Jaelene's danger, he ignored it.

She looked at Konala. "Do you know that thing was whimpering and crying like it was in pain and I fell for it. I've never had an animal *pretend* to be hurt. If Theron hadn't returned from tracking that man, Sandale, I wouldn't have lived to take another breath."

"Sandale?" Rekah looked to Konala to confirm the truth. "He's alive?"

"He is, but he's not himself. We think a Kindred of Mind has altered his personality. He is with the lawbreakers, but Khaos senses that the old Sandale is still inside, struggling with the new personality."

Rekah leaned back against the counter. Holy Bendis! They had hoped he was alive, but if this was true, Sandale had to be in psychic agony.

He had to alleviate his pain. Sandale wasn't just a leader of

Loraleaf, but a trusted friend. Determination overrode all other thoughts. "We must find him and help him."

Konala nodded. "Yes. We have a plan." He nodded toward Jaelene. "Let's discuss it over dinner."

He glanced toward Konala's chosen one. Her look of concern knocked on his heart, but he did what his patients did and refused to examine his feelings surrounding her, Theron, and Konala. He had too many other issues to handle at the moment, the first being dinner. "Have a seat." He turned back to the heat top. "I'll serve."

As they conversed over dinner, Rekah kept sensing the emotions of his companions. Whenever Theron's name arose, Jaelene's love for him was clear. He was both jealous and resentful. When Konala explained the plan to catch Sandale, she was afraid of both their former leader and for Theron and Konala. As for himself, she continued to be nervous, and a bit of physical fear remained. That bothered him the most.

Konala, as usual, was easy to read. He had forgiven Theron and welcomed him back which was not a surprise, and he was completely in love with Jaelene.

Sometimes Rekah envied Konala his ability to accept what life served him, but other times, it felt as if Konala must not care deeply if he could change his emotions so quickly. "What about Star?" It was an inner thought, but he wasn't sorry he voiced it.

Konala frowned for a moment before he grinned crookedly. "To be honest, I'd forgotten about Star."

"What star?" Jaelene's curiosity, obvious from all the questions she asked about Sandale's capture, always invited more conversation.

Konala clarified. "It's not a 'what' but a 'who'. Star is a woman on Earth that Rekah and I were watching as a possible chosen one. Rekah saved her from drowning."

He studied Jaelene closely as she processed the information. How could Konala have forgotten the woman they'd chosen to watch when it was he who had pushed him into it?

He sensed Jaelene's disappointment and withdrawal immediately, and he had to know why. "Yes, I did. Konala was there too, to help her out of the water. She believes in life on other planets and would make a good beloved."

"Oh, I see." She looked at Konala. "I'm not too sure about this whole chosen one practice, but I am glad that I have the final say." She turned back to him and stared him in the eye. "Theron and Konala have chosen me. So we both have a decision to make… eventually."

He bit down on his smile at her blatant challenge. It was the first spark of strength he'd seen in her. It made him more confident in Konala's choice. That she would claim them was a good sign. He may not be a part of their filoz in the future, but he would always want happiness for the brothers of his heart.

Even as the idea crossed his mind, his gut tightened. He was more connected to the social aspect of life in Loraleaf than any other except possibly Sandale. To lose his filoz would be difficult in ways he couldn't contemplate.

Jaelene was correct. He would have a decision to make. He nodded and stood to clear the table.

"Oh, I can do that." She jumped up. "I'm not used to men waiting on me." She grabbed the plates, stacking them on top of each other. "You probably know from studying Earth that in America, the household duties are shared more often than not."

He stopped her from putting the dishes in the basin. "We do know this, but here, it is not our way." He took the dishes from her and set them on the counter. "Konala will clean up while you and I talk."

He motioned toward the living area and she looked at Konala, that fear back in her eyes.

Konala smiled at her then frowned at him.

It wasn't as if he planned to hurt her. She wasn't in love with him. But he wanted to know more about her. Wasn't that why she was brought to meet him?

Jaelene sat on the edge of a chair, worrying her bottom lip. He relaxed across from her, in the large soft chair he used when fellow Edenists came to confide their hopes, dreams, fear, and pain. He *always* helped. It was what he did, no matter how hard it was. "You should go back to Earth."

"What?" Jaelene's eyes widened, then she cocked her head. "I mean, I planned to, but why would you say that?"

"I know you are in love with Theron and falling for Konala, but both men have proven fickle. Both have chosen others before. You will get hurt if you stay."

Indecision crossed over her features before she held up her index finger. "Listen, I don't know why you are so bitter, but I will tell you this. Being bitter isn't going to impress me or Star or any woman. You need to drop the chip you have on your shoulder and get a grip on reality or you'll die a lonely man."

He opened his mouth to rebut her, but she kept talking. "No, it's time to let me talk. You've been baiting me all evening and throwing in snide comments about Theron and I don't appreciate it. If you make Konala and Theron choose between the two of us, you're going to lose."

Jaelene stood. "And as far as my heart is concerned and where I will live, that's my business. I have time yet to make that decision and when I do, you will definitely know. Now if you'll excuse me, I'm going back to my sister's house because there I know I will find people who love me and accept me as I am, namely Serena and Theron. Have a good night."

She turned on her heel and stalked out the front door, her long, silky black hair swishing violently back and forth.

Rekah closed his mouth. By the Crius, the woman had courage! He chuckled. What a pleasant surprise.

Konala stormed into the living area. "What did you say to her?"

He grinned. "Not much. She did all the talking."

Konala frowned at him before striding out of the house.

He clasped his hands together and rested his chin on them. The next few days would prove to be interesting. As Jaelene said, he would need to make some hard decisions, but one concern had been put to rest. Konala and Theron needed Jaelene. There was only one question.

Where did that leave him?

Jaelene lay in her bed at her sister's, staring up at the night sky, so different from her own. She loved that the roof could be switched to clear and she could enjoy the artistry of the universe between the tree leaves.

She discovered many differences in sky patterns and watched Bendis rise to help Selene light up the night with their light. Selene shone a bright silvery white and Bendis was a light pink but just as bright.

She listened to the low tones of Theron and Konala talking to Jahl and Khaos, her sister, like her, having gone to bed. It was a soothing sound to know that there were two men nearby who didn't just want to have sex with her, but liked who she was, quirks and all and even wanted to marry her.

Heck, she'd almost given up on finding a man who would want to have more than a night with her and now she had two!

And Rekah? She sucked her lower lip into her mouth and caught it with her teeth. He confused her, probably because she was so attracted to him physically. His muscles could rival any weight-lifting champion and his eyes, the color of new leaves fresh from the bud, were mesmerizing. And sometimes she caught him staring at her with a soul-burning need in his eyes.

She wasn't Kindred of Heart, but there was something intense about Rekah. She had a feeling that when he loved, it was forever, and when he was angry, something was going to get broken. Rekah could be nice when he chose to and to be so angry must mean he cared a lot. That could be good for Theron, to at least have his friendship back with Rekah.

But when he was holding a grudge he could be a jerk. It was hard to imagine that he and Konala and Theron were close at one time when he acted like that. For someone who was Kindred of Heart, he could be mean.

Luckily, she didn't have to care about what decision he made. She just had to worry about her own future. After just a day in Loraleaf, she felt at home and could easily see how her sister could decide to live on another planet.

Every convenience was available, not through technology, but through the men's abilities and the energy source they called eyllen. Konala said they needed to find more. It wasn't far beneath the ground, but when exposed to air it activated, which made it dangerous. Just a little could power a whole settlement. The problem was, extracting it without harm could be tricky.

Theron was supposed to be the expert in that endeavor, just another reason for her to be proud of him. She had to admit, even if just to herself, she loved Theron. He was so opposite of the macho men she'd been with yet he was built far better than any of them. Plus, he loved her interest in new things and actually enjoyed talking with her.

Konala liked talking to her as well. She sighed. Now *that* was one hot man. While Theron had grown on her slowly, Konala was like being hit by sunshine after a rain shower. His lighter coloring and quick smile had knocked her off her feet. The fact that he could actually communicate with animals was beyond her dreams.

She couldn't be sure if it was just lust or something deeper she felt for him. Either way, she was excited to go to the sitki with him in the morning. There were definitely strange sounding words in the Edenist vocabulary. From the way Konala described the sitki, it sounded like a large barn above the ground. She couldn't wait to meet all the domesticated animals he'd gathered to help supply Loraleaf with food.

Maybe in the next few days, she'd have a better handle on her feelings. She did miss her work and her parents, but the thought of leaving Theron and even Konala, made her choke up.

She rolled over on her side and rubbed her feet together, her socks making her feel at home in such a foreign place. She was too lazy to get up and switch the roof back to opaque.

The sun would be shining through the trees when she woke and that was a sight she looked forward to. She'd love to be able to recreate the look of a night sky or a sun dappled forest on the ceiling of a bedroom at home, but even as she envisioned it, she knew it was hopeless. Just like recreating the look of the cavern in Theron's tunnels would be impossible.

Oh shoot, she still hadn't told him about them. There was always tomorrow.

She rolled over on her other side. If she kept thinking about exploring Loraleaf, she'd never fall asleep. She needed to focus on something else. The sound of Theron's voice filtered through the walls. Now that was something to think about.

She listened to the low sound of his voice until she drifted off.

Theron cuddled her from behind as she grasped Konala around the waist, the heat of the men's bodies keeping her warm without the need for a hesta over her naked body. Lazily, she ran her fingers over Konala's rippled stomach. He caught her hand and pressed it against his hard cock.

"Are you ready for both of us, Jae?"

She shivered as her sensitive skin reacted to his words. "Do you mean the bonding?"

Theron's hand moved from her stomach to the juncture of her thighs. "Of course, but only if you're ready." His husky voice so close to her ear caused her pussy to swell in anticipation.

"Is it like what we just did?" Having Konala pump into her as she knelt on all fours while she sucked on Theron's cock was an amazing feeling.

Konala rolled over to face her, his hand coming up to cup her breast even as Theron's fingers found her clit. Her body turned electric with the circuit completing as Konala's fingers squeezed her nipple. "No, it's not like that. We must each come inside you, one after the other while you come."

She moaned, lifting her leg to allow Theron better access. She wanted this, them. Why deny it? "I do."

"Ah, Khityki, you fill my heart." Theron kissed her back as his large finger dove into her sheath.

She pressed her hips back against him, anxious for more even as Konala moved down so he could take her nipple into his mouth and tease it with his tongue.

Her core ached to have them both as they teased her with fingers and mouth. She felt her body floating on a cloud of pleasure mixed with love from men who adored her. The sensation was so real that she opened her eyes to see if it was possible on Eden.

Rekah stood in the room watching, his green eyes dark with pain and a longing so sharp that she felt it slice through her heart.

"Wait."

Both men stopped immediately and Rekah vanished.

Jaelene jerked awake, her body sweaty, her heart beating faster than a race horse.

"Jae, what is it?" Konala lay on her right, his hand rested on her leg.

"I think it was a dream."

Theron propped himself on his elbow and brushed her wet hair from her face. "You look like you've been crying."

She switched her attention to him. "I was in the dream or I think I was."

"Do you want to tell us about it?" Konala also rose up on his elbow, his brow lowered in concern.

What could she say? Even as she tried to recall it, it faded away, leaving her with an uneasy feeling and a new curiosity about Rekah. She shook her head at Konala. "No, I don't think so."

Neither man spoke as they watched her, ready to help in anyway.

She sat up in the bed. "Tell me about Rekah's past. I already know he is a good man who senses emotions and helps others. He also has muscles on his muscles. But I want to know about his past. What made him the way he is?"

Konala spoke before Theron could. "You mean why he was so harsh toward you?"

She nodded, though she didn't see it as harsh, exactly. It was almost like a wounded animal she wanted to help but that saw her every movement as a threat. She wanted to be friends with the man that was considered a brother of the heart by Konala and Theron. She didn't want it be awkward between them like having unfriendly in-laws.

Then again, for that to be so, she'd have to stay in Eden and agree to being a beloved and bonded. She swallowed. That would be a big leap. She was better with baby steps.

Theron took her attention from her thoughts. "Rekah is Kindred of Heart which means by nature he feels deeply. His ability to sense other's emotions adds to his own feelings in how he reacts to them. Usually, he is kind and empathetic, but there have been a few instances where he hasn't been."

"Like when he met you today." Konala took up the story. "I'm not sure if you noticed but he was both friendly and antagonistic.

Even he wasn't sure how to feel around you. He's angry at Theron right now and not happy with me either. However, he is like all of us, trained from childhood to respect and revere women, but…"

She tried to wait for Konala to continue, but she just couldn't. The residual feelings she had from the dream told her this was important. She'd never felt like this after a simple dream before. Not even after a nightmare. "But what? What happened?"

Konala looked at Theron, so she did too. "Tell me."

"It is Rekah's mother." Theron paused, once again obviously looking for the right words. "She showed him a side of women none of us had been aware of."

"Damn it, Theron, just spit it out. I'm not a child. I can take it."

Konala chuckled behind her, and she frowned at him until he stopped. "Well?"

Theron nodded. "Rekah's mother was the beloved of his three fathers, but she did not love them in return, at least not like they loved her. She would dole out her sexual favors as rewards for getting what she wanted. She didn't believe her son could tell the difference, but from a very early age, he sensed his mother's feelings, even before he went through the change and came into his special ability."

She could almost picture a young Rekah, maybe seven years old, watching his mother interact with his fathers. It made her heart hurt. "What happened when he knew for sure that his mother didn't love his fathers?"

"He confronted her." Konala continued. "She denied it, of course, as she didn't want her agapaytos to know, but Rekah knew. He was very close to his fathers, but not his mother and since he was an only child, he confided in us."

Theron sat up and faced her. "He was very angry and decided to tell his fathers. We tried to talk him out of it, but he wouldn't listen."

Her stomach suddenly felt uneasy. "What happened?"

"They wouldn't believe him." Theron sighed. "He felt betrayed, but I think it was just that his fathers didn't want to know. Like they didn't want to know that she'd been using earthly birth control to keep from having more sons. She wanted all her agapaytos' attention on her."

Konala took her hand. "It was the final straw for Rekah. He left home and the three of us created our own home. So when Sandale approached him to leave Naralina and make a life here in the jungle, Rekah agreed, yet his love for his fathers had him mourning their loss for months. In Naralina, he could still see them, talk to them, even though he never went home again. Once we left, there was no going back."

"Why?" She looked from one to the other. "That's one of the questions I've been wanting to ask. Why have all these men left the supposed beautiful city of Naralina to live in this jungle, which, by the way, I think is far prettier than any city?"

Konala's lips quirked. "Do you want the short answer," he pointed to himself, "or the long answer?" He pointed to Theron.

She smiled. "I'll take the short, please."

"We left because the leaders of the city were moving in a direction that we were not happy with and luckily, Jahl was able to figure out what was happening ahead of time. We had to sneak out at night without the use of portals. It was all very exciting." He winked at her and she could easily see him smiling through the whole adventure.

"What direction was it that the men here didn't like?"

Konala smirked. "The short answer is that an awkward stratification was beginning in our society. In addition, or because of this, men were being found guilty of breaking the law when they hadn't done anything wrong. Those of us who wished to live equally and not worry about a small group of people determining our fate, left to build what you see here." He raised his arm up toward the ceiling.

She looked to Theron, now wishing she had the long version because she had a hundred questions.

His lips twitched as if he knew what she was thinking and she laughed. "Okay, so maybe next time I will listen to you explain it to me."

"A smart decision."

She was definitely learning a lot as it was though. "So Rekah left Naralina with the brothers of his heart, you two, and built a life here. But then you left," she turned away from Theron and looked at Konala, "and you and Rekah began to look for a chosen one."

"Is Rekah in love with Star and if he is, can he bring her to Eden?" She looked at Theron. "And why did you leave the brothers of your heart? It had to be something very important because when we first met, you said you couldn't stay with me because you were alone."

Theron looked past her at Konala and that man pushed her down. "It's a bit late for all this exploration. Let's save it for tomorrow."

She opened her mouth to object, but Konala's lips covered hers and she had a hard time concentrating. When he finally let her up for air, her tank top was pushed up revealing her breasts and Theron knelt between her legs.

"I know what you're doing here. You're trying to distract me."

"Are you distracted?" Theron hooked a thumb on each side of her panties.

"Not completely. We will continue this conversation in the morning and you *will* tell me why you didn't answer me tonight."

Theron shrugged. "That's because the answer is complicated and we would rather make love to you and then allow you a little more time to rest before morning."

Oh heck, he had her at *make love to you.* "Okay."

Theron grinned just before he pulled down her panties and lowered his head. Her view of his luscious dark hair was quickly obliterated by Konala's lips descending over her nipple. Whatever she'd been wondering could definitely wait until morning.

CHAPTER THIRTEEN

Theron stared at the invisible box he, Paxton and Ware had created. It was in pieces, having failed yet another test. The only way he could make it work was with more energy.

Frustrated, he threw up his hands. "Let's take a break and come back after our midday meal."

Paxton nodded but Ware stayed a moment to ponder some idea before he too walked away, his silent guard behind him as he followed Paxton. Jahl had wanted Ware at his house but with Jaelene there, he had to settle for having Ware one level beneath him.

Theron circled the large trap that had now lost its cohesiveness, a gooey see-through substance coated the platform Jahl had built for them to work on.

If only he could think straight, but after two days of working non-stop, he was frustrated.

Part of it was due to not having time with Jaelene. Konala kept her company as well as her sister, but he wanted to have a conversation with her. Instead, he came in after she was asleep and held her in his arms. It was good, but not the same as hearing her voice and listening to her mind work.

Rekah was another frustration. He hadn't made any contact with them and Theron feared he might be furthering the relationship with the woman named Star. If the man would just give Jaelene a chance, Theron was sure he would love her as much as he did.

He kicked a loose tool out of his way then stalked down the walkway toward the lift. Once he arrived at it, he set the lever and glided upward, his gaze focused on his former home. There had to be a way to get Rekah to give Jaelene a chance. Konala was ready to ask her to bond, but Theron still held out hope for Rekah.

When he reached his leader's home, he avoided the front door and walked around the back to the entrance to Jaelene's room, a room originally built for Serena's friend Toni.

When he entered, he halted. Jaelene was in the process of tying on a wrap. The sight of her awake was enough to get his heart revving. "Khityki."

She spun at his greeting. "Oh Theron, it's so good to see you." She gave him a hug which he quickly turned into a deep kiss. Her nutty taste and scent relaxed his mind and body and filled his soul with peace.

Finally, he released her lips, but not her. "It is good to taste you, too."

She smiled. "That's not what I said, but close enough. When will you tell me what that word means?"

"What word?"

"Khityki." She cocked her head, her eyes alight with interest.

He grinned. "It is our term for baby tigrans and is sometimes used as an endearment. From our first meeting, your curiosity reminded me of them."

"Oh, I like that." She brushed a light kiss on his lips, then leaned her head back and studied at him. "You look tired. How is the box going?"

He loosened his hold on her and took her hand as he sat on the bed. "It's not working. Either I have to add another man's ability or find more eyllen. The problem is I don't know which ability would help and Jahl doesn't want us leaving Loraleaf unless on patrol."

She squeezed his hand. "I know. I heard the patrols found a lawbreakers' blood sign and a dead grapet. Konala was not happy."

"Another one?" There were too many close to Loraleaf. Could it be that Sandale was marking the location of Loraleaf? Even Ware didn't know exactly where they were. "I understand Jahl's need to keep us all safe, but without the eyllen, I cannot make the trap strong enough to keep Sandale's abilities inside."

"Where do you find eyllen?" Jaelene's eyes were lighter as her mind quested for more information.

He smiled tiredly. "It is just below the ground's surface. When it is exposed to our atmosphere it gives off energy, but the process of extracting it is delicate because no air can touch it. Sometimes at night, you can tell where it is if it is closer to the surface. The ground will seem to light from underneath."

"Oh shoot! I never told you about the tunnels. That must be what's glowing there!" Jaelene jumped off the bed, her arms waving. "It's in your cave. I saw it. It's like a thousand stars in the sky only it was a dome, but even before I found the dome there were little specks of light that grew in size along the purple and teal veins in the cave walls. There has to be enough eyllen in there to power all of Eden!"

He stood and grabbed her shoulders. "You aren't making sense. What dome? What tunnels?"

She stopped moving for a moment. "In your cave. While you were sleeping, I explored the tunnel of your damp storage room. You have to stay to the far left and continue past the first cavern, but it's in there. What else could it be?"

He reflexively squeezed her shoulders when she mentioned going into the blackness of his cave, the idea of her never finding her way back to him, a cold reminder of how lucky he was to have her. So much so that he found it hard to concentrate on what she'd said. "And you saw eyllen in there?"

"I think I did. Does it glow orange and occur in purple and teal veins of some kind of black mineral beneath the ground?"

This time, the scientific side of his brain took over. "Yes, it does, though it is extremely rare to see it in those veins since that usually means it has been exposed. You say you saw this in my cave?"

She nodded, her smile wide. "I did."

He embraced her. "You are beyond precious." He pulled back and kissed her soundly. As he tasted the citrusy flavor of ambrosia on her tongue and the nutty flavor that was all her, he almost forgot his intentions, his cock starting to have some of its own. Luckily, his brain came to his rescue and he pulled away.

"Come, we must tell Jahl. I can use the portal to get to the cave and extract the eyllen without any of the lawbreakers knowing I am there." He took her hand and pulled her through the connecting door to the living area of his leader's home.

They found Khaos and Jahl sitting opposite each other on the couches, carrying on a low-toned conversation. Both men stopped talking at their entrance.

Theron wasn't oblivious to the mood and he guessed it had to do with the latest lawbreaker blood marking. He'd seen one of them and it wasn't pleasant, a round circle with an x crossing through it written in blood on multiple trees while a dead, torn-up carcass of an animal lay in the middle.

Jaelene broke the silence. "We've figured out how to get the eyllen we need to finish the trap to catch Sandale."

Khaos lifted an eyebrow and Jahl leaned back against the cushions, his doubt obvious.

Is this what she faced on Earth? Men humoring her or not giving her the credit she deserved? It had his muscles tensing as if knocking down one of his leaders was an option. He had better manners than that. "Yes, Jaelene is very smart and sometimes too courageous." He glanced at her and she shrugged.

"The cave where I made my home has tunnels. I thought them endless and that I'd have years to explore them, so I hadn't done so yet, but Jaelene has."

"Yes." She smiled, completely happy with her discovery. "And I found eyllen, though I didn't know that was what it was at the time. It's everywhere and would be easy for Theron to extract, or rather make it easier than usual."

"And," he continued when she stopped. "I can portal into the cave without the lawbreakers knowing I'm there."

Jahl's face had changed and he glanced at Jaelene with new appreciation. Good, he and all other men needed to know what an asset she was to Loraleaf. When she accepted he and Konala, he'd make sure no one ever ignored her chatter again.

Khaos looked at Jahl then addressed them. "I like this idea. We need to catch Sandale. We've mapped out the lawbreaker blood signs and they are at an exact parallel to one side of Loraleaf."

"I wondered if that was the case." Theron squeezed Jaelene's hand, cutting off her question. "The sooner I leave, the faster I can return and finish the project. I'll grab Konala and go."

Jahl shook his head. "Konala has gone to investigate the latest blood sign. Take Rekah."

"And me." Jaelene held up her index finger even though every man in the room had opened their mouths to deny her. "Theron needs me to find the eyllen. There are tunnels upon tunnels down there."

Khaos looked to him. "Is that true?"

He'd only been to the first cavern but there were many tunnels off it. He struggled with his anger that they wouldn't believe her and his need to keep her safe. "If she says that is the case, it is enough for me."

The smile she bestowed on him was well worth his worry.

"Fine. Then go and come back as quickly as possible." Jahl ground out the words through a very stiff jaw. If anything happened to Jaelene, Serena would never forgive him.

"I will protect Jaelene with my life."

"You better." Khaos gave him a serious look.

"I will." He pulled Jaelene out the front door before her brothers-in-law changed their mind.

When they were outside, she extracted her hand. "I'm so excited. Thank you for believing me."

He embraced her and kissed her lips gently. "Always."

When he let her go, she took his hand and they stepped into the lift together.

~~*~~

Rekah stepped through the portal he opened with Theron and examined the living area. He couldn't help admire the level of living that had been achieved under such difficult conditions.

Theron stepped past him, the small bag wrapped around his wrist with his tools swayed as he checked the front reflection and locked door. Satisfied it still held, he picked up the shiner and handed it to Jaelene. Then he opened the middle door of the three on the back wall. "It's this way."

Jaelene stepped through and waited. Her excitement was hard to resist and Rekah found himself anxious to discover the cavern she told him about when she and Theron had come for him.

She'd changed since he'd last seen her. She was no longer afraid of him, which pleased him. She was also no longer unsure around him. In fact, he felt as if she wanted to know him and he sensed her sympathy toward him. It made it difficult to resist her.

He finally stepped past Theron and joined Jaelene in what appeared to be a storage room of some type.

Theron closed the door behind them, leaving them with only the shiner for light in what at first appeared to be a small room.

"Oh look, Theron. Something has been eating your kerasi fruit." Jaelene held the shiner over a basket with a few of the fruit left on the bottom.

"It must be an animal that lives in the tunnels because the front entrance was undisturbed by any Edenist."

Rekah could feel Theron's love for the small living space and his relief that no intruder had been inside.

Theron took the shiner from Jaelene and then grasped her

hand. "Maybe we'll find the culprit sound asleep on the tunnel floor after eating all that fruit."

She chuckled before looking back. "Come on, Rekah." She held out her hand to him. "The tunnels are wide enough to easily fit the three of us."

His chest squeezed at being included. That was unexpected, but he took her hand. It was so small in his large one that he was careful not to hold too tight. He felt her pleasure at his acceptance and Theron's surprise.

Ignoring the brother of his heart, he concentrated on their surroundings as they walked. It was pitch black, the walls as smooth as cyndistone, but with a shine to them.

When they reached a tall cavern, Jaelene stopped them. There were four tunnels leading from it.

"This is as far as I've come." Theron looked at Jaelene. "Which way now?"

She dropped their hands. "First, I need to put this here." From her pocket, she pulled a piece of broken yellow mug. It looked very sharp.

Theron frowned. "Where did you get that?"

She placed the angled piece so that it pointed back the way they'd come. Smart woman.

She shrugged before taking their hands again. "I may have accidently broken one of Jahl's mugs while making my breakfast this morning."

Rekah couldn't help himself and chuckled out loud.

She smiled up at him and in the shiner's light, her face appeared to glow with warmth. His heart wanted that warmth, but he turned away. She came with Theron, the man that had supposedly been in love with Serena. Did Jaelene know that?

He glanced over at the brother of his heart. How could he be sure this time if he was so sure he'd been in love with Serena that he'd left the men who made his filoz?

They continued walking through the cave, following Jaelene's direction until she pointed out the colored veins in the wall. "See, it's the purple I told you about."

Both he and Theron took a closer look. At first he thought she imagined it, but when the shiner was close, the purple sparkled.

"We're getting closer. After the teal merges with the purple you'll see the eyllen. At least I hope that's what it is." She rubbed her arms. "I forgot to bring a hesta."

Theron enveloped her in his arms, holding the shiner away. "Warmer now?"

She nodded and clasped their hands again and they continued. After the teal veins became prominent, Jaelene stopped them. "Turn off the shiner."

"Khityki, if I do that, I might lose you in this darkness."

She pulled her hands from both of them and faced Theron. "Do you trust me?"

He nodded and closed the shiner.

They plunged into pitch blackness and then Rekah saw it. "The walls. They glow!" As his eyes adjusted, he could see Theron moving closer to the wall.

"This is eyllen. It will be very easy to extract." Theron turned around and swept Jaelene into his arms. "By the Crius, I love you."

Jaelene squealed and gave him a kiss of celebration that lasted a while.

Rekah was torn between joy for Theron and Jaelene, and a longing so sharp he almost doubled over. Even as he watched, he tried to picture himself with Star but couldn't. He imagined Jaelene pulling him down for a kiss and his heart heated.

"Rekah?" Jaelene tugged on his hand bringing him back to his dark reality.

"Yes."

"You have to see this." She pulled him along the tunnel, leaving Theron to inspect the eyllen. As they walked, the glowing pieces grew larger until she stopped them before another cavern. Taking another piece of broken mug from her pocket, she put it on the floor next to the wall, pointing the way back.

Standing straight, she rubbed her arms. "I forgot how cold it gets down here."

He wanted to offer her his warmth, but couldn't get his mouth to say the words.

She strode forward and turned to wave him into the domed area.

He forgot to breathe for a moment as his own awe mixed with the joy Jaelene felt at the sight. The purple and teal veins swirled toward the peak with the eyllen glowing upward.

"It's almost like a domed airline runway only with orange lights." Jaelene spread her arms wide. "Isn't it amazing?"

He stared at her, unable to take his eyes from her face or separate his emotions from hers. He strode to the center of the cavern where she stood and cupped her face with his hands. "Jaelene?"

She smiled at him, her hands coming down to rest on his chest. "Yes, Rekah."

He lowered his mouth to touch hers. The warmth of her heart pulled at him as he gently kissed her lips, so soft and pliable beneath his own. He pulled away and watched her eyes open, curiosity in their blue depths.

"It's okay to forgive." Her words took a moment to register, but when they did, he dropped his hands.

He backed away. She was right. He counselled many a man to forgive, but the pain in his heart wouldn't let go.

Theron's steps heading toward them gave him an excuse to move away to examine the natural underground beauty of the wall.

"You found this while I slept?" Theron's words, spoken behind them, revealed awe and pride and a good dose of concern. "I'm so glad you didn't get lost down here."

"Me too, but I'm smarter than that. Do you think you could warm me up again?"

Theron put the shiner on the floor and pulled her into a hug. Rekah couldn't tear his gaze away. He could be a part of that relationship if he could forgive Theron, but something inside him refused to budge.

As he watched them, the shiner fell over and Jaelene and Theron broke apart. She looked at Theron. "You kicked the shiner over."

He shook his head as he picked it up, a smile on his face. "I think that was you."

Jaelene shook her head and then froze, her pale face growing even paler. Rekah took two steps toward her. "What is it?"

"I forgot. There's something down here. When I was

investigating these tunnels, something brushed by me, but when I turned the light in my cellphone on, there was nothing.

He looked at Theron and no matter what their differences, they were united in one thing—protect Jaelene.

Theron kept his arm around her shoulders. "Let's head back. I can't extract the larger pieces, but near the beginning of the eyllen, I can capture a few smaller ones to take back with us."

Jaelene nodded and Rekah fell in behind them, ready to protect her at all costs.

They returned to the spot Theron needed and he started the process.

Rekah kept Jaelene well back from where Theron worked, his hands on her shoulders as they watched.

Theron worked at the black rock with a sharp tool that was made to break hard surfaces. He started with small chips to be sure to incase the whole piece, then drove the tool hard against the rock. The sound was loud and Jaelene jumped.

She looked back at Rekah. "I didn't expect that."

He smiled. "Neither did I."

As Theron made to hit the rock hard again, his tool flew from his hand. "By the Crius!"

All three of them stared at the inert tool for a moment.

Jaelene whispered. "Is it a ghost?"

There were no such things as ghosts on Eden, but Rekah opened his senses to any emotions in the immediate area.

Anger, fear, deep grief, and a need to survive flooded him so strongly, he pressed his hand to his heart. "There is someone here."

The fear escalated at his words. Whoever it was, understood their language. "We are not here to harm you or the caves. All we wish is to take a couple small glowing rocks from this wall and we will leave you in peace."

Theron and Jaelene stared at him, but he ignored their surprised faces. The panicked fear he could sense lessened a little. "I promise, this is all we will do and you will have this place to yourself again."

The fear lowered a bit more, but it was still too high for him to believe the person would allow Theron to work.

The brother of his heart picked up the tool and looked at him. He shook his head as he tried to focus. He kept getting the impression of a woman but that had to be his connection to Jaelene overriding his concentration. No women were born on Eden and no Earth woman could survive on her own.

"We ask you to allow us to finish. We need this energy to entrap a lawbreaker, one of the bad men that roam the jungle." A flash of pure hatred hit him before the fear subsided to caution. That was interesting. "We will be sure that this man never hurts anyone again."

He sensed doubt but also acceptance, so he nodded to Theron. Jaelene leaned back against him and he wrapped his arm across her chest and held it there. Her faith in his ability to keep her safe filled chips in his heart.

Theron went back to work, carefully chiseling away at the rock and finally extracting the two pieces he needed. When they were covered and put away, he wrapped his tool and inserted it into the bag as well.

Rekah could feel the entity waiting to see if they would fulfill his promise. "We will leave now. Be safe." He didn't know why he wanted only good for the mysterious cave dweller, but he'd sensed a deep sorrow and he understood that. "Be well."

He separated himself from Jaelene and took her hand. Theron grasped her other one and they proceeded to Theron's cave.

He looked over Jaelene's head and Theron met his gaze before giving him a slight nod.

Neither of them would open a portal in the presence of whatever it was that inhabited the tunnels.

Konala sat opposite Khaos in the leader's house. "I've never seen anything like these tracks." He kept his voice low so as not to distract from the conversation being held in the meal room about how to capture Sandale. Theron, Paxon, Jahl, Jaelene and Serena had gathered to discuss it now that the invisible box was ready.

"What did they look like?"

He pictured the tracks in his mind. "They are bigger than a boarox print. They have one large pad and three smaller ones in front, probably to support the toes. There are three deep narrow holes in the ground in front of each pad which is a sign of claws, but there is also a shallow hole in the back of the print as if the animal has a claw back there that only hits the ground as it walks." He shook his head. "We have no animal on Eden with that type of paw."

"Could it be a mutation of an Eden animal?" Khaos opened his closed hands. "Maybe a discoverist's experiment gone awry?"

"I don't know. It could be, but I know Naralina has strict laws regarding experiments of such nature."

Khaos frowned. "Could it be an animal from another planet, like Earth?"

Now that was a serious problem as the rule against the importation of animals from Earth was planet-wide. "It is not an animal of Earth. I know those animals and not one of those could have left this track unless they are also experimenting there and creating a new species. Last I had seen, they were busy trying to save a number of them, not create new ones."

They both sat in silence for a moment, Konala concerned yet excited by the possibility of communicating with a new animal.

"Do you think this mystery animal is in league with the lawbreakers?"

"No." He hated the idea that any animal would work with those of such poor morals, but he needed to be objective. "When I reviewed the site, the tracks circled the area as if the animal had come upon it and was curious, but then it continued by before the tracks disappeared."

Khaos looked at him as if he'd imbibed too many drinks at Libations. "Disappeared?"

He nodded. "Yes, disappeared. It was the oddest set of tracks I've ever followed. First the shape, but then it looked as if someone had attempted to sweep them away and didn't do a good job, yet the ground around the sweeping was devoid of tracks. They just ended."

Khaos shook his head. "Maybe something ate it."

He smiled. "I doubt it. I think this animal is quite large."

A screech came from the meal room and they both stood. Jaelene backed into the living area, shaking her head, her hands out in front of her as if to ward off an attack. "Don't you come near me. You lied to me."

Tears ran down her face, but Konala wasn't sure if she was hurt or angry.

Theron stopped where he was, but her sister continued toward her. "Jaelene, please, you're overreacting."

"Really?" She held up her index finger. "Then why didn't he tell me before we came here? Why didn't you tell me when I first arrived? If it was nothing then you one of you at least would have told me. You're my sister and you *knew*. You knew it was something and something big."

Theron took another step, his hands held out to the side. "It's in the past. It doesn't matter. I was a fool and wrecked my relationship with my filoz, but it doesn't mean that I don't love you."

Jaelene shook her head. "Oh, I don't doubt you love me." She gave a tortured laugh. "What choice do you have since the woman you loved first, my sister, was taken by someone else. I'm the next best thing and the only choice you have. But you know what? I'm tired of being the consolation prize. Thanks to you, I've realized exactly what I deserve and that's to be loved for who I am, not because I'm the next best thing." She turned and ran out of the house.

Konala leapt over the couch and grabbed Theron just as he exited the house.

"Let me go. She needs to understand."

Though his heart ached for Theron, he didn't let go. "No. She won't understand. If I've learned anything from Rekah, it's that trauma needs to be processed."

Theron's eyes widened. "Trauma? Holy Bendis, I never wanted to hurt her."

"I know." He watched as Theron struggled with his need to go after Jaelene as she stepped into the lift and moved the lever down.

He wanted to go after her himself, but Rekah would say to let her be. That she had to get over the initial shock before the healing could begin. Now, more than ever, he wished Rekah could forgive Theron and take Jaelene as his chosen one.

Jaelene couldn't even see where she was because her stupid tears blinded her. Angrily, she wiped at her eyes until she could see.

Who was she kidding? Even without tears she was blind. How could she have ignored the tension when she'd first arrived at her sister's? Theron had loved her sister and left Loraleaf and his filoz because he couldn't bear to be near her when she was married to Jahl and Khaos.

That's why he lived alone in a cave when she met him. And all along she'd thought he'd been in a fight with Rekah.

Her heart hurt so much she couldn't stand straight. Stupid. Stupid. Stupid. How could she believe she'd found love with not one but two men? That they wanted her to love a third had been a bonus.

But that wasn't how she was wired. She would always be second best, not good enough. She was stupid to think she could be. She'd never be first choice. She deserved this pain for thinking she was better. Pushing her fist against her chest, she tried to rub the hurt away.

The lift came to a stop and she exited with no idea where she should go. She just needed to put space between herself and Theron.

Movement out of the corner of her eye caught her attention. Rekah stood outside his house watching her. She turned on him.

"What? Haven't you seen an angry woman before?" She stalked toward him when he didn't answer.

"I want to thank you for not accepting me into your filoz."

"Why?" His expression was unreadable which fueled her anger.

"Because if you had, I would be your second choice. You have Star. She is your first choice. I'm done being runner up. Either I'm loved for who I am, the way I am and there is no one else that came before me, or I will live out my life alone. It's that simple."

Rekah continued to look at her as if she was an odd animal he'd never seen before.

"What?"

He nodded. "I agree. That's one reason why I can't forgive Theron."

"Why?"

He looked beyond her.

She'd drawn quite a crowd and they were all naked. She really didn't feel like seeing a bunch of naked men right now.

"Why don't you come in so the rest of Loraleaf can get back to their duties?"

She hesitated. She and Rekah had mutely called a truce in the tunnels, but their differences might actually be their similarities now that her eyes had been opened. "Okay."

Rekah opened his arm toward his home and she stepped inside. She plopped down on his couch, not really caring what he thought of her anymore. What a difference a few days made.

He sat in the same chair he had the first day she'd met him. She'd been so nervous he wouldn't like her.

Rekah crossed his ankle onto his knee, effectively hiding his package, which she appreciated. Then he rubbed the beard around his chin. "You ask why I can't forgive Theron. It is exactly the reason you can't forgive him. He betrayed me."

"Because he left Loraleaf?"

He smirked. "It's a bit more than that. You have to understand what a filoz is to truly appreciate what he did. The three of us have been friends since we were ten years old and have lived as a family since I was thirteen. We had always planned to find a woman from Earth to be our beloved." He paused.

She had to guess he was remembering the happier times when he and Konala and Theron had dreams. She understood dreams. She'd always dreamed of having a man love her and put her first. She'd thought she'd found it here.

Her heart squeezed and she blinked back tears.

After a moment, Rekah continued. "Of course our plans were delayed when we left Naralina because we had to build Loraleaf and be sure it was safe for our agapayto. Once Jahl and Khaos had success with Serena, they agreed to allow the rest of the filoz to start searching for their chosen ones.

"That's when Theron left, isn't it?"

He nodded, his face grim. "Yes. He offered to take your sister's friend, Toni, to Naralina and told us he wouldn't return. So just as all we had worked for was about to come to fruition, he abandoned us."

She understood now the betrayal Rekah felt. Konala had said he was Kindred of Heart. She glanced at the birthmark on Rekah's bulging left forearm. It was a soft edged heart. "So it was harder for you than for Konala because you are of the Heart Kindred and sense emotions, right?"

"Yes. You should be happy you are not of this Kindred. Relationships with others is my life. I am glad you discovered that Theron had first fallen in love with your sister before meeting you. He should have told you."

"Yes, he should have." She tried to picture what that conversation would have sounded like and when it could have taken place, but it seemed awkward at best. Still, he should have told her, especially by the time they'd reached Haven.

"I'm sure you would have told him if you had loved someone else first. You did have sex before you arrived here, didn't you?"

She would never get used to the bluntness of the men in Eden. "Not that it's any of your business, but yes I did, but I didn't love any of them. I might have if they'd actually spent any time with me, but they only saw me as a one-nighter."

Rekah frowned. "So you never loved a man while on Earth?"

"Of course I did." He made it sound like such a terrible thing. "I love my father."

He shook his head at that.

"And this one man in college, but he didn't know I did. I had the worst crush. I couldn't even say a sentence around him without tripping over my words. After we graduated, I heard he married this really smart girl from my chemistry class."

"I'm glad to hear that." Rekah smiled. "That means Theron is your second choice as well. He deserves that."

She opened her mouth and promptly closed it. What could she say to that? "That may be true, but at least I didn't love his brother first." She folded her arms, pleased that she'd made a solid point.

"Yes. I wonder if Konala feels like he is second choice. Did he say anything to you about that?"

She swallowed hard. Did he feel that way? "Wait, how do you know I love Konala?"

He pointed to the birthmark on his arm.

Of course, he sensed her emotions around him. "So will you ever forgive Theron?"

Rekah's eyes widened at her question. "I don't know."

"When will you know?"

He stared at her then chuckled. "Probably when you know whether you'll forgive Theron."

"How can I? I—"

A knock on the door interrupted them. Rekah rose and opened it. After some hushed conversation, he returned. "I think you should return to your sister's. Theron has found Sandale."

She stood. "None of you will be hurt by capturing him, right? I mean, the plan seemed pretty easy."

He took her hand and led her to the door. "Capturing Sandale will be the easy part. It's the lawbreakers with him that will prove difficult. But don't worry, you will be safe here in Loraleaf."

"And where are you going?"

He looked her in the eye, his green gaze reminding her of the underside of the leaves she saw through the roof when she woke that morning. "I must head to the meeting place to receive my instructions from Jahl and Khaos. Konala and Theron will be there too, so you won't cross their path."

"Oh, okay." Despite her anger and heartbreak, her chest tightened at the thought of the danger all three men would face.

He ushered her on to the lift and hit the lever from outside. "Goodbye, Jaelene."

Jaelene's throat constricted at Rekah's words. They just seemed so final. She blew him a kiss, but he'd already turned and strode down the walkway.

When the lift stopped, she ran to Serena's.

She found her sister pacing through the living room.

"There you are. Are you all right?" Serena redirected her steps to meet her and give her a hug.

She hugged her back then pushed away, too concerned about what their men were about to do. "I'm fine. I was just speaking with Rekah."

"Rekah?"

"Yes, the man is not happy with Theron either so we have something in common after all."

"Jaelene, I'm sorry I didn't tell you the minute you walked in the door. I thought that since it was Theron who had the feelings that he should be the one to tell you. I promise you, I never did anything to encourage him."

She looked at her sister and swallowed the words that threatened to erupt. They were nasty and hateful and she loved Serena. She just wished that for once, she came first. Just once, like with the man she loved.

As if she'd heard her thoughts, Serena pulled her to the couch. "As far as I know, Konala has never loved anyone else, even that Star woman that Rekah picked out to study."

"Konala didn't love her?" She was almost ashamed at the relief she felt, her heart completely taken with the man.

"No, he didn't. He and Rekah had just started to watch her. Some of the filoz will watch for years to be sure. Jahl, Khaos and Sandale watched me for six years before making contact and that was because I was in danger of being raped."

"You never told me that either." She couldn't hide the hurt in her voice.

"I know, I'm sorry. It was all part of meeting my beloved and all this," she swept her hand in a big arc. "I promise to tell you every sordid detail now that you are here, but like I told you, they will want you to choose a filoz or become a Cythera, like Toni."

She wrinkled her nose. She didn't want to spend her day teaching Eden men how to make love to a woman. She wasn't exactly an expert. Besides she'd had her fill of bad sex and no relationships.

"But if you really don't like either choice," Serena lowered her voice, "I think I could convince Jahl and Khaos to sneak you home if you promise not to say anything about Eden, which is really hard. Believe me, I know."

Going home. The idea seemed like a long lost dream, but its appeal had tarnished. How could she not tell anyone about Eden and the boarox and the second moon and—oh, she would have to leave Theron and Konala and even Rekah. The idea of never seeing them again had her heart aching.

"I know you're angry with Theron, but is there any chance you can forgive him?"

Could she? If she couldn't, it meant living without him. "I think the bigger question is can Rekah forgive him? I can't imagine bonding with part of a filoz. I would feel like I was breaking up a marriage. Rekah doesn't even like me in that way." She looked at her sister, her eyes filling with tears. "But I care for all three. Is that being greedy?"

Her sister hugged her again. "No, it's not greedy. It's the Eden way." She pulled backed. "These men are special and I'm not just talking about their hard naked bodies, though I love those, or their Kindred abilities. They have hearts of gold."

She nodded, wiping her tears away. "They are unique. I don't think any man on Earth could live up to them."

Serena nodded, a wide smile on her face. "So do you think, you could forgive Theron?"

Could she? How could she not? She was in love with him. She nodded.

Serena jumped up. "I'm so—"

"What is it?" Jaelene stood up and waved her hand before Serena's eyes. "Serena?"

Her sister blinked. "I'm sorry. Through my bond with Khaos, I can see what he sees if it's intense."

"That doesn't sound good. What was it?"

"He saw Sandale. It was a shock to actually see him when we all thought him dead."

Jaelene processed that. "So by bonding, you can see what your men see?"

"No." Serena settled back onto the couch. "I guess it all depends on the bond and the Edenists involved. I can feel what Jahl feels physically, but only if it's serious like being burned or having an orgasm."

"Wait." Jaelene plopped back down on the couch and faced her sister. "You can feel Jahl's orgasm?"

Serena smiled. "Yes, and it's pretty amazing if we, well, it's a very unique experience."

She couldn't help but wonder what her bond might be with the three men she was in love with. Seeing and feeling had nothing to do with Jahl's ability to control non-living nature though Khaos' ability to sense the future could be a kind of seeing. She was confused. "Did your husbands know what would happen after the bonding?"

"No. No one does, and it didn't happen at the same time with each of them. I have no idea why."

"I wish I had asked Erin what—"

"Ow!" Serena doubled over.

"Serena, what is it? Are you okay?" Jaelene crouched down on the floor to look at her sister's face.

"Yes." She straightened. "But Jahl isn't. Something hit him hard."

Jaelene started to rethink her interest in bonding. "But you don't know what it was or if he's okay?"

Serena shook her head. "This is going to drive me crazy."

She sat back on the couch and squeezed her sister's hand. "I have a feeling this is going to get worse before it gets better."

"When I saw Sandale, there were other lawbreakers with him. They are fighting them. I hope Theron's plan works."

They sat in silence waiting for news through Serena's bond. Twice, through Khaos, she saw Sandale pick up a limp form and throw it, but she didn't know who it was. Then she grabbed her head.

"Jahl?" Jaelene wasn't sure how much more she could take. She wanted to know if her own men were okay.

Serena righted herself. "Yes. I think he's been knocked out, but I'm not sure." Serena's eyes glazed over again and Jaelene waited impatiently, biting at her lower lip until finally Serena blinked. "Khaos found Jahl and brought him to safety, but..."

"But what? Tell me." Jaelene grasped her sister's arm. "I have to know."

"I'm not sure, but it looked like Konala was being dragged away by a tigran. But there were many Therons. Some were on the ground and some were standing. That must mean that he is still conscious."

"I have to get to Konala." Jaelene stood up, but her sister grabbed her wrist. "You can't. You don't even know where they are."

"I don't care." Jaelene felt tears well in her eyes, but she furiously wiped them away.

"Jaelene, listen to yourself. This is Eden. They went to the site via portal."

She stopped pulling against Serena's grasp and nodded. Her sister let go. As soon as she did, she ran for the door.

"Jaelene!"

She didn't care what Serena said. She would find a way. From the conversation in the kitchen earlier that day, she knew that if they needed reinforcements, they would come for them, and she knew exactly where they planned to portal in.

She jumped in the elevator and started it down before her sister made it to the landing.

"Jaelene, wait! I'll come with you."

She ignored Serena and jumped onto the first level before the elevator stopped. Turning past Rekah's home, she ran down to the lab where they had worked on the trap.

As she turned the corner onto the temporary landing, two Edenists came through an open portal carrying another. She checked to see if it was Konala, but it wasn't. Three others talked briefly to those who just arrived and then stepped through.

It was now or never. With the picture of Konala in her mind, she screwed up her courage and followed the men through.

CHAPTER FOURTEEN

The Edenists moved quickly through the jungle making it difficult for Jaelene to follow, but she soon heard noise ahead.

Hiding behind a tree, she viewed the scene through the leaves of a big bush. Sandale, who was Kindred of Heart and could calm people to the point of unconsciousness, was inside the trap trying to get out, which meant no one would be harmed by him. She shivered as she watched the tall blond, well-muscled man try to break free, his face the picture of rage.

She moved her gaze to the left, beyond Sandale, and tried to see the men fighting there, but all she could see was a cloud of dust and dirt. Sounds of men yelling and calling out to each other filled the air, making her want to run, but she *had* to find Konala.

Serena said a tigran had dragged him away. That could mean he'd called the animal for help and he'd only do that if he was hurt. Her heart sank at the thought. As much as she didn't want to, she moved closer to the conflict, careful to stay hidden from Sandale.

She almost missed the track in the floating dust and even then she wasn't sure. She moved toward the back of Sandale's cage.

Yes! There were definite tigran tracks, but they were mostly covered, probably from Konala being pulled along. She followed them until she was at the edge of the invisible box. She waited until Sandale was focused in the opposite direction, then she ran behind him and into the bushes on the other side.

When she peeked back through the leaves, she found him staring at her. She shivered at his violet stare and quickly crawled away, following the trail.

Rekah kept his senses on both his levitating adversary and his friend in the trap. He used Sandale's rage to fuel his own energy as he grabbed the foot aiming for his head and slammed the body attached to it to the ground.

He felt the man's evil intent lessen as he lost consciousness. Rekah quickly focused on Sandale again and found the rage abated. In its place was relief and lust. Lust?

He turned toward the cage to see his friend standing completely still, facing away from the battle. A reflection of Theron strode by, headed toward the lawbreaker that was Kindred of Air.

The maniac spun like the planets but at such a high rate of speed that everything in his path was destroyed. He'd already hurt a number of his own comrades.

Theron's plan was to confuse the lawbreaker and weaken him so that Ware could push the man off his feet. Then they could transport Sandale and leave before any other men were wounded.

So why was Sandale feeling lust?

Rekah strode toward the trap, keeping his senses open. A feeling of anticipation came from behind him and he dove to the left just as a lawbreaker tried to tackle him. He quickly punched the man in the face, staying clear of his hands. He was Water Kindred and Rekah had seen him pull the water from one of their men before he'd been separated from him by the winds of the maniac.

Rekah had seen enough to know he had to avoid the lawbreaker's hands. The man shook his head to clear it and Rekah gave him a solid kick to the gut before he hit him hard with his right fist. The lawbreaker crumbled to the ground.

Not wasting time, he refocused on Sandale and sensed his disappointment just before the rage returned and with it the agony. But there had been lust and only one thing would cause that and that was a woman. Did the lawbreakers have a woman among them?

He'd walked to one side of the cage when he caught a whiff of a nutty scent. Fear tried to obliterate every other sense and with difficulty, he pushed it away. Jaelene could not be at the battle site. She was safe at her sister's waiting for them. It must be another woman.

He tracked the scent and footsteps around Sandale's cage and up a small hill, parallel to the fighting. From his vantage point, he could see the major concentration of dust and the unconscious bodies on the ground. He could also see at least five Theron images. The frustration of the maniac grew.

Rekah refocused on his path, reaching out ahead of him with his senses. Finally, he felt her and she was worried and scared… and she was Jaelene.

He recognized her from her emotions, their telltale back and forth. By the Crius, how did she get out here? He ran, his senses focused only on her. As he broke through a dense salis bush, he saw her.

She stood frozen in fear as the maniac barreled toward her.

"No!" Rekah ran forward and leapt. He grasped her in his arms as his body hit the ground and they rolled away from where she'd stood. Debris buffeted him and he tucked her beneath him, protecting her with his body as rocks and ground cover cut into him.

The out of control maniac continued on his way as if he had no control over his own abilities.

Theron ran to him. "Rekah, what happened?"

He rolled over, still cradling Jaelene in his arms, his heart beating out of his chest, pounding the pain of his cuts. "Jaelene."

Theron fell to his knees. "Holy Bendis, is she hurt?" He brushed her hair away from her face.

Her eyelids fluttered open. "Konala."

Rekah felt her worry. "Where is he?"

"Dragged away by a tigran." Her words were but a whisper and she started to shiver.

Rekah held her tighter and looked at Theron. "You find Konala and I'll get her back to Loraleaf."

Jaelene jerked her head. "Tracks."

Theron kissed her on the forehead. "Don't worry. I'll find him." He stood, his gaze on Jaelene.

Rekah watched him and waited. Finally, Theron's gaze met his own. He nodded and immediately felt Theron's relief that he accepted Jaelene.

"I'll be home soon."

Home. Their filoz united and with it their chosen one. Rekah watched Theron until he disappeared into the bush then he pulled Jaelene into a sitting position and carefully stood with her in his arms. Despite Ware's watch over the fallen lawbreakers, Rekah would not risk any of them waking and hurting her.

It had taken almost losing her to break down his pride and accept what his heart already knew.

He made a wide path around the battle scene and moved toward the portal location. There he found Khaos, who directed the retreat. When he saw Jaelene in his arms, he stopped him.

"I see a great happiness for you with her, but you must ever be vigilant."

Rekah smirked, his heart finally at peace. "I wouldn't want it any different."

He walked to the portal entry and turned back toward the battlefield to take a last look. Jahl had undertaken the transport of Sandale, Paxon gathered the remaining men from Loraleaf and somewhere out there Theron searched for Konala.

He turned and stepped through the portal and onto the landing in Loraleaf. As soon as he had Jaelene safe, he would help Theron search. They weren't a whole filoz unless they were together.

~~*~~

Jaelene woke to the sight of an elseire bird perched on a branch over the ceiling above her. The green feathered bird slowly leaned forward, spreading its wings and showing its bright purple under-feathers, but it didn't take off. It stood like that for a few seconds before a large green blob hit the outside of the ceiling.

She laughed as the bird refolded its wings to blend in with the jungle leaves.

She sobered. The view was not the one she was used to. Turning her head to the left, she found another bed. Her room had only one. On her right was yet another.

Throwing off the hesta, she discovered she was naked. Shoot. Where were her clothes? The hesta was see through, she needed to find—Oh no, Konala!

As her brain woke up, so did her worry. Where was everyone? Were Theron and Rekah okay?

"Everything is fine, Jaelene." Rekah strode into the room, a platter of food on a tray in his hands.

As the savory scents wafted toward her, her stomach growled. "How long have I been asleep?"

Was it her or did Rekah color at her question. He placed the platter on the small table next to the bed. "It has been two days. You needed to rest."

"Two days? No, it can't be. Konala."

He sat on the bed next to her. "Is fine. We found him with Talia."

Her heart slowed with her relief. "And Theron? Is he okay?"

Rekah smiled which was not the expression she expected. "Yes, he is also fine. All men from Loraleaf who battled the lawbreakers are fine, or will be soon." He picked up a cup and gave it to her. "Though I cannot say the same for Sandale."

She shivered at the thought of the wild man in the invisible box, but the smell of the kafez had her taking a sip. He'd watered it down perfectly for her. "What will happen to him? Where am I? How did you find Konala? Did you bury the hatchet with Theron? How do you clean the roof because an elseire bird just shit on it? Is—"

Rekah's laugh made her pause. She'd never seen him laugh. He always frowned or scowled or gave no expression. She'd caught a few smiles here and there, but his actual laugh made her grin. "You should laugh more often."

"You're right, but you are the only person who makes me laugh so easily. I guess you'll have to stay."

She swallowed the kafez in her mouth quickly. "Stay? Do you mean with you?"

He nodded. "And with Konala and Theron. We would like you to be our beloved."

She opened her mouth to tell him how she felt, but he raised his hand, his face serious again. "This is an important decision. I'm going to leave you while you eat everything we made for you. When you are done, we will return for your answer."

"And if I have any questions?"

His lip quirked up. "I'm sure you will. We will be happy to answer them." He rose from the bed. "One question you might have, I can answer for you now. I tried to resist you because you were Theron's and my heart had been trampled by him. But I couldn't. You are all I ever wanted in an agapayto." He looked off into the distance as if seeing a scene in his head. "When I saw your life in peril, I realized how stupid my hurt was and that it could never heal without love."

He paused as he moved his warm green gaze back to her. "I love you, Jaelene."

Oh shoot, she was going to cry.

"Now finish your meal and we all will talk." Rekah turned and strode out the door, the massive muscles in his shoulders and back distracting her from his words for a moment.

But it was only a moment. She took another sip of kafez and smiled. He loved her. Konala loved her. Theron loved her. And she loved all three of them.

She'd always dreamed of having a husband who would put

her first like she would him. Having three men willing to make her the most important thing in their lives was beyond any dreams she could have had.

That they were kind, loving, muscle-bound men who had special abilities was a bonus. Heck, having them at all was amazing.

She looked up through the ceiling, around the crap, at the branches above where the sun shined between the leaves. She knew where she was. She was on the planet Eden where her sister lived. She looked at the beds on either side of her. She was in the house where Konala, Rekah and Theron lived.

She was home.

She took another sip of kafez and pulled the platter onto her lap. At her first bite of egg and what tasted like bacon, she groaned softly. That her men could cook this good meant she would get fat. Maybe she could do something a bit more physical than design the inside of houses. She wouldn't change a thing about the inside of the homes in Loraleaf.

There was so much food on the plate. She wasn't *that* big. Then again, they may be used to cooking for men. She ate everything that was hot and left what looked similar to croissants and muffins for later. She was anxious to tell her filoz of her decision.

After finishing her kafez, she threw her legs over the side of the bed and stood. She looked around the room for something to wear, but there was nothing. Not even a towel.

What did she expect? She lived on a planet where being naked was the norm. Her sister didn't do it, at least not in front of her. If only she had the guts to walk around naked. Maybe she could learn, slowly. Then her men would be really proud of her.

The first step would be to walk naked in her own home.

She studied the bedroom. This would be *her* home. Erin told her she could visit her parents anytime. Serena had. To live in this wonderful place and learn all there was to learn about abilities and animals and the city was beyond exciting—just like her men.

She couldn't wait any longer and with no choice left, she bolstered her courage and walked down the hall where she found a bathroom. She vaguely remembered using it a few times, but her last two days were a fog. She had a suspicion she'd been given something stronger than kerasi fruit.

Past that was the doorway to the living room. She could hear voices so she took a deep breath and stepped in.

No one was there.

Really? A bit disappointed that her grand entrance wasn't so grand, she strode through that room and walked into the kitchen.

All conversation stopped as three pairs of eyes turned to her.

Rekah stood with his ass against the counter, a cup of kafez halfway to his mouth. Theron sat at the table, his elbows resting on it, his mouth open. Konala sat opposite him, his chair tipped back as he balanced it on the rear legs and wore a wide grin on his face.

Their shocked but admiring stares reminded her of her nakedness and she felt a flush heat hit her cheeks and neck. "Hi."

Theron recovered first and stood. "Khityki." He didn't say anything else, just looked at her with love in his eyes.

Rekah put down his cup and pulled himself away from the counter to stand straight, taller than them all. "Jaelene."

Konala let his chair down and slowly rose. "Jae, I hope your undress means that you are willing to stay with us and not simply because you couldn't find your clothes."

She grinned, though both Theron and Rekah frowned at him.

"Konala." Rekah's voice sounded exasperated.

She straightened her shoulders and stood proud, ready to take on her new life. "Rekah, what do you feel from me?"

His eyes half closed. "I feel love."

She nodded. "Yes, I love each one of you. I couldn't imagine my life without you. I want to stay here in Loraleaf and be your beloved, if you will have me."

Konala shouted, jumping in the air and Rekah laughed.

Theron stepped up to her and took her hand. "We promise to cherish you forever."

"I know you will." Her heart felt as if it had grown two sizes in two minutes.

Konala grabbed her from behind and turned her around for a kiss. The second her full naked body was up against his, her heart began to pound and her nipples hardened. He must have felt it too because his gentle kiss turned passionate as his tongue swept into her mouth.

No sooner had her knees gone weak than he passed her to Rekah. The big man gathered her into his arms gently and pressed her body against his massive one. His large hand cupped her head and his mouth touched hers.

He explored her mouth with his tongue, learning her. She let him do as he wished, enjoying every moment, even the press of his hard cock against her tummy. Her sheath was flooded by time he separated his lips from hers. She hoped he didn't expect her to stand.

She needn't have worried because Theron took her from Rekah and propped her on the table, spreading her legs so he could step between them and pull her close. He cupped her face in his palms. "Khityki, we want to bond with you. This is beyond a simple Earth marriage. It is spiritual and magical. It can never be broken. So I must ask you. Are you sure?"

Theron's eyes were black, proof his emotion was strong. She had no doubt in her mind. "I'm sure. I want to bond with you." She looked to his right where Rekah stood. "And with you." She looked to his left where Konala was. "And with you."

When she looked back at Theron, his eyes were sparking. Tiny flecks of light bounced against each other and disappeared.

Her heart hitched at the sight of his love.

He didn't hide his eyes. "I love you." His words were said against her lips before his mouth took hers.

His kiss was passionate and she met him with her own. Her breasts, crushed against his chest, were ready to be touched and her pussy was wet and needy. She wrapped her arms around his neck and tugged his hair. He moaned and she pressed her mons against him as best she could, but it wasn't enough.

Sensing her need, he broke their kiss and rested his forehead against hers. "Do you know what happens during the bonding?"

She took a moment to catch her breath before she pulled her head back and looked at Rekah and Konala who were watching, Konala with a grin and Rekah with a slight curve of his lips.

"Each of you will have to come inside me one after the other, but I must come each time as well, right?"

Theron took a deep breath as if she'd just sucked on his cock and he was trying to maintain control. "Yes, that's correct."

"And if it doesn't work the first time, we can keep trying until it does, but we won't know if it worked until days, maybe a week later and then we will have to discover what particular connection we have, but I won't have the connections all at the same time and—"

Theron's finger on her mouth stopped her from continuing, or rather his frown did.

"Are you nervous?" Theron's concern touched her.

Rekah wrapped his arms around her from behind and chuckled. "No, she's not nervous, she anxious to get started."

"My kind of woman." Konala pulled out a chair by her side and sat.

"Come, lay back." Rekah tugged her gently.

"What? Here on the table?" She didn't know why, but the idea of having sex in the kitchen sent her libido racing. As if having three men in a row wasn't enough!

Konala stood. "Would you like a head puff?"

"A what?" It sounded like a new hairdo. What did that have to do with sex on the table?

"A head puff. What we use under our heads to sleep at night."

Rekah nodded. "Yes. It will be more comfortable for her."

He slowly lowered her back to the table, the hard surface revving her up more. Rekah held her head in his hands and she looked up at him. He was staring at her breasts.

Shoot, where was Konala with that pillow? If Rekah wanted to play with her little breasts, she didn't want to delay him.

Theron's hands pushed her thighs wider, catching her attention. He had to see her wetness.

Konala came back in and placed the pillow under her head while Rekah supported her. "Comfortable?"

She nodded and watched him sit back down. Holy guacamole,

the man was going to watch *everything*. Of course, what else was he going to do, watch television until it was his turn?

At the thought of them taking turns, her core started to ache. She looked at Theron who was staring at her wet pussy. "I'm ready when you are."

Konala chuckled beside her, but didn't say anything.

She focused her gaze on Rekah above her. He was a very handsome man when he wasn't frowning.

Theron's cockhead brushed her opening and she snapped her gaze to him. "Please, now." She tried not to sound too needy, but she was going to come faster than him at this rate.

His eyebrows rose, but he placed his hands around her waist and pushed his cock into her in one long glide.

Her heart pounded at the feel of him and her sheath tightened around him. She wanted to tell him not to take it slow, but somehow he knew and pulled out to push back in. He started a steady rhythm and she slid back and forth on the table.

Rekah's hands came down on her shoulders. She thought he would keep her in place, but instead he accented Theron's thrusts by pushing her toward him. She grabbed onto his forearms so he could pull her away as well. The double force of Theron's penetration had her arching in pleasure.

Every nerve ending was tightening as he pumped into her, winding her tighter and tighter, Rekah's control of her body making her feel loved, helpless but safe.

Theron's hands tightened on her waist and she knew he was close. She turned her head as the tension escalated, bringing her to the edge. That's when she saw Konala, his face tense as he watched her body moving back and forth across the table.

He reached his hand across as if he'd been waiting for just the right moment and pressed two fingers against her clit as Theron's come filled her.

Her orgasm barreled through her like a runaway twister, spiraling upward in ecstasy and breaking her into a million pieces of delight before settling back down to lay about the ground, or table as the case might be.

She opened her eyes.

Theron, still inside her, leaned over and kissed her gently. Rekah waited then lowered his head and took over her lips. It was no gentle kiss this time but a promise of what was to come.

When he was done ravishing her mouth, she was as limp as a rag doll.

Theron pulled out and she moaned, her body feeling the loss of him.

Rekah gently rolled her over and slid the pillow under her tummy, her feet barely touched the floor. Then he crouched down in front of her. "You want more, don't you?"

She winked at him, too relaxed to form the words. He nodded and she felt a hard cock lightly trace the line of the crease of her ass before pushing forward past her opening to rub against her clit.

She came up on her elbows at the spike of pleasure that ran to her core with that move and quickly looked behind her. Konala grinned. "You liked that."

Oh yeah. She nodded before turning forward again. In front of her was Rekah's hard cock. She licked her lips at the sight before Konala pushed his cock against her clit again.

Her eyes closed of their own volition and she tilted her hips up. She heard steps leaving the kitchen. Hopefully, Theron would come back quick. There was something about three men playing with her body that had her hotter than a piece of eyllen.

Konala teased her clit again with his cock and she pushed back with her hips. Theron's footsteps sounded on the kitchen floor. "I brought the shilla."

"Good." Konala's voice behind her sounded excited.

She turned her head to see what shilla was, but Rekah's hands turned it back before she could look.

She frowned at him. "What is shilla? Why can't I see it?"

He stroked the side of her face. "Don't you want to be surprised?"

"I guess." She wasn't completely sure, but she was sure that she trusted them, so she focused on Rekah's cock in front of her. Just the idea that it would be inside her soon was enough to have her heart racing again.

Konala's cock moved from her clit to her opening and he pushed in about an inch. She tensed with anticipation, her sheath anxious to feel him.

A cool liquid ran between her ass cheeks and her stomach tightened. That was shilla. What did they plan?

Konala grasped her ass and spread her. More cool lube flowed down her crease to where Konala kept himself barely inside her.

She didn't move. Her body was sensitized with anticipation. A finger ran down between her ass cheeks. It had to be Theron. Unique zings of pleasure pulsed up to her clit.

More lube flowed and Theron moved his finger down again, but this time he stopped at her anal star and pushed against it. "Relax, Khityki. I won't push my cock into you here until another time."

At his words, her body turned to mush and his finger slipped into her hole. It felt strange as if it tightened everything else, and as Konala slipped farther inside, she was proved right.

Her body was on fire, edging toward another orgasm and Konala hadn't even started.

His hands moved to her hips. "Ready, Jae?"

She managed to squeak out a single word. "Yes."

Konala's cock pushed all the way in and she thought she'd come, but her orgasm stayed on the edge. As he pulled out and pushed back in, so too did Theron's finger. Her hips rocked up of their own accord.

Again and again they pushed her toward the edge but not over, Konala's breathing growing loud enough for her to hear him over her own pants. She closed her eyes, letting her body enjoy the new experiences as excitement zigzagged between her legs and ass.

Rekah's fingers on her nipples had her opening her eyes. He pinched them lightly. "Lick me."

She opened her mouth and he pushed the tip of his cock inside, not releasing her nipples as she sucked. Her body rocked back and forth between the men, every sexual nerve screaming with pleasure. But she remained on a high ledge, one she'd never reached before, waiting, enjoying myriad sensations running through her.

Konala's fingers found her clit and played as he rocked into her. The pleasure was constant, her body rejoicing from every place until Konala came.

She screamed around Rekah's cock. Her body splintered as joy filled her and pulsing thrills swept through her until satisfaction blanketed her soul. She lay face down on the table, her body limp, her heart full.

Konala's hands ran down her back, lightly massaging as they went. He was still inside her, but Theron had pulled away as did Rekah.

The big man crouched once again and brushed her hair from her face. "One more." His husky voice wakened her pussy, but the rest of her body was wiped. She really needed to start exercising if just to keep up with her men.

When Konala pulled out, she couldn't believe that once again she felt empty. How could that be? Would she always feel like that?

Oh, would she always be having sex? If Rekah was helping someone and Theron was on patrol, would Konala want sex and when he left to go to the barn and Rekah was done would he then want sex?

Her body started to hum at the thought. Maybe sex would be enough exercise.

Konala lifted her to standing but her knees buckled and she caught the table. She needn't have worried because Konala had her.

Rekah smiled slyly at her. "Bring her over here." He pointed to the blank outside wall. She hoped he didn't expect her to stand for long. Maybe they should go in the bedroom if he didn't like the table.

Theron came around the table and between he and Konala, they held her upright. She looked up at Rekah. "Sorry. Guess I'm a little out of shape."

"I think your shape is perfect."

"Really?"

He nodded. "And you don't have to do a thing except let me in."

Her breath stopped for a moment at his words.

Rekah moved closer to her. Once his body was against her, he pushed her back until her back hit the wall. "Oh."

Then before she knew what he was about, he picked her up and wrapped her legs around his waist. She automatically wrapped her arms around his neck.

He shook his head. "Theron, Konala, take her arms."

Each man held an arm to the side while Rekah pushed her higher up the wall, his hands under her ass.

Shoot, the man was strong.

He lowered his head and sucked on her breast. Her body responded eagerly to this new onslaught of titillation.

Rekah's tongue and teeth played with her nipple while keeping a steady suction. She arched. The thrills he sent to her core revved her body up and caused her to moisten once again.

He let go of her breast and blew on it, causing it to pebble up hard. He grinned then lowered her. Theron and Konala continued to hold her arms to the side, partially holding her up. She was very happy with the support.

Rekah pulled his hips away from her and bent his knees.

His cock pressed into her opening, stretching her as he straightened, spearing into her, claiming her as his as well.

He held her there for a moment, pinned against the wall by his cock.

Her body flooded him with her juices.

He pulled back and pushed in again, his hands on her ass gripping her hard, tilting her hips to take him deep. Her nipples brushed against his hard chest, fueling her need.

Rekah lowered his head and whispered. "Come for me, Jaelene." His lips descended on to hers and his tongue delved into her mouth, taking it like his cock took her body.

She tried to grasp him, but they held her arms away. All she could do was take what Rekah offered, his body, his heart, his seed. He groaned into her mouth as he pressed against her, rocking her against the wall, driving his tongue into her mouth, pumping his cock deep inside her.

Her heart thrilled as if it knew their bonding would be complete. The joy inside her tightened her sheath again and as Rekah thrust upward, her orgasm crested.

Rekah released her mouth and yelled as his own hit, sending his seed to join with the seed of the brothers of his heart. She welcomed it, welcomed their love.

When he slowed, giving one last push to his hilt, Konala and Theron released her arms.

She wrapped them around Rekah's neck and he walked with her to the bedroom, Konala and Theron following. She smiled at them, not sure why she was so confident the bonding worked, but she was.

Rekah sat on the bed with her on his lap, his cock still deep inside. Konala and Theron sat on each side and took a hand.

Konala spoke first. "Each life converges to some centre, Expressed or still; Exists in every human nature, A goal,"

Rekah continued. "Admitted scarcely to itself, it may be, Too fair, For credibility's temerity, To dare.

Theron squeezed her hand. "Adored with caution, as a brittle heaven, To reach, Were hopeless as the rainbow's raiment, To touch."

Rekah smiled. "Yet persevered toward, surer for the distance; How high, Unto the saints' slow diligence, The sky!"

Konala brought her hand to his lips and kissed her palm. "Ungained, it may be, by a life's low venture, But then, Eternity enables the endeavoring…Again."

The words of the three men were so poetic, her eyes watered. They sounded like wedding vows. "That was beautiful. Did you three write that?"

Theron shook his head. "No. It is a poem by our late high poetess, Emily Dickinson. All Edenists are very familiar with her writings."

"Wait a minute, did you say Emily Dickinson, as in the recluse of Amherst, Massachusetts in the 1800s from Earth?"

He nodded.

"Heck. Was she here before us? How did she get here? Who was her beloved? Did she do the bonding? Is that why she never married on Earth? How long did she stay? Is that why she never went out because she wasn't home? Did she live in Naralina? If we went there, could we see her house?"

The three men stared at her a moment then broke into laughter.

She grinned, her heart filling with happiness. Now she would have a lifetime to learn all she wanted to know about this Eden she'd discovered, including everything there was to learn about the three men who filled her heart.

EPILOGUE

Theron watched Jaelene from across the room as she talked to her sister, explaining how his tigran had heard Konala's call for help and brought him to his cave. She loved telling that story and her sister was happy to hear her version of it.

He was proud of his beloved as she sat on the couch naked while Serena still wrapped herself in cloth. It had only been three days since they'd bonded, and Jaelene didn't leave their home that way, but she was getting used to it, at least among family.

When *he* left home without her, she always knew exactly where he was, thanks to one of her new senses since they'd made her their agapayto. And just yesterday, she'd discovered by accident that Konala could communicate with her. She'd been in the living area when she'd heard his thoughts as he swung home anxious to see *all* of her. Theron was pretty sure he would be seeing her blush a lot.

As he looked at the two women, he couldn't believe he'd ever loved Serena. The two sisters, though alike, were very different. What he saw as the biggest difference was Jaelene's new found confidence. He hoped he and the brothers of his heart had something to do with that.

He did not regret falling in love with Serena. If he hadn't, he would have never left Loraleaf and wouldn't have been there to hide Jaelene from the lawbreakers. Though his actions had caused a lot of pain, he'd do it all again if he knew he could have her in the end.

The door opened and Rekah walked in with Jahl and Khaos. From the look on Rekah's face, it wasn't good news. The women stopped talking and immediately rose and walked over to join them.

Jaelene took Rekah's hand and then his. "What is it?"

Rekah shook his head. "We've tried everything. We can't separate the immoral mind from Sandale's. He can't live this way anymore. He's asked us to erase his memory."

"What?" Serena looked at Jahl and he nodded. "Khaos?"

"I foresee no other conclusion."

Rekah sighed. "Saphr tried to erase only the thoughts of the lawbreaker, but whoever did this to Sandale, interconnected the psyches of each man. They are fused together."

"No wonder the man who did that was cast out of Naralina." Jaelene scowled at Jahl. "Did Sandale actually talk to you? Are you sure it isn't the criminal talking?"

"It is Sandale." Rekah touched his hand to his chest. "I can feel his agony. We can save the physical man, but he will have no identity and will even need to learn how to use his ability over again."

Jaelene looked at her sister. "I'm sorry."

Serena didn't say anything, but the tears in her eyes made her feelings clear.

"Saphr will do it tomorrow." Jahl looked at each of them. "We will say goodbye to the man we knew this evening." After that pronouncement, he turned Serena toward the door.

Khaos followed and the solemn trio left.

Jaelene let go of their hands and turned to face him. "If they were able to separate Sandale from the criminal and he was himself again, could he join Serena's filoz?"

"No. The bonding can only take place once for every Edenist."

"Oh, so maybe this is not totally terrible. I mean, if Sandale was back to his old self and he was part of Khaos and Jahl's filoz, he wouldn't be able to rejoin that. That would be heartbreaking, especially since he had been with them when they chose my sister. I know she feels guilty over his being hurt when they saved her, but can you imagine if he was back?"

Theron widened his eyes then looked at Rekah. The brother of his heart pulled Jaelene into his arms. "And I have to be thankful that Theron left us because otherwise we wouldn't have you."

She laid her face against his chest. "I have to agree with you. Also, Sandale would have taken me and who—Oh, Konala is on his way and he has a surprise for me."

Theron looked over her head at Rekah and grinned. They were well aware of what it was.

"Hey." Jaelene raised her index finger. "You two know what it is, don't you?"

Rekah shrugged but couldn't seem to keep the smile from his face.

"You have to tell me. I'm dying to know." When Rekah shook his head, she looked at Theron. "You'll tell me, won't you?" She sidled up to him and batted her lashes. "Please?"

He laughed and she pouted. He loved it when she stuck out that full bottom lip of hers.

The door to their home opened and Konala stepped in. "Sorry I couldn't get here any faster. I was delivering kits."

"What?" Jaelene ran over to him. "Without me? I told you I wanted to help with any births, sickness, or broken bones."

He ran his hand through his hair. "I know, but this was an unexpected one. Talia had three kits."

"Three? Is that normal? Is she feeling okay? Should we bring her some food so she is healthy for the nursing?"

Konala pulled her against him and kissed her to stop the questions.

"Hmm, I like that." She looked askance at him. "You do know that I'm well aware that you will kiss me if I go off like that, right?"

At Konala's surprised look, Theron laughed. It seemed even the brother of his heart underestimated their beloved.

"So what's my surprise?" Jaelene perched on the edge of Rekah's stuffed chair, her legs crossed over the area they all loved so much, but her breasts were upright and lovely to gaze at.

Konala looked at him then back at her. "Talia has agreed to let you befriend one of her kits when they are old enough."

Jaelene's eyes grew wide. "Do you mean like a pet, but still free to live in the wild?"

"Yes."

"Eeeeee!" She ran to him and hugged him then picked him up off the floor.

Theron and Rekah moved toward her, but she still held Konala aloft as she hugged him, much to his consternation.

Theron touched her shoulder. "You can put him down now."

"What?" She let go of Konala and the man came down with a thud. She stared at him then looked at her arms. "I can't do that."

Silence reigned until Theron noticed Rekah starting to smile. "Rekah?"

He gazed at Jaelene, the love in his eyes matching the love they all had for her. "It's the bond." His voice was just above a whisper. "You've gained my strength when you feel strongly."

She cocked her head. "So if I try to lift him now, it won't work because I not super excited and only very excited?"

"Yes." Rekah looked at him and Konala. "This means if she is ever in danger, and realizes that," he gave her a quick frown, "my physical strength will aid her."

"Oh wow." She plopped down in Rekah's soft chair. "That means I don't have to do any exercising, well except…" Her voice trailed off as her gaze roamed over each of their "manly parts."

Konala laughed. "I think you are in need of more exercise right now."

Her gaze came up at that and she winked before scooting behind the chair. "I hear running is good exercise, too."

Konala headed for one side of the chair and she ran out the other way, only to be picked up and thrown over Rekah's shoulder.

Her squeal ended in laughter and she slapped his ass.

"Oh, you're going to pay for that." He tapped her ass in retaliation and strode from the room, Konala following.

Theron touched his hand to his chest. His heart was not only whole again but full with love. He was home and he had his beloved. He was content.

"Theron!" Jaelene's yell was pure pleasure.

He strode out of the room and headed for their bedroom. "I'm coming."

Jaelene's laughter followed his statement. "No you're not. At least not yet."

For updates, sneak peeks, and special prizes, it's easy to sign up to receive the latest news from Lexi at http://eepurl.com/D3MqT

EDEN – ENGLISH GLOSSARY

agapayto – wife, but more, woman with a connection with every man in the filoz

ambrosia – mango, coconut tasting drink with a trace of spice in the aftertaste

Bedia – endearment meaning "beloved"

beloved – less formal name for agapayto (wife), a woman can refuse to be a beloved

Bendis – the large moon with pink light often called the second moon

blood sign – marking of lawbreaker band, a circle of blood with an x over it.

boarox – as big as a bison with no hair and black splotches on its legs, large droopy upper lip that covers mouth full of white shark teeth

bonding – the sexual act that connects a beloved with her filoz if she is on Eden

breast binding – bra

brother of his heart – best friend who will share a beloved

burning ceremony – celebration of an Edenist's life with everything the deceased liked from food to songs to favorite free time activities. Then the dead is placed on a pyre and burned. People take turns watching the fire so the man is never alone as his spirit rejoins Eden

caball – bird with blue feathers

chosen one – like finacée, but the Edenists choose with no agreement from the woman

cold box – referigerator

Criuson Law – law set up by the original settlers of Eden

crossover – the first time the chosen one goes through the portal to Eden

cyndistone – teal, granite-like stone

Cythera or **Cys** for short – women of the Pleasure Temples

daemond – honey bee

decods – like leaques (3 miles is a decod)

Dickinson Law – laws instituted after the Fullamush when the men fought over women

direlot – ferocious and cunning animal most closely resembles a wolf

discoverists – scientists but not only in the scientific field

Eden day – 22 hours

Eden month – 40 days

elseire – Bird with purple wings when in flight but folded up looks green

eyllen – energy rock source

feroon – big beast with tusks, furry and as large as an elephant but no trunk

filoz [filous] – group of men (2-5) who are close like a family

Fiya – endearment closest to sweetheart

Fullamush – the great war that almost destroyed the planet but the women and Emily Dickinson brought peace (story in Unexpected Eden)

grapet – purple vegetable that havling pigs like (used as bait)

grendal – like a wild boar but larger, has tusks and squeals, travels in herds

Haven – new walled settlement founded by Nassic and Wareson who escaped Naralina and gathered other "lawbreakers" who were falsely accused to form a society

havling pig – smaller pig-like animal that wanders alone

head puffs – pillows

heat top – stove

Helios – Sun

henny – chicken like bird

hestas – blankets made of see through material that is very thin, but quite warm

Holy Bendis – expression of surprise, frustration, anger, etc.

Holy Crius - expression of surprise, frustration, anger, etc.

idonee – nightingale

inducer – microwave

infragile vine – unbreakable a day after it's cut from its live piece

ithio – idiot

jump-off ledge – in Loraleaf where men pick up the vines left on a hook to swing across or down.

kafez – coffee but stronger

kerasi – mild sleep inducing fruit (cherry flavored) red

Khityki – kitten

Kif – Capital of Eden

Kindred – a broad group that every Edenist is born into but doesn't know his specific abilities until his transition. A family will have multiple kindreds within it.

Latzeran Sea – large body of water known for its depth

lawbreakers – what the Edenists call criminals, those exiled from cities

layfeenya – dolphin like creatures with much bigger tails

living area – living room

logar – horse

Loraleaf – an older settlement in the trees founded by Jahl, Khaos and Sandale as an alternative to the city of Naralina which contains men who followed them from the city

meal room – kitchen

Naralina – white and gold walled city that men of Haven and Loraleaf hail from

pander bush – bush with large dark green leaves

racide – poisonous plant

rhoade – like chicken with chickpea, a mild curry, mild garlic, coriander maybe, a strong flavored potato and a tinge of hotness, maybe a tiny amount of red pepper

rhybat – small rodent with super large ears, afraid of its own shadow

Ruling Circle of Naralina – the oligarchy government of 5 for the city of Naralina

sable worm silk – thread

salish bush – looks like a small weeping willow

Samuvian desert – large cactus filled desert

savinstone – gold

Scrat – swear, like "shit"

Selene – moon with silver light

sherry flower – light pink flower with strong scent that grows on a thin stem (very fragile)

shilla – lube

shiner– lantern powered by eyllen

siris webbing – silky soft webbing made by large caterpillar type creatures often used for head puffs

sitki – barn

Stass! – whoa!

table cover – table cloth

Talia – tigran Theron befriended while living in his cave

Hermday – Wednesday

tigran – sabretooth sized cat with chameleon abilities, loves to be petted

villain's mark – blood sign

waterhole – swimming pond or stream

welchet – animal the size and look of a porcupine though the quills are actually soft with small tusks that grow down from the bottom jaw, has 6 legs and if the tail is touched he'll disappear quick because he's fast

yenea – filoz with a bonded woman

Read on for an excerpt from *Passion of Sleepy Hollow* Re-releasing September 2016

Chapter One

Present Day, Sleepy Hollow, NY

"Brom." The tortured whisper escaped Katrina Van Tassel as she stared at the back of the man waiting by the reception counter of her inn.

He must have heard because he started to turn in her direction.

Panicking, she retreated two steps and swung around the corner of the hallway, plastering herself against the floral wallpaper. Her heart beat faster than the wings of the monarch butterflies of summer, and she folded her arms across her stomach as a chill filled her soul and tears blurred her sight.

It couldn't be him. He was dead. Long dead. It was someone else, a Newtimer, that's all. But his build was so exact that she didn't want to see the front. What if he looked just like Brom? She would faint. Yes, she was sure she would. No, she wasn't. She'd never fainted. Of course, there was always a first time.

Brom had been her first, her only, her intended.

Her gut twisted at the remembered pain of sitting on the church steps realizing something terrible had happened. That was long ago. Too long ago. She needed to get a hold of herself.

Ignoring her agitated pulse, she stepped away from the wall, tucked stray hair back into her braid and straightened her shoulders. This man was probably lost. That's all. No reason to make a mountain out of a molehill. She brushed down the apron on her cotton dress.

The little bell on the counter rang again.

"Well, hold your horses," she murmured under her breath as she strode around the corner to face her visitor. Her feet slowed of their own accord. The striking man with amber eyes and the build of the only man she ever loved tapped his long, blunt fingers on the counter. He looked so much like Brom, and yet not.

Irritation with herself and him brought her heart back on track. Stepping behind the counter, she nodded once, her lips refusing to smile her usual welcome. "How can I help you?"

"I need a room."

She ignored his smooth baritone and the goose bumps it sent along her arms. "I don't have one."

He had the audacity to raise one eyebrow. "Really. I see three rooms right here."

"That would be the parlor, the breakfast room and the kitchen." She glanced down, searching for the stool she used when dusting, wishing she could step on it now to meet the man eye to eye. She settled for craning her neck and catching his gaze. "I'm sorry. I thought you wanted a bedroom."

His brows drew downward, giving him a menacing look, but he didn't say a word.

She didn't even blink. She hadn't been running the Sleepy Hollow Inn by herself since her grandmother's death because she backed down from a little conflict. Besides, staring at him was pure pleasure. Like her former betrothed, his face had all the right masculine angles from his straight nose to his shaded chin. His dark brows, lowered as they were, set off warm, amber eyes, and his short black hair gave him a good-boy look that Brom never had. The fact that this man was just as tall and broad as her only lover proved she still found that physique attractive. More than attractive, if the warmth suffusing her body was any indication.

The man's mouth quirked to one side, causing her heart to stutter. His lopsided grin could melt ice. "I am looking for a bedroom." He sighed and ran his hand through his hair. "But I can sleep in the parlor if I have to."

Oh Lord, he needed to stop being nice or she would be ready to give him the whole darn inn. She shook her head. "I'm sorry. I'm full, but you can find a room in town or even try Tarrytown. That's just down the road and they have a lot of inns."

"No. I already checked. They're full too. I didn't know this festival thing was such a big deal." He rubbed one side of his face with his large hand.

He had no calluses. Just another way in which he was different from Brom. She simply had to keep finding differences until he left, and he needed to leave soon. His continued presence was shattering her nerves. She pulled out her reservation book. "It's always this busy. That's why people book rooms so far in advance." She turned the page. "If you like, I can check to see if I have a room available for the next festival."

His hand came down hard next to hers, effectively covering all the names listed there. "I need a room tonight. Just tonight. I have to play at being this stupid Headless Horseman at midnight."

She snapped her head up, her voice barely a whisper. "The Headless Horseman?"

At her undivided attention, he squirmed and glanced away.

"Yeah. Stupid, I know. But my brother asked me and since he can't do it, I promised him I would."

Kat's hand on her book gripped the pages into a crumpled mess as she croaked, "You're Stephen's brother?"

"Hey. Are you all right?" He covered her hand with his, its warmth relaxing the muscles between her fingers, as well as those around her heart. All she could do was shake her head.

He took her hand and kneaded it. "You aren't going to faint on me or anything, are you?"

"Is Stephen hurt? I know he loves being the Headless Horseman. He wouldn't miss it. He'd move mountains to get here. Something must be terribly wrong." She squeezed the man's hand like she wrung out the laundry, but she couldn't help it.

Stephen's brother wouldn't look at her, but his face had definitely closed off that conversation.

"What's your name?"

"My name?" His gaze found hers again and his devastating smirk returned. "I'm Braeden Van Brunt, temporary Headless Horseman, only as you can see, I have my head."

She dropped his hand. "Braeden Van Brunt?" Brom Van Brunt. "But you look nothing like your brother." Not even slightly. Yes, his brother had dark hair and was tall as well, but that was where the resemblance ended. Stephen had a softer face, was small-boned and very thin. Even his eyes were hazel, which had made her think he was a distant cousin of her Brom. But Braeden, even in the loose garment he wore—

"Yeah, we get that a lot. He takes after our uncle and I take after our dad." He stood straighter, his whole body stiffening. "Stephen had open heart surgery and asked me to fill in. I'm guessing no one will mind who rides tonight as long as there is a Headless Horseman."

Kat's mind tried to grasp Braeden's words, but her heart beat too loudly for her to focus. Stephen's heart? Kind, sweet Stephen's heart was bad? His brother, Braeden, so like Brom. She didn't want this. To feel like this again for him. No, not for him. For Brom. For—Argh. His baritone words finally penetrated her thoughts.

"I have to stay here. There isn't enough time to find another place." Braeden ran his hand through his hair again.

"Fine." The word was out of her mouth before she could stop it.

"Fine?" His voice softened. "You'll let me stay?"

She shook her head but refused to meet his gaze. "Wait here." Without checking to be sure he remained, she spun on her heel and headed down the hall to her room. She needed to remove herself from his presence to find her brain again.

Once behind her closed bedroom door, she looked around. *God in de Hemel,* what was she doing? She had no rooms available. Her inn was filled with Oldtimers every festival because Newtimers simply couldn't stay at the Sleepy Hollow Inn. But Braeden was the Headless Horseman. If she turned him out, the festival wouldn't be complete. He had only asked for one night. One night shouldn't hurt. As long as he didn't want to stay Sunday night, it would be fine. After midnight Sunday the whole village disappeared. That secret could never be revealed to a Newtimer, or so it was said.

Kat glanced around her room, the only room not occupied— well, not by a guest. Worrying her bottom lip, she took a shrewd inventory. She could have the room made up in an hour.

Then what? How could she let a Newtimer, who reminded

her so much of Brom, stay in her room? How could she let a descendant of Brom sleep in her bed?

How could she not?

Braeden leaned back against the check-in desk, his elbows resting on the wooden surface. The diminutive innkeeper was his biggest surprise of the day. At least a foot shorter than his six-foot-five frame, she had the curves of a larger woman packed into a concentrated package, easily assessed in her historical outfit. Her pale golden hair didn't like to stay in the loose braid she wore and it teased her round blue eyes as they danced with her changing emotions. Too bad he couldn't tell if he irritated her or attracted her, though he had a hunch it was the former. That in itself was strange. He couldn't remember the last woman he irritated, not counting his mother. After high school he'd found his ridiculous muscles attracted women. He hadn't minded that until he'd lost his best friend, or rather half of his best friend.

Why hadn't his brother suggested he stay here? Because it was always full? He could sleep in his car tonight if he had to, but he'd be sore tomorrow. He hadn't ridden a horse in over a year.

Braeden surveyed the tiny interior of the inn. He doubted it had more than eight bedrooms. The parlor had two settees and an armchair. The breakfast room, as she had called it, was only set for six. The entire building was like a dollhouse. He straightened. Maybe the beds were small too. He'd never fit anyway.

"Just great." He glanced at his Rolex and tensed. It was already past nine. He wanted a shower before putting on the costume Stephen had designed. He still couldn't believe he'd let Stephen talk him into this. If his brother hadn't been in the hospital, he would never have caved. But seeing his brother sitting in bed wearing that crappy hospital gown with his wife and four kids all in the room with them, he couldn't say no. He might not see his brother in person very often, but he'd do anything for him, even be the Headless Horseman for a night.

"I have made the arrangements." The innkeeper's voice had him turning as she strode up the hallway toward him, hips swaying with purpose in the full skirt of her dress. "You can have a room in one hour. If you want, you can go next door to the pub until then."

Not likely. His bulk tended to challenge smaller men, especially when they were drunk, and the last thing he needed was a fight tonight. He glanced at the parlor as a possible place to wait, but when he looked back at his hostess, it was clear she wanted him out. Not wanting to push his luck, he nodded. "Great idea. I'll be back in an hour, Miss…"

Silence greeted his polite inquiry. If she pursed her lips any tighter, they might just disappear altogether.

She glowered. "Do you want a room or not? Now go while I get it ready."

He turned away before she caught him smiling at her. It wouldn't do for her to see he found her interesting. She appeared immune to his physique, a breath of fresh air for him. That was at least one bright spot in his day.

Striding out the door without looking back, he walked by the building next door and glanced in the window. The bar was dimly lit, but even so, it was clear there were plenty of people inside. Ignoring the inviting feel of the place, he continued along the darkened dirt road.

He didn't like having to be out among so many people. Luckily, not many strolled around the village. Most seemed to be at the other end of the road where tall lanterns shed light over stalls and tents. He should check in with the stable. His brother had told him where to retrieve the horse, but never said how much it would cost.

Braeden strode farther down the road until he spotted a wooden sign touting a horseshoe. Since his brother had been playing the Headless Horseman for years, the least the organizers could do was provide a horse free of charge, but since Stephen had a soft heart, Braeden doubted the man ever suggested it.

Stepping into the wide opening of the wooden stables, he stopped and took a deep breath. Despite his best intentions, the scent of hay and old wood had excitement growing in his chest. Anticipation built at the remembered feel of a horse beneath him. It had been too long.

"Do you need somethin', sir?" A bulky man with a balding head and a large nose emerged from the shadows to the right of him. Some kind of suspenders held brown knickers up over a white shirt with the sleeves rolled up to the elbows.

Braeden turned and the man stopped, both hands out in front of him, shaking his head. "No, don't come no closer. I be a good man."

Braeden looked behind him to see what caused the man's fear, but there was nothing. "What are you afraid of? There's no one there."

The man lowered his hands and stepped forward hesitantly, squinting. "Who are you?"

"I'm Braeden Van Brunt. My brother Stephen rides as the Headless Horseman?"

The man broke into a smile. "Ah yah, Stephen is a good man. You are his brother, huh?" He took a lantern off the hook and brought it closer, holding it high. "Hmm, I don't see much 'semblance."

"Yeah, I know. We look different. I understand I don't have much time, so I thought I'd better make arrangements to pay for a horse to ride tonight."

The man reached out his hand. "I'm Ludo Van Ripper and you don't pay for the horse. You just ride it. You know how to ride, yah?"

Braeden shook Ludo's hand, the hard calluses on the palm telling him this was a hardworking soul. "Yes, I do."

"Good. Come. You need to meet Daredevil."

Braeden followed Ludo down a short row of stalls. The man lifted the lantern and pointed. "This here's your mount."

The huge black stallion lifted its head high before bringing it down in short bounces.

The blood sped through Braeden's veins at the sight of the beauty walking toward him. The horse lifted its head over the stall door and sniffed him. Braeden didn't blink. Now, this was a horse. Braeden stepped forward and lifted his hand slowly, so as not to spook the animal. When the horse nudged him with its nose, he stroked its neck.

"I'll be a barn swallow's baby, I never seen Daredevil take to no one like that except his master."

Braeden continued to stroke the majestic beast, sensing its need to run. "We'll be out soon, boy. Just a bit longer." He gave the horse a final pat and turned to Ludo. "Didn't my brother ride Daredevil?"

The older man shook his head. "Nah, he couldn't get near him. He always rode Gunpowder."

Braeden followed the man's nod to see another black beauty across the way, but that horse stood at least a hand shorter and was smaller-boned than Daredevil. Daredevil took the opportunity to nudge Braeden's shoulder. He grinned and gave the horse another stroke.

"Yah, that is the horse you need to ride tonight." Ludo ambled away. "Yah, it's a right match, it is." His chuckle hung in the air and despite his loose cardigan, Braeden felt a chill.

Zipping up, he returned his attention to the horse. "We'll have a great ride tonight, Daredevil. I promise."

Passion of Sleepy Hollow
(http://www.lexipostbooks.com/passion-of-sleepy-hollow/)

ALSO BY LEXI POST

Sci-fi Erotic Romance

Cruise into Eden

Sci-fi television employee, Erin Danielson, boards a nude cruise to get lucky, and boy does she ever because Nase and Ware have ripped bodies, enticing accents, and hearts of gold. In fact, they are out of this world…literally.

Unexpected Eden

Jahl, Khaos and Sandale easily save their chosen one on Earth, but convincing pyrotechnics expert Serena Upton to stay on Eden is going to be a lot harder.

Coming 2017

Eden Revealed

When Toni finds herself in over her head in Naralina, she receives help from the most unlikely men, but who will protect her heart from a relationship that can never happen?

Paranormal Erotic Romance

Masque

Rena Mills plans to turn an abandoned abbey in Nova Scotia into a haunted bed-and-breakfast, but Synn MacAllistair, the self-proclaimed Ghost Keeper from the 1860's has other plans that include taking her through the seven Pleasure Rooms and freeing 73 ghosts.

Passion's Poison

Beatrice Rappaccini refuses to fall in love because she's cursed with deadly orgasms, but when she meets Zach Woodman the chainsaw artist, her heart refuses to obey. To protect the only man she's ever loved she will have to make the ultimate sacrifice…if he doesn't beat her to it.

Pleasures of Christmas Past

Though Jessica Thomas is thrilled to land the job of novice Spirit Guide, she's been assigned a hot, arrogant Scottish mentor who confuses her heart. But what should concern her more, is will he protect her soul?

Re-release Autumn 2016

Passion of Sleepy Hollow

When present day headless horseman Braeden Van Brunt meets the original Katrina Van Tassel, he cannot resist her pull on his heart, but her own heart may still be with his look-alike ancestor. How can he love a woman living in a different time period and put the past to rest, especially when the dead don't rest in Sleepy Hollow?

Contemporary Cowboy Erotic Romance

Cowboy's Never Fold
(Poker Flat Series: Book 1)
Cowboy's Match
(Poker Flat Series: Book 2)
Cowboy's Best Shot
(Poker Flat Series: Book 3)
Cowboy's Break
(Poker Flat Series: Book #4)

Christmas with Angel
(Last Chance Series: Book 1)
Trace's Trouble
(Last Chance Series: Book 2)
Coming Soon
Logan's Luck
(Last Chance Series: Book 4)

About Lexi Post

Lexi Post is a New York Times and USA Today best-selling author of romance inspired by the classics. She spent years in higher education taking and teaching courses about the classical literature she loved. From Edgar Allan Poe's short story "The Masque of the Red Death" to Tolstoy's War and Peace, she's read, studied, and taught wonderful classics.

But Lexi's first love is romance novels. In an effort to marry her two first loves, she started writing romance inspired by the classics and found she loved it. From hot paranormals to sizzling cowboys to hunks from out of this world, Lexi provides a sensuous experience with a "whole lotta story."

Lexi is living her own happily ever after with her husband and her cat in Florida. She makes her own ice cream every weekend, loves bright colors, and you will never see her without a hat.

www.lexipostbooks.com